SERVING
GREEN
LAKE

DUSTY NICOLE SANDERS

MILTON & HUGO L.L.C.
4407 Park Ave., Suite 5
Union City, NJ 07087, USA

Website: *www. miltonandhugo.com*
Hotline: *1- 888-778-0033*
Email: *info@miltonandhugo.com*

Ordering Information:
Quantity sales. Special discounts are granted to corporations, associations, and other organizations. For more information on these discounts, please reach out to the publisher using the contact information provided above.

Library of Congress Control Number:	2025906798	
ISBN-13:	979-8-89285-515-0	[Paperback Edition]
	979-8-89285-514-3	[Digital Edition]

Rev. date: 04/03/2025

To my husband, Allen. Thank you for believing in my dream to write a book. I wouldn't have done this if not for you. I love you.

To the readers picking up this book. Thank you for taking a chance on a debut author.

Welcome to Green Lake!

Chapter

1

Annella's day could be described in three words: great, crap, and WTF!

Great—she finally landed a catering job for a family reunion, meaning there was money going *into* her bank account instead of *out of* it.

Crap—a large barbeque sauce stain on her favorite purple chef's jacket and her hair tie snapping with no replacement.

WTF—the red and blue lights flashing behind her as she sped home.

She gripped the steering wheel so tight her knuckles turned white and pulled to the side of the two-lane road, her van's tires thumping on the rumble-stripped pavement as she slowed down and came to a stop to wait for the officer. She pulled her driver's license from her wallet and the insurance card from the center console and waited.

She listened to her favorite song, admiring the postcard-like landscape of the flower-covered hills rising over the lake where the town got its name. The normally calming effect was not working though, and her patience dwindled by the second.

"What is taking this cop so long?" she murmured out loud as she looked behind her to see if there was anyone getting out of the cruiser. She was hot, even in the cool air conditioning of the van, she was tired, and she was *hangry*.

She popped the lid to her little purple cooler and pulled out her post work snack, chocolate-covered peanuts, savoring the salty sweet combination still waiting on Officer Slow Poke.

She catered the Peterson's family reunion lunch earlier today where she received glowing feedback on her smoked chicken, but she could have done without the stain courtesy of little Jimmy Peterson.

She stripped off her jacket before getting in to drive home to use her stain stick, which was not in her oh shit bag, leaving her in her teal sports top. She just wanted to be done with this nonsense so she could drop the leftovers at the community center before taking a long, hot shower at home. Maybe she was going slightly over the speed limit, but not enough to warrant being pulled over for it. Wasn't there some type of grace rule?

—⁂—

Officers Max Thorne and Cal Roberts had just pulled into their favorite hideaway to wait out the rest of their shift in peace and have their pre-workout granola bars when duty called, or rather sped, right past them.

Max flipped on the lights and pulled out onto the highway swearing as he tossed his un-opened bar back into the cubby. He followed just close enough so that whoever was in the awful purple van could see that they were being pulled over but not so close that he would hit them if the person slammed on the brakes. He slowed down as the driver did and pulled in behind them, kicking up a cloud of dust as his tires left the pavement of the shoulder and hit dirt.

Neither officer wanted to work the stop as the temperature on the dash read almost triple digits and Max wouldn't pull rank on Cal, so they settled the decision the same way as they had when they were kids. Rock, paper, scissors, best two out of three. They held up their fists and pounded their palms while running the license plates.

"Son of a bitch, it's hotter than the seventh circle of hell out there," Max said, grabbing his hat and getting out of the SUV after getting beat by a paper to cover his rock in the final round.

"Have fun," Cal said, leaning back in his seat to watch the show in the comfort of the blasting AC. It was always eventful when Max stopped someone speeding.

Who would paint their van the color of an orchid, Max thought as he walked the four feet between vehicles, sweat already dripping down his front and his back. He had pulled over every color of vehicle imaginable, but this was a new one. He looked back at Cal and saw his honey-blond hair blowing in the air.

"What a dick," he said, even though he knew Cal couldn't hear him.

Seriously, though, purple? He approached the window, got his first look at the offender, and felt his blood pressure rise instantly.

Annella waited until the officer made it to her window before she rolled it down letting in the heat of the spring day in Green Lake and the smell of sandalwood and cedar.

"Do you know why I've stopped you?" Max started his speech.

The woman flung her documents at him before he could ask. He reviewed them in stiff silence, already writing out the ticket in his head, as his stomach decided to declare its anger at the missed snack.

Annella tried to stay mad, but laughter bubbled up her throat until an un-ladylike snort broke free making her laugh even harder. She clapped her hand over her mouth, but her shoulders shook with amusement. Max raised a chestnut brown eyebrow and gave her his no-nonsense cop face, the one that would make actual criminals slink down in their interrogation chair, but that didn't stop the giggles.

"Chocolate-covered peanut," Annella asked extending the bag to Max.

Max thought back through the day and wondered how he had pissed off Karma so much that this was who she threw at him.

"No, thank you," he snapped. Okay, maybe he was a little cranky, his gas station hot dog and chips was too long ago, and he had burned it off already.

He pinched the bridge of his nose and tipped his head back, trying not to let this woman rile him. He had seen her type so many times in his years with the Green Lake Police Department, nails done, make up applied perfectly, curls spilling down to her amble breasts, the princess type. He could predict exactly how this was going to go.

"Please sit tight while I go run your information," Max said, only out of duty. He was nothing if not a polite police officer.

"And here I was thinking of trying my luck with a high-speed chase to liven the day up," Annella replied.

"Cute." Max tossed over his back as he turned toward the cruiser.

"I know, but thanks for noticing," Annella chirped, still giggling. Max stalked back to the SUV and flung open the door, immediately wanting to strangle his partner.

Cal sat in the passenger seat the picture of relaxation, no sweat dripping down his face or ass crack or other parts of his body snacking on Max's protein bar. Not bothered by the scowl that Max was currently leveling at him.

Max tossed Annella's ID to him as he shoved his face into the air vent. "Who's the culprit that has you so worked up?" Cal asked while he pulled up Annella's information on the computer. Cal whistled at the picture staring back at him from the screen. "She's hot."

"She's not hot." Max sighed as the cool air ruffled his hair. "She's just a spoiled princess who thinks she's above the law. Ten bucks says she's going to cry or try to flirt her way out of this.

"I'll take that bet." Cal pulled out a ten-dollar bill and laid it on the dash looking at her again on the computer. *I'd let her flirt her way out of it* he thought. Max laid his own soggy money on top of Cal's. "She's not going to get off with a warning no matter how tight her sports top is." The cool air did nothing to bring down Max's anger.

Max didn't see the point in speeding if there was no emergency? Speeding just equaled death, in his opinion. Max never sped anywhere unless his lights were on.

How am I going to get out of this? Annella wondered while munching her snack. *I've already ruined my chance to flirt my way out when I laughed at Officer Cranky, but there must be another way. Think Annella.*

As she popped another nut in her mouth, licking the melting chocolate off her fingers, the saying about a man and his stomach came to her. She snapped at her genius idea. She just had to get him to try her food. One bite, and he'd let her go.

Annella's information came back clean, meaning it was time for the fun part. Max chuckled, thinking about the fake tears he was about to see and wondering what sob story she would attempt. Some days, he really loved his job. As he approached the window, still wondering about the color choice of her van, he didn't hear any crying, real or fake. Damn, Cal was probably going to win.

As he looked in the window, he noticed the smidge of chocolate melting on her lower lip. His thoughts betrayed him wondering how that chocolate would taste if he licked it off her lip or...other places. He brought his thoughts back to the present, he was not going down the heartbreak road again.

"I am so glad to see you taking this seriously. Who has a snack during a traffic stop?" Max all but yelled.

Annella didn't rise to his anger, to her surprise. She looked at him with her best customer service smile and dropped some extra sugar in her voice when she said, "I'm sorry that I was speeding and caused you extra paperwork at the end of your shift, Officer," she squinted at his name tag, "Thorn. If you'll allow me to get out of my car, I can at least fix you some food to quiet your stomach." Annella batted her eyelashes at him for good measure.

Max raised an eyebrow and scoffed.

"You, fix something? What do you know about fixing anything besides your hair?"

Man, what was *wrong* with him? Why did this woman get under his skin so bad? He was still trying to figure those questions out when her annoyed voice butted into his thoughts.

"I can fix more than my hair, I assure you. I'm a caterer, and I just left an event where not everyone showed up. I still have enough food in the back to feed the entire Green Lake football team since I never learned how to only cook for the exact number at my events which has saved my ass more times than I can count. Who doesn't remember to RSVP? Sorry, I'm rambling. Anyway, I have plenty. Please let me fix you a plate as my way of apologizing."

"What kind of food do you serve? I'm not sure if you've noticed, but it's going to take more than kale salad and carrot juice to fill me up."

Annella raked her eyes over him. Even with the height of her van his head was in line with the top of her window and built like a superhero action figure—biceps that said he clearly worked out often accentuated by his tight uniform shirt—soft chestnut hair and eyes that resembled a nice, aged whiskey. Not that she was *really* looking.

"Does your nose work, officer? Do I smell anything like kale salad and carrot juice? Or are you smelling smoked chicken, baked beans, and potato salad so good you'll lick your plate when you are finished then hunt me down for seconds?" At the sound of the menu, Max's stomach agreed with her. Annella bit her lower lip, trying not to laugh at the sound again.

"Get out slowly, and don't make any sudden moves." Max opened the door and kept his focus on her hands. Just because she was a woman didn't mean that she wasn't carrying a weapon of some type. His focus lasted for about five seconds after she got out of the van, and he saw her fully.

She was a little tyke coming barely to his chest. Curves that he wouldn't mind frisking if she did something dumb. Shapely legs that her black tights clung to, and her curly, auburn hair reminded him of a fall sunset.

"Don't you know you're not supposed to trust a skinny cook?" He laughed at his own joke as Annella looked up and up and up and rolled her eyes at him.

Max followed her to the back of the van and glanced over to see Cal sitting as close to the windshield as possible. Max shook his head signaling he didn't need backup. "You're going to be begging to eat more than your words after just one bite." She reached up to open the back, and Max's stomach growled again.

Annella turned around and looked at his stomach, wondering if his abs were as impressive as the rest of him. "I know you're hungry. I'm working on it." She could feel Max's intense gaze on her as she opened the back of the van.

Piece of cake or chicken, Annella mused as she jumped in. *I'm so not getting a ticket now.*

"You don't have to fix anything large. I have a workout session at the end of my shift." Max was still trying and failing to watch her hands to make sure she didn't go for a large kitchen knife or cast-iron skillet. But he couldn't take his eyes off her plump ass as she made him a to-go container with a piece of beautifully smoked chicken, beans, and potato salad.

Annella handed him his plate and a Styrofoam cup with her business information on it filled with ice-cold, homemade sweet tea before she hopped down from the van and noticed for the first time that he had someone in the car with him.

"Oh, you have a partner with you. Would they like a plate too?"

Annella would feed the whole police department to prove how good her food was if that's what it took to wipe that look off Officer Thorne's face.

"Him? Oh, he ate my snack while I was busy dealing with you, so fuck him," Max said as he took a step back so she could close the van doors.

"Enjoy your snack and have a nice day."

Annella began to walk back to the driver's door congratulating herself for her quick thinking as she heard angry footsteps follow her.

"Do you really think you can just throw food at me and get away?"

"One taste of my food, and you'll forget all about me speeding. You'll be thanking me for giving you the best food you've ever had. Go ahead and try it. I'll wait."

"Cocky, aren't we?"

Max followed her down the length of the van and stopped as she whirled back to him. She crossed her arms under her ample chest and glared at Max.

"Not cocky, just confident. Besides, you don't have a free hand to write a ticket." She uncrossed her arms and climbed inside.

"Hold it or wear it," he said as he shoved the food through the driver's window forcing her to catch the food and drink or be covered in her own creation for the second time. He wrote out the ticket with a practiced hand, slipped it in her lap, and took his food back from her, watching her mouth gape open.

"I gave you food, and you're still giving me a ticket? WTF?"

Annella threw the ticket in the passenger seat and glared at Max.

"Be glad I'm being nice and only giving you one ticket instead of two since you did try and bribe a police officer." Max laughed as he sauntered back to join Cal in the SUV, the sound of the woman groaning about the ticket following him.

"I didn't see any tears when she came back this way and you don't look like a man that just got flirted with by a pretty girl. Looks like I won. What is that?" Cal said pointing at the container and cup in Max's hand. He grabbed the winnings off the dash and tucked them in his pocket.

"Were you even looking at her face?" Max asked. "This." He held up the food and cup. "*This* is how she tried to get out of her ticket. She's a caterer and thought food would set her free."

Cal smelled the aroma of the tangy sauce and spicy beans, his mouth salivating. "She's hot. She gave you free food, and you *still* gave her a ticket?"

"She was speeding, and she laughed at me. You're damn right I gave her a ticket. And since you've already snacked, you can drive while I eat."

"I can't believe you didn't get me a plate," Cal complained, getting out of the car.

"Next time we pull over a hot caterer, you can get humiliated and get your own food," Max said, getting out and going around the car.

"So, you're admitting she's hot. That's interesting," Cal said as he went around to be the driver.

"Shut up, Cal," Max replied as he shut the passenger door and took a bite of the chicken, moaning.

"You're the boss," Cal said as he pulled a U-turn to get back to their hideaway.

Annella smiled, watching the officers switch seats.

I knew he couldn't resist my food, she thought, pulling back onto the highway and heading once again to the community center. That slightly made up for the ticket.

Chapter

2

Annella was still in disbelief about getting her first Green Lake ticket when she pulled up to the community center and beeped her horn to alert Lauren she was there. She had called her best friend after one group of the Peterson family didn't show up and told her there would be plenty of food for the community meal today.

In the three weeks since she moved to Green Lake from Pure Springs, she had met eight people, now nine, if you counted the cranky cop, and the reviews were mixed. Lauren, she liked instantly, though with her small frame, short blonde hair, and energy for days. They were peas in a pod.

Lauren owned a consignment shop, Twice is Nice, and had been approached by the town council to take over running the community center when the previous coordinator retired to Florida at the beginning of the year. Annella always believed in giving back to the community as much as possible so one of her missions was to ask about donating her extra food to help feed the community.

When Lauren heard this, she jumped up and down and hugged Annella so tightly she couldn't breathe for a minute. The two had been friends ever since.

Lauren came out of the back door to help Annella unload and greeted her with that same air-stealing hug. "How did it go?"

Annella hugged her friend back and walked to the back of the van. "It was great! Everyone loved my food, and it made my heart happy to hear all the laughter and love. I could have done without the ticket on my way here, though."

Annella told her the whole saga of her run-in with Green Lake's finest and her friend doubled over laughing so hard she was crying.

"Oh, Annella. I'm sorry I haven't told you not to speed around here." Lauren lifted her tear-filled emerald, green eyes up, still chuckling. "Speed Trap Thorne is always watching."

Annella opened the back of the van to start handing Lauren foil pans of deliciousness. "Thanks for the tip now. And here I was thinking you'd be on my side, so we could bash officer tall, handsome, and grouchy together."

Annella handed Lauren a pan of food and climbed down to unload her sweet tea.

"I would love to bash Max with you, but there really isn't a nicer person in town. Wait, you thought he was handsome?" Lauren held the back door open, leading into the kitchen portion of the center with her hip.

"Yes, I thought he was handsome. I'm pissed, not blind. The man looks like he just stepped out of a superhero movie and the way his uniform fit him like a second skin." Annella bit her lower lip thinking about his figure and how appropriate his first name was. Everything about him that she has witnessed so far was to the max. "He must reserve that niceness for his friends, because what I just saw was full-on crankiness."

The friends worked together to get the rest of the food unloaded while Lauren chatted the entire time about Sadie and Cody's upcoming wedding. They were people Annella hadn't met yet, but she laughed along with her friend when she talked about the not-so-bad maid of honor dress that she could wear again.

The Green Lake Community Center was one large room with a sectioned-off kitchen. It was a bit dated with wood paneling on the walls from the eighties, linoleum tile floor, and tables that had seen better days, but people still loved to use the space for receptions, showers, and town meals.

"Can I convince you to stay and help serve?" Lauren asked, holding out a serving spoon to Annella with her best-begging smile.

"You can, but only if you have an extra shirt." Annella pointed to her teal sports top. "Little Jimmy thought my chef's jacket needed a healthy dollop of sauce to make it look better, and I didn't have a spare shirt."

Lauren beamed at Annella's agreement to help and headed through the kitchen to the back parking lot.

"I feel bad for Mrs. Honeycut in August when he starts her kindergarten class. That one will be two handfuls. Come on, I have extra clothes to take to the shop after we're done here in my car. I'm sure there's a shirt for you in one of the bags." Lauren walked out the door and headed to her silver compact.

She dug around a few bags and finally handed Annella a Property of Green Lake Cheer Squad shirt with lots of glitter and pom poms on it, claiming it was the only one that was her size. Annella didn't mind as she slipped it on over her sports top and felt the fabric. It had been washed so many times that it was soft as a cloud.

Annella went over to the van and put her non-slip tennis shoes back on so that she wasn't in her flip-flops while serving food. Properly clothed, the girls went back inside to start serving the early dinner. Green Lake wasn't a large place, so it didn't take long to feed everyone that came in.

There was *still* food left over, so they sent everyone away with to-go boxes in case they got hungry later or wanted it for breakfast. Barbeque was good at every meal, in Annella's opinion.

"Do you need any help getting the clothes to the shop?" Annella asked after they had cleaned up and were heading out the door.

Lauren waved her off with a content smile.

"That's alright. I've hired Ginny to work at the shop part-time. She can help me when I get there, but thanks, though."

Annella knew it was hard for Lauren to find help for both the community center and the consignment shop. The teens that were working age didn't find her shop "cool," and the older generation was already in their own careers, retired, or happy as domestic chiefs of staff, so she was happy knowing that Ginny was there.

"You get home and relax," Lauren said as she gave Annella another hug before she headed to the van and climbed inside. She waited while Lauren locked up and checked her phone for the first time in several hours. She only had one message from Travis Ashwood about dinner.

Travis had been her introduction to Green Lake three weeks ago. She had answered a post on social media advertising for a head chef position at his family's restaurant, The Black Tie. Travis interviewed her first via phone and all but hired her.

He invited her down for an in-person interview with his parents and Annella fell in love with the quaint town as soon as she arrived. The older Ashwoods put a stop to her dream though, when they interviewed her. They claimed that she wasn't "skilled" enough in the culinary arts to accommodate the elite clientele that frequented The Black Tie.

Annella thought that was BS since Green Lake was a smaller town. The customers in The Black Tie were the same type of customers that Annella served at her job in Pure Springs. Travis had asked her on a date that night, and since she didn't know anyone and she didn't want to be rude in case his parents changed their minds, she accepted.

He took her back to The Black Tie and proceeded to tell her all about the chef they did hire. Annella smiled and listened, but inwardly, she wanted to scream that she didn't care.

That was when she decided not to work for anyone else, traded her red compact in for a large van, and sank most of her life savings into turning it purple and starting her catering business in Green Lake.

She texted Travis back: *Just leaving the community center, meet you at the restaurant in an hour.*

She didn't need to ask which restaurant. They only ever ate at The Black Tie. She waved to Lauren and finally headed for home, but instead of the long, steamy shower she had planned, it would have to be quick so she could get to the restaurant on time.

She did the speed limit the whole way home and smiled at her house as she pulled into the driveway. It wasn't perfect, but she loved it anyway. With the bright red roses emitting a sweet smell out front and the cobalt blue door, it had charmed Annella as soon as she saw it.

It boasted an amazing chef's kitchen thanks to the owners, Tom and Paula. When Tom showed her the house, he explained that they owned The Buttered Biscuit bakery in town. He and Paula had lived in this house before moving to the outside of town. He wanted her to be able to bake anywhere she wanted, so he remodeled the kitchen for her before they decided to move.

Tom and Paula were great people, and Annella wished her own parents were more like them. Tom had commended her courage to strike out on her own and move to a strange town. Paula encouraged her to create tasty food as often as possible in the kitchen. It was the kitchen of Annella's dreams with commercial grade appliances and black granite counter tops.

The rest of the house was more modest. A comfy living room, a half bathroom, and an office were also on the bottom floor, while upstairs housed the master suite and two bedrooms with a Jack-n-Jill bathroom.

Her own parents had never understood her desire to cook for a living and told her that she wouldn't make any money from it. She wrote them off as soon as she could afford to move out with a roommate that she met at her first line cook job.

Annella used the upstairs bedroom space as her personal library. She loved to read and always wanted her own library. Now she lived in a house big enough to have it.

Annella got out of her van and smelled her roses on her way to unlock the house and start getting ready for her date. She dropped her keys in the cream, scalloped bowl on the entryway table and set her purse beside it, locking the door behind her. Some habits were hard to break, no matter how small the town was.

She was a very meticulous woman, so everything was always in its proper place. She had been told, more than once, that she couldn't be lived with because of it. She walked through the kitchen to the laundry room to put stain fighter on her jacket before heading upstairs.

She turned on the shower to warm up while she undressed and put her clothes in the hamper. She made a mental note to get the top back to Lauren as soon as it was clean and to add a stain stick and extra hair ties to her oh-shit bag.

With the shower full of steam, she stepped in and sighed as her muscles relaxed under the hot water. She didn't care if it was six degrees or one hundred and six degrees outside. Her shower always had to be hot. She finished getting ready, grabbed her keys and purse and headed out to have some mediocre scampi.

Chapter

3

"Dude, you're seriously not even going to share one piece of chicken? She gave you three," Cal whined. He parked them back in their favorite hideout as Max continued eating what was, hands down, the best chicken he'd ever had.

"Not sharing, get over it."

Max and Cal had been through their whole lives together, from kindergarten to graduation, then college and the academy. While they couldn't pass for brothers physically, everyone in town knew they were family.

"I'm keeping my eyes open for her van every shift and hope her foot stays heavy."

Cal took another longing look at Max's food and blew out a huff of air. "What do we even know about her?" Cal asked, looking at her license picture on the computer to write up the report.

"Everything I know about her is on that screen," Max responded, around a mouth full of potato salad.

"Thirty-six, brunette, five feet and six inches, one hundred thirty-five pounds, and she's renting Tom and Paula's place."

"That's not a lot to go on," Cal remarked, transferring it all to the paper form.

"I'm willing to bet her favorite color's purple," Max chimed in. "I have to give her credit for originality. I've had attempted bribery with everything from baseball tickets to the shirt off someone's back, but never a full plate of food. I almost feel bad for the ticket, almost."

Max polished off the rest of his snack and poured his lukewarm soda over his leftover ice. He noticed her business information printed on the side of the cup in purple and wondered about the name Grace Squared Catering. Maybe he'd ask her about it if he ever saw her again. The odds were in his favor in a town this size.

—⁂—

The rest of their shift was a typical day; four out-of-towners who didn't know enough to always slow down for small towns and a fender bender with Mrs. Johnson and Old Man Martins— he really needed to stop driving. They wrote the speeders and Old Man Martins tickets before heading back to the station.

"Not a bad shift," Max commented as they pulled into The Green Lake Police Department parking lot and found their space.

"Easy for you to say," Cal grumbled. "You didn't spend the last hour of the shift starving."

"Well, your stomach is going to have to wait a little longer, gym time."

"Damn it." Cal's shoulders slumped as they walked inside and headed for the locker room.

"We *can* go one day without working out, you know."

"Maybe, but I have to work off at least some of that second lunch," Max said, holding open the gray metal door. Max loved working out. It was a way for him to shut down his brain for at least an hour and forget about everything except the next rep.

They couldn't take the day off if they wanted to be ready for the town's annual Muscles for Money fundraiser for the first responders. It was the town's biggest event of the year. There was a big block party with food, bounce houses, jail lockups for an hour, and other great fun. At the end of the night, for every dollar raised, the response team had to do pushups.

"An hour in the gym won't kill you, Cal. I'll even buy dinner after." They had changed clothes and made it to the station's workout room.

"Dinner on you?" Cal asked, suddenly full of energy. "The Black Tie it is." Cal rubbed his stomach as he walked to the treadmill.

"It's not as good since Kevin quit, but if that's what you want, then fine," Max said, grabbing the machine right next to him. They finished their workout in record time since Cal barely stopped to breathe and then hit the showers. Max was the first one out of the locker room after his cold, refreshing shower and getting dressed in his jeans, navy blue collared shirt, and boots.

He walked over to chat with Danielle, the dispatch officer, while he waited on Cal. He popped a hip on the edge of her desk. "How was your shift?"

Danielle's blue eyes sparkled as she looked up. "Not as eventful as yours. What did she give you to try and get away?"

Max rolled his eyes. "A plate of food. How did you know about it?"

"Cal told me about the whole play-by-play on the radio while it was happening. It was just like a daytime soap opera."

Danielle shook her head and answered the non-emergency line at the same time. Cal finally came out dressed and ready for food. "You're worse than a woman," Max told him as they headed out of the station, down the front steps, and to their trucks.

"I hope we don't have to wait long," Cal said as he hopped, literally, into his fire engine red, long bed.

Max was more relaxed climbing into his tan, four-door truck. I guess that's the difference between the one who's buying the food and the one eating for free, he thought as he started the truck and followed Cal to the edge of town where the restaurant was. He couldn't believe it when he pulled into the parking lot, and there sat a familiar purple van.

Max backed into a space behind the van and got out. Cal came out as he walked up to the large black, smoked glass door of the restaurant.

"Tammy said it'll be a twenty-minute wait. I grabbed us a couple beers to have while we waited on the patio."

"How long have you been here? I didn't drive that slow."

Max grabbed his beer and leaned on the patio railing. "The woman from earlier is here eating with Travis. Do you think she has any food left in her van?"

Max wasn't sure why, but that bothered him. It wasn't his business who she ate with, but damn it, why Travis?

—⚏—

Annella was filling Travis in on her day and couldn't help but compare him to Officer Thorne. Travis had an aristocratic look on his face, jet black hair, that she suspected was not his real color, dark brown eyes, medium build, but he was on the short side as he was only about three inches taller than her. She glanced up as the hostess showed two men to their table.

"Speak of the devil," she mumbled, and cold fury filled Travis's eyes as he looked up to see who she was talking about.

"Thorne was the officer you gave food to after he gave you the ticket?"

"To be fair, I gave him the food before he gave me the ticket."

Annella stabbed her salad, the only part of the meal she liked, a little harder than necessary as Travis stood so fast he knocked his red velvet chair over.

"What are you doing?" Annella asked as Travis stalked away from their table.

She followed behind, trying to hide the embarrassment creeping up her face.

"Thorne, Roberts," Travis said, nodding to Max and then Cal placing his hands on his hips. "You need tell Annella to tear up her ticket."

Max stood and glared down at Travis from his six foot seven height, loathing everything about him "Not going to happen. She needs to thank me for only giving her one ticket. I could have also cited her for bribery of a law enforcement officer, but I felt like being nice."

"I can't believe you would be such an ass." Travis snapped dropping his hands into fists by his side. "She's barely been here for a second. She doesn't know your crazy obsession with speeders," Max swore Travis was about to stomp his foot for good measure.

"What better way to figure it out than firsthand. Hey, don't speed through my town." He said to Annella over Travis's shoulder.

Annella rolled her eyes. "Thanks, I've been warned now."

Annella stood watching the pissing contest between the two fully grown men and decided it had gone far enough. She didn't think Max would rise to a physical altercation, but she wouldn't put it past Travis.

Looking for any change to the subject, she reached for Cal's hand and said, "Hi, I'm Annella Lindly." She pasted a smile on her face as Cal stood and grabbed her outstretched hand and shook it.

"Nice to meet you. I'm Cal Roberts. That meal you gave Max sure smelled good today."

Annella beamed at the praise. "Thanks! You're so much nicer than this one," she jabbed her thumb in Max's direction, "Why couldn't it have been you to speak to me at my stop?"

Cal suppressed a laugh at the look on Max's face. "I beat him in Rock, Paper, Scissors so I got to stay in the car."

"I did try to fix you a plate, but Officer Thorne said you were eating already and didn't need it."

Now it was Cal's turn to glare at Max.

"Not to worry though. I finalized all my permits recently to start my food van business next week."

"What's a food van?" Cal asked.

"It's like a food truck, but I don't have a truck so I'm creating a new craze, food van. All my info was on the cup I gave Officer Thorne earlier. You come find me, and your first meal is on the house."

"Free food, I'll be your first customer," Cal said as his sapphire blue eyes lit up with excitement for more free food.

"Come on, Travis." Annella grabbed his arm and forced him back to their table. He gave her an angry shake-off and glared at Max, taking his seat one more time.

"When were you going to tell me about the food van?"

Annella had never seen a mature man sulk, but that's exactly what Travis was doing right now, sulking at not being the first to hear her news.

"I was about to when you decided to play the white knight even though I didn't ask you to."

Annella pushed her salad plate away as the waitress sat the plate of scampi on the table. "What's the deal with you and Max anyway?"

Travis sneered and clenched his fist. "Some of us will always be jealous of the starting quarterback," was all he said in response to her question, taking a bite of his chicken alfredo.

"Don't let him get to you. Ashwood has and will always be a pompous ass." Cal picked up a slice of garlic bread and took a huge bite while Max digested his anger about Annella calling him Officer Thorne.

"I'm good. I stopped letting him get to me a long time ago," Max said, grabbing his own bread and thinking about shoving it down Travis's throat.

He'd had the pleasure of giving him speeding, parking, and littering tickets, but those only came with a fine and maybe community service. The one time Travis had been in a cell and should have stayed there forever, Mommy and Daddy Ashwood got him out.

He watched Annella leave as the waitress sat their steaks on the table. "What's she even doing with him? He's an asshole to women, which is why he had to wait for someone new to move in to have a date. All the women here know how he is. She needs to find a better man," Max told Cal as he cut into his steak.

"And are you saying you're that better man? You stared at her the whole time we've been here. You can't tell me you're not attracted to her now." Cal took a bite of his own steak. "You were right, not the same since Kevin quit. I don't blame him, though. I wouldn't want to work for Ashwood either."

—⟊—

Out in the parking lot, Annella unlocked her van and opened her door while Travis stood there. "I'll text you later," he told her as he went to give her a kiss. She turned her head at the last minute, so his lips landed on her cheek. She saw his nostrils flare in anger as she climbed inside.

"I'll see you later," she said, shutting the door and starting the engine.

"Don't speed, don't speed, don't speed," she told herself as she headed for the parking lot exit, excited to go home and get into her comfy clothes and unwind.

Chapter

4

Travis stood rooted to the pavement as he watched Annella drive away. He knew she would eventually meet Thorne, but he had hoped to have a little more time to cement an actual relationship status with her before that happened.

Fucking Thorne. He always gets what he wants. He thought as he turned and headed for his extremely large, expensive, black truck with it's massive grill guard on the front.

Sure, Max hasn't had a date since Brenda left, Travis continued his musings, *but the smell of fresh blood might bring him out of his shell. Fuck!*

Travis had to think of something and fast or he would lose to Thorne again and he was sick of that shit. It had been happening since they were little kids playing flag football and Max got to be the quarterback even though his family donated the money for all the equipment and uniforms.

I just have to make sure that she is always focused on me that way she can't focus on Max Fucking Thorne. Travis's evil grin spread across his face as he pulled up to The Tavern to find him some company for the night since Annella wasn't giving him what he needed. That would all change after he put his plan into place.

He hopped out of the truck and walked into the bar with a lightness in his step and a plan in his head. *I will not lose again.*

—⚌—

Max and Cal finished their steaks, had one more beer, and Cal slid Max the check when the waitress placed it on the table. They walked out of the restaurant, Max taking an extra scan of the lot for a purple van before he said, "See you Monday," to Cal, heading for his truck.

"Have a good day off," Cal said as he headed in the opposite direction.

I'm so glad tomorrow's Sunday, Max thought. No work, extra sleep, and no thoughts of an auburn-haired caterer.

"Want me to grill us better steaks tomorrow?" Max called after Cal causing him to stop and turn around. Max fished his keys out of his pocket while waiting for an answer.

"I'll be there," Cal said and turned around again and headed for his truck.

Max got in his truck and headed for home to put those steaks in the fridge for tomorrow.

—⚌—

Annella was ready for the quiet of her house and that relaxing thing Lauren advised her to do earlier.

She changed clothes and heard her stomach make a sound much like the one she heard from Max earlier. She didn't have much of an appetite after the incident at The Black Tie, so she just pushed her food around until it was time to leave.

Travis was too tied up in his own anger to realize that she hadn't eaten, but now she was hungry. Annella could cook herself some better scampi than she would have gotten at the restaurant but settled for a grilled cheese, some wavy onion chips, and a bottle of water.

Fully supplied for her night, she grabbed her violet fleece blanket off the back of the couch, tucked her feet under her, and picked up her latest fantasy read. She was just getting to the good part about the fae queen riding into battle on her dragon when her text tone sounded.

She cringed, thinking it was going to be from Travis, but smiled when she read it was from Lauren.

Sorry about dinner. Tammy told me about the part of the stand-off she overheard. It's not a big deal. She wrote back. *How about you come over to brunch tomorrow at 10:30 and I'll fill in the gaps Tammy left. Brunch at your place, yes please. I'll see you at 10:30.*

Annella was already planning the menu as she went to bed.

Chapter

5

Sunday was always the day Annella looked forward to most and today was extra exciting. Brunch with Lauren meant pulling out all the stops. Travis had texted her bright and early giving her a lame excuse for his actions last night that she ignored. She was not going to be distracted while having a nice time with Lauren.

Annella had the food ready and displayed perfectly at 10:30 when Lauren rang the doorbell after trying to just walk in. Her dark wooden table covered in a springy floral tablecloth was set with elegant white dishes and her antique silverware. A few of her roses from out front added a sweet smell to the air that blended with the syrup. She clapped her hands in excitement and went to unlock the door hearing her laughing friend.

"You know, I think you're the only person in town that locks your doors."

"You're probably right, and it's still a foreign concept to me that you Green Lakers don't." Annella smiled and stepped back to let Lauren in and receive her best friend's hug.

"Oh! Everything looks beautiful like it belongs in a magazine," Lauren said as she tuned into the eating portion of the kitchen and sat down.

"Thanks, I took some photos of it to post on my website so that potential clients can see I don't just make barbeque." Annella sat down across from Lauren and started serving her friend generous portions of all the delicious treats before making her own plate.

Annella loved having Lauren around any time she could. In the time that they spent together, she could imagine what it would have been like to have a sister instead of being an only child. She recapped her dinner disaster from last night filling Lauren in on the pieces that Tammy didn't tell her.

"I don't think I've ever been that embarrassed in my life. Everyone was staring at us as Travis's voice got higher and higher. He has been texting me all day already. I had to put my phone on silent." Annella placed a large slice of golden French toast on her plate and drizzled sweet maple syrup over it.

"Don't worry about it too much," Lauren said placing a fruit kabob on her own plate before continuing. "Those three have never gotten along all the way back to elementary school." Lauren slipped a piece of juicy watermelon off the skewer and popped it in her mouth.

Annella ate another bite of toast piecing together a picture of a younger Max throwing a pass to Cal while Travis watched from the side of the field.

Lauren wiped watermelon juice from her fingers on the yellow linen napkin. "Travis's problem was that he thought he had to be in charge. Max and Cal didn't work like that, though. They went with the flow. Whatever the day, situation, or challenge was they faced it together. He is still envious of their bond."

"That's more than I got out of Travis last night and makes a ton more sense," Annella said scooping up a bowl of strawberry yogurt topping it with granola.

As they ate, Lauren told her more stories of the Max and Cal show that had her rethinking Max being a jerk.

"I'm so full. If I eat before lunch tomorrow, it will be a miracle," Lauren said, prying herself from the chair to help Annella clean up and put away what little food was left. The girls put a healthy dent in the brunch.

"I know exactly what you mean. I don't think I could eat another thing."

The two made quick work of the cleanup and settled into the couch and comfy tan chair in the living room to watch/nap through their favorite rom-com.

—◇◇—

Annella woke up later to the sound of the credits playing and Lauren's deep, even breathing. Despite the filling brunch they had consumed earlier, she found her stomach growling with hunger again. She got up quietly, so she didn't wake Lauren and slipped into the kitchen. She had already prepared for this exact situation and went to the refrigerator for the two charcuterie boards located inside.

She added two different types of crackers to each board, fixed two glasses of sweet tea, put it all on her silver serving tray, and went back to the living room. Lauren was just waking up when she spotted Annella with the tray full of food.

"I'm retracting my previous statement about not eating until tomorrow," Lauren said, sitting up straighter and stretching her arms overhead.

"I figured you would." Annella sat the tray down on the table and handed Lauren a bamboo board with pepperoni, turkey, ham, two types of cheese, more grapes, nuts, and crackers.

"Did you make it to the end of the movie?" Lauren asked as she took the board and the tea from Annella. She placed the board on her lap and the tea on a coaster on the end table.

"Not at all. I made it to where they were picking out a movie to rent, and that was it." Annella picked up her own food and sat back on the couch with her feet propped up on the table.

"I didn't even make it to the house swap." Lauren laughed.

"Did I sleep through most of the movie and you fixing more food?" Lauren made a stack with crackers, pepperoni, and mozzarella before popping it into her mouth.

"No," Annella responded building her own cracker stack. "I already had these made. Just had to add the crackers and fill the tea glasses. It was probably the tinkling of the ice that woke you." Annella ate her snack savoring the spicy pepperoni with the mild cheese.

"Did you take pictures of these to add to your website too?" Lauren asked as she picked up her phone and took her own pictures. She wanted to be able to spread the word of Annella's food and having pictures would be a plus.

Annella nodded sipping on her tea.

"Are you excited for your first day with the food van?" Lauren put her phone back on the end table and picked up a grape.

"I'm nervous-excited. I haven't been here that long, so not many people know me, and I know how small towns are with outsiders." Annella wrung her hands together second guessing herself.

"It's going to be great. I've already started telling everyone about it, and as soon as I see your post, I'll share that, too." Lauren popped the grape in her mouth with a satisfying crunch.

"You're such a good friend, Lauren." Annella blew out her breath and rested her head back on the couch.

"Right back at you," Lauren said, picking up her sweet tea and taking a big gulp.

"Do you need any help with the prep for it?" Lauren asked, finishing off her grapes. Annella was snacking on the salted cashews, running through her mental to-do list.

"Thanks, but I'm in a good spot with everything. Just promise me that you'll come eat so I have at least one customer."

"Of course," Lauren said with a nod.

They kept the TV on for noise while they finished their food and talked like they had been friends forever instead of just a moment. Lauren stayed to help Annella clean up the living room and only left after Annella had reassured her three more times that she didn't need any help with the prep for tomorrow.

It was still early, and Annella had so much nervous energy, so she decided to be productive. She made sugar and chocolate chip cookies to hand out to her customers. Hopefully, they wouldn't know that she didn't make them from scratch.

She could cook with the best of anyone, but baking was like a whole other language to her. She baked three dozen of each and set them out to cool while she rinsed the baking sheets and put them in the dishwasher. They were still too hot to package, and Annella had cleaned all she could, but she still had so much extra energy thanks to that nap earlier.

She knew what she needed to do to calm her body and mind, a nice long run. She was already dressed for it, just needed to grab her shoes from upstairs. She sat on the edge of her bed to put on her black and red shoes and headed back downstairs.

Annella grabbed her spare house key from the bowl so she didn't have to carry all her keys for the whole run and slid her phone into the side pocket of her yoga pants. She popped her wireless earbuds in and walked outside to the fading evening sun.

She did a quick warmup session before she started running toward Green Lake Park setting a nice easy pace. She was happiest during this time of year; she wasn't cold all the time, and the days were longer, so she could take her runs outside in the evenings. She was soaking in the beautiful oranges, yellows, purples, and pinks of the sunset, making the half-mile run to the park pass quickly. Another thing Annella loved about the town of Green Lake was the mile-long running/walking loop that was around the lake in the park.

The tall trees with the draping branches created a fairy tunnel for her to run through. As she made the turn at the half-mile point, she looked out over the lake. She saw families soaking in every minute of sunshine, splashing in the shallows, couples on the cute bright blue paddle boats taking laps on the lake, and a group of teens getting ready to have a fire in the brick fire pit.

This...Annella thought, *this is what I was missing in the city.*

Annella had lived in the city of Pure Springs her whole life but never felt like it was "her place." She was always considered the outcast during her school years, preferring to spend her free time at home cooking instead of out partying. She graduated culinary school at the top of her class because all she did was study and practice her dishes and techniques. She was hired as a sous chef at the most prestigious restaurant in the city, Sky, where she was constantly surrounded by at least a hundred people, but she still felt alone.

Annella had had enough of the busy city and not knowing her neighbors, so she started searching for new opportunities. She thought she had found it when she saw Travis's advertisement, but now she knew The Black Tie wasn't where she belonged either. She was cautiously optimistic that her catering/food van adventure was right where she needed to be.

Annella finished her loop and let herself simply walk back home. Her thoughts had settled, and she wasn't as nervous as she had been when she started her run. Endorphins were wonderful like that. She marveled at the sunset the entire way home and sat on her bright yellow porch swing to soak in the last of the day.

When the first stars appeared in the ink-black sky, she walked inside for a bottle of water and some yoga stretches on the enclosed back patio to keep the bugs away.

She loved the quiet of the nights in Green Lake since most everyone was settled down at home by the time the streetlights came on. She finished her last child's pose and sealed her practice with a namaste. She got up, rolled up her lavender-decorated yoga mat, and placed it on the hooks above her yoga blocks.

She walked back inside to package up her cookies in the purple cellophane baggies and tie them with a little white bow. She loaded all her non-perishable items in the van just as the sky was turning full black. After she made sure everything in the van was exactly as she wanted it, she wandered her way back inside and picked up her book to read until it was time to get the smoker warmed up and the meat cooking.

Annella read a solid four chapters before her alarm went off, letting her know it was time to start the meat. She walked out to the part of her patio that wasn't screened in where she had her smoker/grill set up. She was going to keep the menu simple tomorrow with chopped and sliced brisket and sausage links. People would be able to have them either solo, on a sandwich, or in a wrap.

The sausage wouldn't have to go on the fire until early in the morning to just warm and get the smokey flavor, but the brisket had to go low and slow. She put the briskets on and inserted her Bluetooth meat probes. They connected to an app on her phone that would alert her when the briskets reached 205, and it was time to wrap them.

Having done everything possible to be ready for tomorrow, Annella went upstairs, changed, and went to bed to try and sleep.

Chapter

6

Max rolled over and checked the time on his phone, hoping that it was at least past 8:00 so he could say he slept in and was shocked to see 9:00! He hadn't slept that late since high school. It had helped that he was dreaming of a petite, auburn-haired caterer that cooked like a goddess feeding him directly from her fingers so his body was reluctant to wake up.

He yawned and stretched thinking if he was going to get his run in, he needed to get to it. He threw off his hunter-green comforter and climbed out of his king-sized bed, making his way to the bathroom around the disaster that was his bedroom. He didn't bother making his bed because he was just going to sleep in it again later, so what was the point?

After relieving himself and brushing his teeth he went into his closet for his running clothes. Max picked up a pair of gray running shorts, gave them the smell test, and deemed them clean enough to run in before putting them on.

He walked to a different pile in the back and fished out a well-worn Green Lake Police Department shirt that had once been white. It was now paint and food-stained, had holes in both sleeves, and a ripped bottom hem, but it was still one of his most prized articles of clothing.

He pulled the shirt over his head and went in search of matching-ish socks. After an embarrassing amount of time, he finally had socks, one red and one blue. His running shoes were easy to find after he tripped over them and landed on his bed.

He sat up on the corner and put his shoes on, grabbed his phone off the charger, and headed outside into the bright, already warm morning. Max worked through his warmup routine before heading toward the park for his three miles.

He jogged toward the park passing Cal's house and then turned around chuckling as he went to get his partner for some running company.

Cal was going to kill him, but Max didn't care as he jogged up the steps and banged on the dark wooden door out of courtesy before walking in. He thought for a split second that Cal might be in his bedroom with company but still walked in anyway.

"Morning, Cal," Max bellowed, turning on the switch and flooding the sparsely decorated room with light.

"I'm going to arrest you for breaking and entering and cruel and unusual punishment."

Max leaned against the door, crossing his arms. "Yeah, but I know a guy on the force and have a good attorney, so I don't think the charges will stick."

"Why?" was all Cal said as he pulled the covers up to block out the light.

Max pushed off the door frame and pulled the cover down from his face. "You want that steak later? This is the price of it."

Cal lifted his head and looked at Max with sleepy blue eyes. "Are we having baked potatoes?"

"What am I? An amateur, of course, we are, but only if you're up and ready in five."

"I really hate that you always use food against me." Cal grumbled that and a few other words as he got out of bed that Max chose not to take personally.

Max walked out to the living room to wait for Cal and started the timer on his phone for five minutes. He kept moving so his muscles wouldn't get cold and shouted at Cal that he only had sixty seconds left. Max looked at the three pictures Cal had hanging on his wall, probably taken from his mom and dad's house.

There was a snapshot of Cal and his brother Danny on the day Danny graduated from the fire fighter academy. Another showed Cal and Danny with their parents in the fall leaves, and the last was Cal and Max at their academy graduation.

Cal came out of the bedroom looking mildly annoyed in his faded Green Lake Mustangs shirt that had seen better days, black, silky long shorts, and black running shoes. The jerk even had on matching socks.

"Ready sunshine?" Max asked, turning from memory lane and walking toward the door.

"I don't really like you right now," Cal said stretching his arms over his head.

"Just keep your mind on the food, and we'll be finished in no time." Max replied as he headed out the front door

"You get dressed in the dark?" Cal asked, pointing at Max's mismatched socks.

"I might need to do laundry," Max said as he joined Cal in his warmup routine before they took off for the park.

"Remind me to start locking my doors." Cal grumbled between breaths as his feet hit the pavement.

"You could do that, but I have a key." Max said cheerfully.

The guys made it the two blocks to the park and then kicked into another gear as they made their way down the trail. Max thoroughly enjoyed Sunday morning runs. No one was out yet, so he and Cal had the park to themselves. Max knew it wouldn't last long, though, as Sundays were when the mom joggers came out with their running strollers and neon shirts.

The moms jogged a full lap and then spread blankets out in the shade for the littles to play while they caught up on the gossip from the week. The comradery was one of the things Max loved about this town. He loved thinking about all the life things those little ones would experience together. That's how it had been for Max and Cal, their parents had been and still were best friends. Max couldn't think of a single memory that didn't have Cal in it.

As Max and Cal made the turn to begin their second lap, they saw all the moms stretching in the soft green grass before they started.

"Hey, Max. Hey, Cal," they all said as the two guys ran past.

"Hi, ladies," they replied and kept running.

"I think I'm going to move and not give you my new address," Cal told Max as they finished their second lap and started on the third.

"You could do that, but I'd find you. You know you'd miss my face."

"I wouldn't miss it for long, we do still work together."

Cal's second wind kicked in, and he thought he might just make it to the end. The guys finished their run and found the shade of a large elm tree for their cool-down stretches.

"I hope we don't get in any foot chases tomorrow. I'm going to be sore."

"I don't think there's ever even been a foot chase in the history of Green Lake, so I think you'll be safe."

Max stretched his hamstrings while Cal stretched his calves against the base of the tree.

"Ready to go?" Max asked, shaking out his left leg and then his right.

"Considering I didn't want to come in the first place, yes."

"I know, but aren't you glad you did?"

Max and Cal headed for the sidewalk that would lead them back to their block and waved at the moms as they passed.

One of them offered the guys some water that they accepted graciously, and Cal had half of his drank before he spoke.

"I will be glad when I get my steak and potato later."

The two walked their way home, talking about Max's brother Cody and his upcoming wedding and what was happening with Danielle's pink highlights.

"I really hope Annella has her food van out tomorrow and that we are free to swing by for lunch. I love a free meal."

"I noticed," Max said, stopping on the sidewalk as Cal broke off toward his house.

"See you later," Cal said.

"Come by whenever you feel like it," Max called back and walked in silence the rest of the way home.

Max and Cal had rented this house together when they were both rookies. It was a small three-bed and two-bath, but for just the two of them, it was perfect. They had lived together until the end of last year when Max became Lieutenant and Cal made sergeant. It felt weird sometimes, still being in the house all by himself, but it wasn't as if Cal went far.

Max let himself in and headed immediately for a nice, cool, refreshing shower. The day was going to be another hot one, and Max was drenched in sweat. He picked up a mostly clean towel from the floor and hung it over the shower rod where his sapphire blue curtain was hanging on by three of the eight loops that had once held it.

He turned on the water and went in search of more clean adjacent clothes to put on after his shower. He found a deep green T-shirt, some jeans that didn't smell like they had gone too many days without being washed, a pair of blue cotton boxer briefs, and the other red and blue socks.

Figures, he thought.

He stepped into the cool water and made quick work of getting clean. He grabbed the towel from the shower rod and dried off then slipped on his bachelor clean clothes and padded down the hall to the kitchen. Max heard the cabinet door slam and reached for his weapon, only to realize that it was still on his nightstand. He tip-toed back to his room and reached for the pistol. At the same time, he heard a familiar voice call his name.

Max walked back to his kitchen, leaving his weapon where it was, and saw his younger brother, Cody.

"What are you looking for?" Max asked, causing his brother to startle and his head to connect with an open kitchen cabinet.

"Shit. Hello to you too. I found the whiskey I was looking for but couldn't find a clean glass. I guess I'll have to wash one if I'm going to have a drink. You know it's not illegal to own more than two glasses, right?"

Cody picked up a tall, square-bottomed glass and a dish sponge to wash the glass before filling it with two fingers of Max's finest whiskey. Aged twelve years with a smoky, cherry aftertaste.

"Everything is just how I like it," Max said as he walked past his brother and pulled a bottle of water from the fridge. "Why do you want whiskey? It's a little early, isn't it?"

"It's five o'clock somewhere, and I'm in a crisis."

Cody downed the first glass and poured another as Max looked at his kitchen. It wasn't *that* bad. Three cabinet doors were standing open, the sink was full, his to-go cup from Annella was tipped over, the mail was strung all over the counter, and he wasn't sure what that smell was, but he knew where everything was this way.

Cleaning wasn't his cup of tea, and it seemed like every time he started, his phone rang, calling him to work. By the time Max finished the view of his space, Cody had taken three small sips of liquid courage.

Max took his water, walked around the piece of the counter that created the eating space, and sat on a wooden bar stool. Cody didn't bother sitting down, his long legs eating up the wooden tile floor as he paced Max's kitchen.

Max knew his little brother well enough to know that Cody would talk about whatever his crisis was when his lawyer brain worked out the way he wanted to say it. Max downed half the bottle of ice cold water and tried to work out what had his little brother so worked up.

It wasn't until after he finished the second glass of fire water, looking very put out that it was empty again, that he spoke.

"It's bad, Max," was all Cody could get out at first.

Max's cop brain kicked in, preparing for anything but what came out of Cody's mouth next.

"The caterer we had hired for the wedding, the one that everyone always uses from Star Oak, just had to cancel on us. They had hired a new office assistant about the time we were booking our date, and she double-booked them. The other couple was there first, so that's too bad for us."

Max and Cody both looked to the front of the house at the sound of the front door opening and closing.

"Hey, Max," Cal called, walking the path that led from the door to the kitchen. "What have you been doing to this place since I—" Cal broke off when he stepped into the kitchen and saw Cody. "Hey, Cody. I didn't realize you were here. Where's your car?"

"Hey, Cal," Cody said rubbing a hand over his face. "I walked over. I needed time to think."

"Must be a hell of a problem. It's a two-mile walk." Cal leaned on the door jam and waited for Cody to talk.

"It's the worst dilemma I've ever had to deal with, and that includes taking the bar exam with the flu. Sadie is beside herself; she didn't sleep last night, and I haven't been able to get any food down her either." Cody kept pacing, running his hand through his dirty blond hair. "I finally got her to calm down and take a nap when I told her I would handle it for her."

39

Cal gave Max a confused look and slid onto the stool next to him. "The caterer they hired for the wedding double booked, and the other couple was booked first."

"Ah, thanks for catching me up," Cal said with a grin. "Continue, Cody."

"This is no light matter, Roberts. I have to find a caterer, but I've called everyone within fifty miles, and everyone is booked or doesn't want to travel for the event."

"I get it," Cal said. "You would do anything to make Sadie happy." He turned to Max and saw that same mischievous twinkle from when they were kids playing a prank on Cody or some other poor, unsuspecting soul.

"Are you going to tell him about Annella before or after we have to revive him from a panic attack?" Cal asked Max.

"I was getting there. Just letting him get it all out so he would listen."

Cody stopped pacing in the middle of the kitchen and glared at Max, nostrils flaring, face turning red.

"Calm down, little brother, and pick up that cup lying on the counter."

Cody shot one more dagger at Max and gingerly picked up the cup with bright purple writing.

"Grace Squared Catering," Cody read aloud ignoring the sticky feeling on the cup from he didn't want to know what. "You've had a caterer's information this whole time, and you let me go through all that? What a dick," Cody said and pulled his phone out of the pocket of his black jogging pants to take a picture of the information. "That's the third time I've been called that in twenty-four hours. I would be offended if I thought you all meant it, but I know only one person did."

"How do you just happen to have a caterer's information handy?"

Cody put the cup back on the counter right side up and his phone back in his pocket. "We pulled her over yesterday," Cal supplied, getting up to get his own water since neither Thorne brother had offered him a drink.

"Yeah, pulled her over on Route 30. She made Max a huge plate of food, trying to get out of her ticket, and he didn't even share." Cal opened the fridge and took in the mediocre supply of anything. They had lived like bachelors when he had lived here, but it wasn't this bad.

"Did you let her go?" Cody asked finally looking relieved and took his first full breath.

"She was speeding," Max said, finishing off his water.

"So that's a no," Cody said, eyes going soft. "Look bro, I miss Heather too, but Max, you can't fix the past by stopping everyone that speeds through Green Lake."

"I can try." Max tossed his empty water bottle in the pile on his counter telling himself he'd clean it up later. "I didn't give her a ticket for trying to bribe me, but I should have given her a ticket for being on a date with Travis."

Cody's lip turned up in a snarl. "If she wouldn't have been speeding, was the food good enough to have gotten her off with a warning?"

"The food was good enough that she almost didn't get a ticket."

Cody's brows shot up. *That must be some damn good food,* he thought.

Max started the grill while Cal prepped the potatoes, and Cody washed enough dishes for everyone. After the guys finished eating, Cal walked back to his house, and Max took Cody home so that he didn't have to walk so far again.

Chapter

7

Annella was already awake and going over her checklist again by the time her alarm went off.

She prepared for her first day with the food van in an organized manner, the only way she did anything. Dressed for success in her stain-free, thanks to her work with the stain-fighter, purple chef's jacket, black tights, and black tennis shoes.

She packed her "oh shit" bag with the Green Lake Cheer shirt to give back to Lauren, a Grace Squared Catering shirt in case she got more stains on her jacket, first aid kit, extra hair ties, bright pink flip flops for after she was finished, AND a stain stick.

Out in the backyard, Annella could tell it was going to be another beautiful but hot day. She pulled the briskets off the smoker and replaced them with the sausages before going inside to rest the meat Eventually, Annella wanted to have her own restaurant, but she would be grateful for what she had.

She finished prepping all the meat when her third alarm went off, telling her it was time to go. She looked at herself in the entryway mirror as she grabbed her keys and purse and told herself again that today was going to be great. She was a badass chef, and everyone was going to love her food.

Annella chuckled as she locked her door, hearing Lauren's voice tease her about doing this in a town so small. She fished her purple polarized sunglasses out of her purse and put them on as she got into the van and started it. She cranked up her favorite country station and drove to the convenience store for a ton of ice.

"Good morning," the clerk, Neal, according to his name tag, greeted her with a warm smile when she walked in. There were three convenience stores in Green Lake, but this was the only one that carried her chocolate-covered peanuts, so she made it a point to come here whenever she needed something quick.

"Good morning," Annella called back as she walked to the back of the store for her ice. She carried two large bags up front and then went back for three more.

"That's a lot of ice. Are you making a home for a penguin?" Neal asked as he began to ring her up.

"Nope, it's to keep my potato salad cold and cups filled for lunch." Annella giggled in response.

"You're the girl Lauren was talking about? The one with the food van." Neal asked as Annella pulled out her debit card.

"That's me. Annella Grace." Annella held out her hand.

"Neal Schwartz," he said as he shook her hand.

"Nice to meet you, Neal." Annella said grabbing a box of her snack from the rack below her.

"Likewise. Where are you going to be set up?" Neal had finished ringing her up, and Annella swiped her debit card.

"I'll be at the picnic area across from the clinic and police station. I'll be there from eleven to whenever the food runs out or four o'clock, whichever comes first."

Neal handed her the receipt for her ice. "That's perfect. I get off at one, so I'll make sure to come get a plate."

Annella put her debit card back in her purse and picked up the first two bags of ice. "Here, let me help you." Neal came around the counter and grabbed the other three bags.

"Thanks. I appreciate the help."

"That's a lot of purple," Neal said as they walked outside and he saw her van.

"Yeah, it's my favorite color and I thought it would make me noticeable." Annella stepped into the back of the van, and Neal handed her the ice to dump into the waiting coolers.

"I gotta get back inside, but I'll be by later." Neal waved, turning to go back to work as Annella closed the back doors and got back into the driver's seat.

She texted Lauren: *Thanks for spreading the word.* Annella saw the three dots pop up, so she waited to read Lauren's response.

You're welcome! Good luck today! I'll see you later!

Annella started the van and thanked modern technology for the gift of air conditioning as she backed out and drove to her spot for the day. It was the perfect place to be, cheap, already set up with tables, shade, and a view down at the lake in the park. She thought back to her time in the full, enclosed, loud kitchen she had worked in previously and breathed a sigh of happiness.

Gone were the days of her boss yelling at her, kitchen staff running over each other, and the smells of sweaty bodies. Now she delighted in the sounds of the birds chirping, the wide open, beautiful, sunny sky, and the smell of the wildflowers blooming around the picnic area.

She set to the rest of her checklist and quickly had her service tables set up and covered in her signature color cloths with covered pans of meat, the dispensers of tea, lemonade, and water, to-go containers and glasses, and a bright yellow basket with her cookies.

She had the cold items in coolers at the very back of the van, so she didn't have to bend over a million times throughout the day. Annella knew she might be criticized for her lack of options, but it was the first day, and her food choices were delicious, so they could like it or leave it. She would take the critiques and adjust where needed later.

She pulled out her phone and took photos of her setup, the lake view, and a fun selfie, and posted them to her social media account and website with the caption that she was ready for hungry customers.

Not even a full minute later, she had alerts that Lauren and Ginny had shared her post and commented that they would be coming later for lunch. Those two knew almost everyone in Green Lake, so she was grateful for their share.

Annella paced behind her set up and checked her phone for the fifth time—11:25. Twenty-five minutes and not a single customer. She started to panic and doubt herself when she heard a car. She walked back to the center of the table, but the blue sedan kept going. She pulled out her camp chair that matched everything purple and sat down to breathe and wait.

It was 11:30, and still no customers. Annella was contemplating packing up and donating the food to the teachers for teacher appreciation week. She could drop Cal's free plate at the station, and Neal's to him at the store on her way to the school. She was scrolling through her phone, looking at people who were having a better day than she was, when she heard another car.

She didn't bother looking up, figuring that it was just another person driving by, but the sound of gravel under tires drew her attention to the gray minivan pulling in. She hopped out of her chair to greet Lauren and Ginny.

"Hey, girls!" Annella waved, excited to finally have customers and to see that they were friends.

Lauren stepped around the table and hugged Annella.

"Thanks, I needed that," Annella told her letting go and turning back to the table and Ginny on the other side. "I was about to give up and donate all of this to the hungry teachers when you pulled up."

Annella pulled on her purple latex gloves and picked up a plate.

"Why would you do that? Everything smells amazing, and I can't wait to eat!" Ginny said glancing at Annella's menu.

"These are the first plates I've sold all day. I started overthinking it—maybe I'm in a bad spot, or maybe people are too into their own lunch routines and don't want to take a chance on new food."

"Honey, deep breath," Lauren told her and led Annella through some deep inhales. "It's still early. Most people here wait until right at noon to eat."

Annella exhaled for a count of four and gave Lauren a tentative smile.

"I hope you're right. I can't afford today to be a huge failure. Little failure, sure, but not a huge one."

"Well, we're here to get you started," Ginny said, rubbing her hands together in anticipation of her lunch.

"Thanks, Ginny. Now, what will you have?"

Ginny looked again at Annella's teal chalkboard. She couldn't find purple, and she didn't have time to paint it.

"Sausage wrap with potato salad, cheesy chips, and lemonade. Please" Ginny responded pulling her wallet out of her purse.

"That sounds great. Make it two," Lauren said, pulling out her wallet and motioning for Ginny to put hers away.

Annella fixed their orders and handed the boxes to Ginny. She took them and went to sit at a picnic table that Annella had already covered in purple plastic tablecloths.

"I feel weird taking your money. I didn't realize that it was going to feel different serving my friends." She pulled off her gloves so she didn't get the tangy sauce all over the bills Lauren was handing her.

"You shouldn't feel weird about taking my money or anyone else's. Now take this, and here's your tip." Lauren said patting her hand when Annella tried to giver her the change.

"You're going to make me cry. I'm going to have to frame one of these dollars as my first food van dollar and hang it next to my first catering dollar." Annella sniffed and rubbed her nose looking up to keep the tears away.

"You earned it, and I hope your day picks up. I'll come say bye before we go." Lauren picked up the Styrofoam cups and headed towards the table where Ginny had their plates waiting.

Annella looked over and watched them both take pictures of their food before eating. Fingers clicked away, and a few seconds later, Annella's phone dinged that she had been mentioned in posts.

Annella went into the van to pull out the shirt for Lauren that she had washed so she wouldn't forget to give it to her. When she came back out, there were three nurses in black scrubs waiting for her. They greeted her as she stepped down from the van and put on fresh gloves.

"Hey! Welcome to Grace Squared Food Van. I'm Annella Grace. What can I get for you?"

"I'm Mitch," said Nurse One. He was about Annella's height with curly, dark brown hair, tan skin, and dark green eyes. "I'll have a chopped sandwich with plain chips, potato salad, and water, please."

Annella handed him his order and used her phone to swipe his debit card.

Annella went back to the other end of the table to help Nurse Two. She was five foot with red hair and freckles. "I'll have a half-pound brisket plate with cheesy chips and sweet tea, please."

Annella made her plate and swiped her card before going back to help nurse number three.

"Hey! I'm Abigail. Can I please get the two-meat plate with sliced brisket and sausage, potato salad, sour cream chips, and lemonade?" Abigail was a touch shorter than Annella, with raven black hair and island-tanned skin.

She handed Abigail her plate and told them to make sure they grabbed cookies before they went back to work. "My way of saying thanks to my customers." They grabbed their cookies and walked back to the clinic.

—∞—

Business really picked up after the nurses left, and Annella was so glad everyone was patient with her as she prepped food and drinks, took payment, and chatted with what she felt was most of Green Lake. She said goodbye to Lauren and Ginny when they came to get the shirt and their cookies.

"See, I told you it would pick up," Lauren said, stealing a side hug.

"Thank you for tagging me. You started the trend. That shirt from the other day is clean right there," Annella said pointing as she prepped a chopped sandwich.

"You deserve this and more. I'll talk to you later." Lauren picked up the shirt and walked to the van to join Ginny, giving Annella one final thumbs-up before they drove off.

Annella lost track of the time and how many people she served by the time the crowd thinned out. She only knew it was after one when she served Neal his sausage wrap, plain chips, and sweet tea. She knocked a few dollars off his meal to say thanks for the help with the ice, which he added to her tip, and she gave him two cookies before he left.

—∞—

Max and Cal were having a slow morning. They were driving around their assigned beat, looking for anything unlawful. They only found an abandoned truck that they marked for towing.

"I'm glad it's easy today, I'm so sore," Cal told Max from the driver's seat.

Max glared at him. "You know you just jinxed us, right?" Max kicked back in his seat. You were never supposed to say the shift was easy or slow.

They were backed into a cove of trees that they called "Max's mile" to wait for any unsuspecting speeders. This was the best spot for waiting on the edge of town so people either sped up too early or slowed down too late. Drivers always just assumed once they left the town, they could go however fast they wanted.

Max and Cal had issued many tickets in this stretch of highway, so it was only a matter of time before they caught someone today.

"I know we won't be pulling Annella over right now. Lauren shared her post about being set up for her first day with the food van."

"I suppose that's where you want to have lunch?"

Max sat up and pulled out his phone to look at Lauren's post.

"Absolutely! It's free food. And don't act like you don't want to see her again," Cal teased as a bright yellow sports car with windows tinted too dark blew past them.

"Damn it, looks like I have to wait for my free meal."

Cal pulled out of their spot as Max hit the lights and siren and called it into the station to tell Danielle to show them in pursuit.

Cal was going 90 MPH, and still, the driver was not pulling over. Max hit the siren again grinding his teeth so hard he thought one would crack. Cal scooted over to the left to ensure that the driver could see the lights in his mirror, but the driver still didn't pull over. Max bumped the siren a third time, and finally, Cal was gaining on the car.

After two miles, the speeder finally pulled over and stopped. Max was bouncing his legs in anger, about to get out of the car, when Cal pointed at him and said, "Let me work this. You stay here and keep Danielle updated."

"Fine," he grumbled. "But don't let him go."

Cal stepped out of the cruiser and walked up to the driver's window, which was still annoyingly up and tinted too dark to be legal. He tapped on the window, and the driver finally lowered it.

"License, insurance, and proof of registration," Cal told the kid- maybe nineteen if he had to guess.

"Hello, officer, of course. Here you go." He flashed his bleach white teeth, charm and entitlement oozing out of him.

"The reasons I've stopped you are your speed, the tint on your windows, and your failure to pull over. Is there an emergency that requires immediate attention?" Cal was going to give the kid a chance first, unlike Max, who would've already had him in cuffs in the cruiser.

He could hear the wheels turning in the boy's head, trying to come up with something, but in the end, he said, "No, sir. I just didn't think any cops would be out here."

At least he had manners, Cal thought.

Cal looked at his documents and made sure they were valid. "Okay, Connor, you sit tight while I go run your information. I'll be right back."

Cal could see the anger still on Max's face as he walked back to the car. This kid is screwed, Cal thought as he opened the door and climbed inside.

"What the hell was his problem?" Max screamed before Cal could even close the door.

"Young kid, new car, if I had to guess," Cal said, typing Connor's details into the computer.

"He still should know better," Max fumed. "No other hits on his license."

Cal looked over to Max. "Are you sure we can't just give him tickets for speeding and window tint and go to lunch?"

"He was going more than twenty-five miles over, so that's reckless driving. He resisted pulling over, so that's evading. His windows were too dark for us to see what he was doing. He's got a trifecta. No way is he just getting tickets."

"You're the boss," Cal said opening the door to go tell Connor the bad news.

"But you're doing the paperwork when we get to the station."

"Alright, just go get the kid off the street." Max picked up the radio to tell Danielle that they were bringing in the kid for booking.

Cal hung his head, closed the door, and walked back to Connor's window. "Here are your documents back," Cal told him. Connor took the papers and put them away, looking smug. Connor was just finishing putting his ID back in his wallet when Cal said, "I'm going to need you to cut the engine and step out of the car."

He reached for his handcuffs causing Connor to drop his wallet to the floor. "What are those for?" Connor squeaked.

"People don't get arrested for speeding. This is a joke, right?" Connor's face turned white and sweat started to bead on his forehead.

"No joke. You were going more than twenty-five miles over the posted speed limit with no emergency. That's considered reckless driving, and I have to take you in." Cal reached for the door handle to open it himself, but Connor jerked it back closed.

"You can't take me in. Write whatever tickets you need to, but please let me go. My parents are going to freak if I call them from jail." Connor still had the car running and tightened his hands on the steering wheel.

"I know what you're thinking, and that's going to make this even worse for you. Just cut the engine, get out of the car, and come with me," Cal told him, watching his hands carefully. Connor debated his options for another half a minute before lowering his platinum blond head and turning the car off.

"Bring your wallet and keys," Cal told him as he stepped out of the car. "Turn around and place your hands behind your back." Cal thought Connor was about to cry as he recited his Miranda Rights and placed the cuffs on him.

"I'm going to give you a quick pat down before we get in the cruiser. Do you have anything dangerous on you?"

Cal moved Connor to the rear of the car and had Connor spread his legs a bit wider.

"No sir," Connor replied with a sniffle.

Cal performed the pat down and walked Connor back to the car and placed him inside. Cal looked at Max and judged him calm enough now that Connor was no longer driving.

"I'm going to put his tow tag on, be nice." Max's only reply was a sarcastic-looking smile. Cal came back and got in to drive Connor to the station. The good thing was Annella was set up just across the highway, so after they dealt with Connor, he could still get his free lunch.

Cal pulled into his parking spot out front of the station and checked to make sure Annella hadn't left yet before opening Connor's door and helping him out. "Make this quick," he said to Max as he handed Connor over and followed the two inside.

Cal left Max and Connor at the booking desk and headed to chat with Danielle while he waited for Max. "I'm seriously going to be in so much trouble," Connor said after Max uncuffed him for his fingerprints. "Maybe you'll think about this before you endanger your life and the lives of others again," Max said as he started filling out the paperwork. Once he had Connor in custody, he went to find Cal so they could go get lunch.

He found him at Danielle's desk, retelling the arrest, making it sound like they were in an action movie.

"Somebody should give you a trophy for that performance. Hey Danielle," Max said to the pair from his spot, leaning against the wall.

"You seem more settled than the last time I heard your voice," she said to Max.

"I am, now that 'lead foot' is locked up. You ready for lunch?" Cal pushed off Danielle's desk.

"Are y'all going across the street to get lunch?" Danielle asked. "If I give you some money, will you please bring me a plate with sausage, potato salad, cheesy chips, and lemonade?"

"I will, but keep your money. It's on me."

Cal gaped at Danielle. "He wouldn't even bring me a plate when Annella was giving them away. How do you do it?"

"I'm cuter," was all Danielle said in response. "You're eating for free today, so stop complaining."

Max pushed off the wall and turned to walk out of the station. Cal winked at Danielle and followed Max, still gripping that Danielle was getting free lunch.

Annella had just sat down from serving Neal and was drinking some water and snacking on a piece of sausage when she heard footsteps and looked up to see Max and Cal walking across her lot. She stood up and put on a new pair of gloves as they reached her serving table.

"Hey, Cal." She smiled at him. The look she gave Max was not as polite. "Officer Thorne." She nodded.

"Hey, Annella," Cal said cheerfully while Max waved as he looked over her menu. "How's it going? We meant to get here sooner, but we had an exciting chase. This kid was speeding and wasn't pulling over. I thought we were about to get to call in a high-speed pursuit, but he finally stopped."

"It's going great! The lunch rush was fun, and now it's just a few customers here and there. That's crazy about the chase. Did you give him a ticket?" she asked Max.

"Nope. Put him in a holding cell to wait for his parents." Max said, still not looking up.

"That poor kid. You really don't like people speeding, do you?"

"Nope."

Max's monosyllabic answers grated on her nerves, so she turned back to Cal who was bouncing with excitement to order his free lunch.

"I'll have a chopped sandwich and two sausage links, potato salad, barbeque chips, and a sweet tea, please. If that's too much for a free lunch, Max will cover the rest." Max shot daggers at Cal with his look.

"It's totally fine," Annella told him as she fixed his order and listened to more of the chase story feeling bad for the kid ending up in jail.

Max just stood there, arms crossed, rolling his eyes as Cal embellished the story. "Make sure you get two cookies for keeping our streets safe," Annella told Cal as she went back to help Max. "Are you going to speak in long enough sentences to order your food, or do I have to guess?" Annella didn't feel guilty for being feisty to Max thinking back to his smug expression as he wrote her ticket.

"Let me have two plates with sausage, potato salad, cheesy chips, lemonade, and tea."

"Wow! He speaks," she joked and moved to make his plates. Max reached for his wallet.

"I ought to charge you double now that I have a ticket to pay." Annella laughed, and something inside of Max shifted at the melodious, lilting sound.

"You could, or you could thank me for passing your information to my bother that needs a caterer for his wedding. He'll probably be calling you soon."

The shock of him doing something nice for her showed on her face and now she felt a little bad for being feisty. Max only swiped his card on her phone and left her a decent tip. Cal had already opened one of his cookies and moaned at the light, sugary texture.

"These are amazing."

"Thanks. Don't tell anyone, but they are break and bake," Annella told Cal.

"Your secret is safe with me." Max put his wallet back in his pocket and looked at the boxes and drinks, trying to figure out how to carry everything.

"Hang on. I think I have a plastic bag in the van that will help you carry everything."

Annella climbed around the coolers and came back out with a white bag adorned with a smiley face. She bagged up Max's containers, and he looped the handles around his wrist. Annella made a mental note to price more bags later. Max picked up the drinks and told Annella thanks, turning around to go to the station.

"Have a nice day, Officer Thorne," Annella said, causing Max to flinch. "Bye, Cal," she said before she took off her gloves and sat back down.

—◁▱▷—

The rest of the afternoon was slow. The doctor from the clinic came over with the receptionist and two more officers.

At 3:00, Annella had gone for forty-five minutes with no customers, so she decided to clean up and head home. She bagged up all her trash and loaded the serving pans, tables, and chalkboard into the back of the van.

Annella looked around the space to make sure she didn't miss anything and nodded off the next thing on her list—have a kick-ass first day. She got into the van and started it, turning the AC to max.

She was celebrating her success, dance-driving to the country hits on her way home and not paying attention to her speed. Something in her rearview caught her eye, forcing her to look down and notice that she was once again speeding in Green Lake and getting pulled over.

You've got to be kidding me, she thought as she pulled over and got ready to receive her second ticket in forty-eight hours. She had her window down, waiting, hoping that it was Cal and not Max who would come to the window. Maybe Cal would let her go with a warning.

—m—

Max was grinning from ear to ear when he pulled in behind Annella. "She makes it too easy," he said to Cal as he put the cruiser in park and got out. He got to the window, and she already had her documents hanging out for him.

"If I didn't know any better, I'd say you're following me on purpose, Officer Thorne."

"Don't flatter yourself. Just doing my job," Max said as he took her documents from her. "It's not my fault you're easy to see in the orchid on wheels."

"I *am* trying to be noticed, so I guess it's working."

"It's working, but not in a good way. If you insist on speeding, I suggest a vehicle that's more inconspicuous."

"Like that would help with Speed Trap Thorne lurking around every bend in the road. You'd still find me and give me a ticket."

"You're right about that. I'll be right back."

"Ugh!" Annella ran her hands through her hair and leaned her head back on the headrest to wait for Max.

Annella texted Lauren that she got pulled over, *again*, and was getting another speeding ticket. Lauren's response was an undesired laughing emoji.

She texted Lauren back: *I guess I should have listened to you harder.*

"Have you ever tried putting a block under your gas pedal?" Max ripped the paper from his ticket book and handed it to Annella with her license and insurance card.

Annella sneered at Max and jerked the paperwork from his hand. "Have you ever thought about taking a chill pill on people that are *barely* speeding?"

"Not going to happen." Max responded vehemently. "Now slow down and have a good day."

"You made sure that good part of my day was over, Officer Thorne." Annella threw her documents into the passenger seat and slowly pulled back onto the highway.

Max flinched again at her farewell annoyed that she never used his first name like she did with Cal.

Max got into the cruiser, slamming his door and running a hand over his face. "I've never seen a girl get under your skin so bad."

Cal grinned at the aggravation on Max's face. "I don't know why she bothers me so much, but I've got to stop being so rude before she reports me to the Chief."

Max put the car in drive and made the block before heading back to the station to end their shift. "It's because you like her, and you don't want to like anyone."

"Shut up, Cal." Cal sat back and closed his eyes, remaining quiet the rest of the way back to the station.

Chapter

8

Life settled into a quiet routine. Annella's food van was considered the hot spot to have lunch, and she was thrilled. She either sold out of food or had very little left at the end of each day.

She had been out with Travis once more but kept finding reasons to avoid him and ended the date early. He kept texting her incessantly, but all she could muster up were one word or very short answers. He was past annoying, and she was about to ghost him if he didn't let up. All he did was talk shit about Max giving her two tickets no matter how much she insisted it was fine. Cody had called, as Max said he would, to ask about hiring her for their wedding since they didn't have any other options. Annella tried not to take that part personally and they agreed on a date to taste the menu they discussed.

She added the appointment to her calendar immediately, curious to find out if the younger Thorne brother was as cranky as the older. Every night, she went to bed exhausted, and every morning, she woke up excited to do it again.

Today was the perfect day for outside food, Annella thought as she set up for her day. The temperature was comfortable, and the clouds in the sky kept the sun dimmed enough that she left her shades in her purse.

Since her first day, she had adjusted her times to get set up by 11:30 instead of 11:00. It was working perfectly since, typically, her earliest customers were tellers from the bank at around 11:40 each day.

Annella was just adjusting the cold coolers in the back of the van when she heard footsteps over the gravel parking lot. She turned around with a smile ready to greet her first customer of the day.

"Hey, Annella!" Dr. Sullivan said coming up the last five feet of the parking lot, bubbling with excitement. She was always upbeat and perky, which made Annella understand why the people of Green Lake loved her as their general practitioner. She had the ability to put you at ease when you talked to her with her dazzling smile and kind eyes. Today she was dressed in sage green scrubs that made her green eyes pop with her light brown hair curled up in a high ponytail.

"Hey, Dr. Sullivan. What can I get you?"

"Lunch for my staff, please. Once a month, I treat them, so I wanted to get here before I got busy. Not that the clinic is the ER in Pure Springs, but the afternoons are always crazier than the mornings."

"You are such a nice boss." Annella pulled on her purple gloves and waited for the order.

"It's the least I can do for all their hard work. They are the best batch of nurses I've worked with. Can you fix up everything on this list for me, please?" She handed Annella a prescription pad with the list of food she needed. "It was the only paper I could find handy." She laughed as Annella took it and began pulling out to-go containers.

"Not a problem. I'm just glad it's not prescription handwriting, or this might take a bit longer." Dr. Sullivan laughed with Annella.

"While you're working on that I wanted to ask your availability to prep Abigail's birthday lunch. It's next Monday so if it's too late I understand. I completely dropped the ball on lining you up earlier, and I'm sorry. It's not a large thing, and you won't even have to stay and serve or anything. I wanted to do a taco bar set up for the staff, Abigail's parents, and boyfriend."

Annella finished prepping the plates with everything and moved on to get the drinks ready. "That's not a problem at all. As soon as I get these drinks ready, I'll put it on my calendar and get you a price. What are you wanting to have on the taco bar?"

Annella bagged up the food in her pretty new purple bags and tossed in everyone's cookies, plus a few extra. She looked at all the doctor was going to have to carry and got into the back of the van for an empty box and her tablet.

She came back and put everything in the empty silverware box she found and put the event on the calendar. "Nothing crazy. Brisket and shredded chicken tacos, rice, beans, sweet tea, and lemonade? Is that too much on such short notice?"

"Of course not! I'll throw in some chips and salsa, too."

"That would be perfect. Now, about the cake."

Annella threw her hands up in the time-out motion at the mention of hard baking. "I'm touched that you think I can bake, but my talents do not extend to cakes."

Dr. Sullivan laughed again and told her not to worry, that she would order the cake from The Buttered Biscuit. "I'll pick the cake up on my way over on Monday at least."

"I would appreciate that."

Annella gave her a price for the party, and she told Annella to add it to her lunch total. She swiped the doctor's card and handed over her phone to sign.

"Enjoy your lunch," Annella said, taking back her phone.

"We will. Thanks for saving me with Abigail's party."

Annella made sure that Dr. Sullivan made it back into the clinic without dropping anything, then went back to arranging the coolers before her lunch rush hit. She had learned that the people of Green Lake were a rather predictable bunch in both what they ate and when they ate it.

The only group she really couldn't time was the police officers. They showed up anywhere between opening and closing. Hazard of the job, one deputy told her when she asked about it.

It must have been a slow day for the police force of Green Lake because she saw all the officers by 1:30. Max and Cal were the last two that came over. "Hey, Cal, Officer Thorne."

"Hi, Annella," Cal said with his usual happy smile.

"Hi," was all Max ever said to her. She rolled her eyes, wondering why he was still so cold to her. She hadn't broken *any* laws lately, so it didn't make any sense.

"How was your morning?" Annella asked, fixing their usual orders.

"Not as exciting as the chase, but we still protected and served the good citizens of Green Lake."

Max hated the way that Cal and Annella chatted like they were old friends almost ignoring him completely.

It must have been the full moon coming up or temporary insanity that had him opening his mouth. "How has your day been, Annella?"

She whipped her head up from scooping potato salad with a confused look on her face aimed at him, her heart twisting in her chest at his friendly tone.

She recovered quickly and schooled her face into a smile. "It's been good! I got contracted to fix a birthday lunch for Abigail on Monday at the clinic so I'll need to grocery shop on Sunday. It's a taco bar setup."

"Will you still serve lunch or do we have to crash Abigail's party?" Cal wanted to know.

Max held his breath waiting for her answer. He didn't know when it happened but seeing her for lunch had become an important part of his day.

"It's not a full catering gig. I only have to drop off food and the cake. You'll still get your lunch and cookies." Annella piled meat and potato salad into Max and Cal's plates then pulled off her gloves and reached for her phone.

Cal held out his hand with his debit card extended.

Annella gaped at him equally as shocked as she was to hear Max ask about her day. "Did you lose a bet?" Annella swiped his card and handed Cal her phone to sign.

"Ha, no, lost a coin toss," he laughed scribbling something that did not look like any of the letters in Cal Roberts on her phone.

"Do you guys ever settle anything in a normal way?" Annella pocketed her phone and tidied up her table. "Rock, paper, scissors to see who has to write the ticket. Coin toss to see who pays for lunch. Have you ever liked the same girl? How did you decide who got to date her?"

"That's an easy one. Whoever called dibs," Cal responded.

"I see, and have either of you called dibs on me?" Max's face turned so red it was almost purple and Cal laughed out loud. Annella raised an eyebrow waiting for a response, but neither of them actually answered her and the silence stretched on.

"See you later, Annella." Cal grabbed his bag and headed back across the street.

"Bye, Cal," Annella called after him. She looked at Max, staring at his feet, stalling at picking up his drink. She didn't know what he was waiting for, maybe for his face turn return to its normal color. "Have a nice rest of your day... Max."

He looked up from his boots, the pupils of his eyes dilated in surprise at hearing his name in her voice. He nodded to her, not trusting himself to speak at that moment, and tuned around to join Cal grinning.

"This is an odd look on your face after an encounter with Annella. I like it. I wonder, though, what you would do if I did call dibs on her?"

"Shut up, Cal."

—⟡—

Annella finished her day after serving a couple driving through town the last two helpings of brisket. She cleaned up her serving tables and re-packed the van while they enjoyed their lunch at the picnic table. She sat and waited for them to finish their meal, catching pieces of their conversation while scrolling on her phone. They loved the town and the view of the lake. They even said the food was perfect and that they would have to stop on their way home from vacation for round two.

Annella loved hearing that people enjoyed her food. It was why she decided to pursue culinary arts in the first place. The way food had the power to connect people and create memories was always miraculous to her. BBQ was a passion project for her that she discovered after a solo trip through Texas. Sky cuisine ranged from poached salmon to veggie risotto, so Annella had to perfect her craft outside of the restaurant.

The couple picked up their trash when they were through, and Annella gave them the last of her cookies for the road before they left. She did one last check of the area to make sure everything was in order and left to tell Lauren the good news.

Annella got to the community center for the town meal, bubbling with excitement that only grew once she saw her friend.

"What's your sunshine?"

Lauren grabbed her in the customary hug greeting that only made Annella happier. Annella grabbed a plastic serving apron and some gloves from the supply closet and filled Lauren in on Abigail's birthday lunch and the fact that Max spoke to her for something other than to order his food or write her a ticket.

"The taco bar is going to be amazing and I'm glad you're getting to see Max's nice side." Lauren gave Annella a wink and a coy smile as they walked out of the kitchen.

Annella followed Lauren to the serving line adjusting her apron. "Don't give me that look. It's not like he declared undying love for me, but it will be nice not to feel awkward around him."

Lauren went across the great room to unlock the doors while Annella took up her spot on the service line, ready to give back to her community.

She had gotten to know the regulars in her time helping Lauren and loved that they were so welcoming to her. When she first started helping, she was shy, only serving the food and saying a quick hi.

Now, once they finished serving, she mingled with Lauren. She learned about the people of the town and listened to their stories. Laughed and sometimes cried with them. She couldn't believe that she went from a corporate restaurant to a food van/catering business, but she absolutely loved it. She had friends that felt like family, and a place where she felt like she belonged.

The clouds had cleared, revealing the sun just beginning its descent to the horizon when Lauren and Annella stepped outside. Annella's phone started ringing, and she glanced down, rolling her eyes as she read the name.

"Travis?" Lauren asked, making a face like she smelled two-day-old salmon.

Annella hit the decline button and put her phone back in her pocket. "I've been ignoring him for the last week, but he keeps calling."

Lauren sat on the steps of the building and rested her elbows on her knees. "You're going to have to be very direct with him and tell him to move on."

Annella ran her hand down her face and joined Lauren on the step. "I know. I know. I just keep hoping he'll get the hint to go away."

Lauren turned to Annella with a serious look that Annella didn't normally see on her face. "Travis isn't going to just go away. He's dated every available woman in town but is still a bachelor." There's a reason for that."

Annella pulled her hair tie out wincing as a few hairs came out too and tried to think of being direct with Travis.

Lauren stretched out her slim legs rolling her ankles around. "I can't say that I wanted you to date him, but I was hoping he would be different this time. Sorry, it didn't work out."

Annella digested the information and wondered if everyone included Lauren. Before she could ask Lauren continued.

"Yes, I dated him too. In a town this size it was pretty much a guarantee that it was going to happen."

Lauren laughed at Annella's shocked expression and wondered how long it would be before she gave in and admitted she liked Max. Max had said he would never love again when Brenda Green dumped him to move away after Heather's death. She said she couldn't live in a town or with a man who was so sad all the time, but Annella was getting to him. She knew it in her soul.

Annella texted Travis that she was heading home to shower and sleep, hoping that he wouldn't call twenty more times before she got her goodbye hug from Lauren and slid into the van to go home. She didn't want to go for the hat trick and get her third ticket, so she drove the speed limit the whole way. She backed into the driveway and unloaded the coolers, putting them in the yard to drain the melted ice.

Annella was wheeling her empty coolers up to the porch when she noticed her neighbors, Brock and Olivia, sitting on their porch glider, enjoying the cooler evening. She contemplated going over to visit wondering if she would interrupt them, wondering if they would be upset that she did, but Olivia waved her over and smiled.

The whole time she lived alone in her one-bedroom apartment, she had never once met her neighbors. It was weird but good to be able to wander to her neighbors' house and chat.

Olivia taught home economics at Green Lake High, and Brock was a firefighter.

"Hey, neighbors," Annella greeted as she sat in a white rocker in the corner of the porch.

"Hey, Annella," Olivia said while Brock smiled and waved. "Can I get you a glass of wine?"

"Annella slipped off her flip-flops and crossed her legs underneath her, leaning her head back on the rocker. "Wine would be great, but I can get it." Olivia was already up and heading inside her honey-brown curls bobbing behind her.

"Nope, you stay right there and rest. I've got it."

"How was your day with the van?" Brock asked in his deep voice, itching his large, tan bicep.

"I sold out of everything and didn't get a speeding ticket, so the day was a win in my book."

Brock laughed as Olivia came back with Annella's wine. "You're going to get a building named after you with all the money you're paying in fines." Oliva said as she handed Annella her glass of red wine.

"I wouldn't complain about a building dedication, but I'm hoping two tickets is my limit."

Annella took a sip of her wine and closed her eyes in appreciation of the cool sweetness on her tongue.

"How's your off-rotation going?" she asked Brock.

"Pretty good. Olivia has had me busy with my honey-do list, but nothing has been too hard."

Annella breathed in the floral scent of Olivia's hibiscus flowers letting the knots unkink from her shoulders. "That's good. Are you ready for summer break?" She asked Oliva, taking another sip of her wine.

"Absolutely!" Olivia drank more of her wine while Annella filled them in on Abigail's birthday lunch and Cody and Sadie's wedding tasting.

"A taco bar sounds delicious, and I know Abigail will love that. Cody and Sadie will love your food, too. That's going to be a big event. They know everyone in town, so pretty much everyone will be there."

Annella finished her wine and stood up, heading to put her glass away. Olivia took it from her and put it on the table. "Don't worry about It." You go home and get some sleep."

Annella stepped down from the porch. "Goodnight. Talk to you guys later."

She pulled her coolers up the steps as she went inside and showered off her day, then curled up with her book on the couch. She must have fallen asleep because her phone woke her up an hour later with a message from Travis. Dinner or lunch tomorrow? She rolled her neck before responding that she had a full day of grocery shopping and prep work to do.

Travis didn't respond, and Annella didn't know if that was a good or bad sign after what Lauren had told her earlier. She decided she didn't care and went upstairs to bed.

Chapter

9

No matter how much he tried Max could not sleep late. Even in his younger days when he would tie one on the night before and stay up late his body still woke up early, maybe hungover, but still early.

He laid on the soft mattress, the cool sheets soft beneath his bare chest, looking at the ceiling thinking of a certain auburn-haired chef and how he had been nicer to her yesterday confused as to why he had done that.

Max blew out his breath and swung his legs over his bed kicking a black dress uniform shoe out of his way to stand up. He used his typical smell test to find clothes he deemed good enough to wear on a run, dressed, and headed for the park. Maybe a long run would clear Annella out of his head.

—∞—

Annella woke up, smiled, and stretched her arms over her head. Her Egyptian cotton sheet pooled at her waist as she stretched down to her toes. It was finally Sunday, and she was ready for a day off. Sure, she had to hit the grocery store, do a load of laundry, and wash and straighten up the van, but she didn't mind.

She slipped out of bed and grabbed her phone on her way to the bathroom, groaning as she unlocked the screen and saw three missed messages from Travis.

Why are you blowing me off? I know my parents didn't hire you, but you don't have to be a petty bitch about it. You're going to want to stay in my good graces, or life can get more difficult for you.

She closed her text app without responding and put on music to drown out his voice in her head while she got ready to head to the grocery store. She decided to skip her usual Sunday brunch and picked up a banana on her way out of the house, trying not to let Travis's messages stay in her head. The more she tried not to think about them, the more she did.

—⚋—

Annella had been ignoring him lately. He had been ghosted before, so he was familiar with the process. She was hoping that with time, he would just go away, but that wasn't going to happen. Fucking Thorne. She talked a big game about hating him for giving her the tickets, but she would fall for him eventually. They all fell for Max, leaving him behind.

In a town the size of Green Lake, all the guys chased the same girls, but Max or Cal were always the ones the girls wanted. Cal had a different girl every week, and Max left a string of broken hearts when he took up with Brenda seriously.

He had started following Annella after she blew off their last date. Max wasn't going to win this time.

Normally, he followed her on her run or watched her smile at her customers while she wasn't thinking about him, but today, he followed her to the grocery store.

—⚋—

Annella wandered down the spice aisle of the only grocery store in Green Lake. It was small, but she never found it lacking the ingredients she needed, and if she got there early enough, the place was mostly hers. Travis's threatening messages were on a loop in her head while searching for cumin when she came to a sudden stop.

She turned her head from the spices to see what she bumped into, hoping no one saw her but saw that it wasn't a what she ran into, but a who. A very tall who with soft chestnut hair.

Max turned around with his hands on his hips, nostrils flaring in anger. She opened her mouth to apologize, but Max spoke first. "Are you fit to operate anything with wheels?"

Annella forgot all about the apology as heat flooded her face. "I've had a perfect driving record until I moved to a town with Captain Speed Monitor."

"It's Lieutenant Speed Monitor, and Green Lake is one of the safest towns because of it." Max took a step back to remove the cart from his leg and really looked at Annella, his cop sense tingling. *Something is off* he thought.

"Whatever you say, Officer Thorne. Are you going to ticket me for failure to stop?"

Max cringed that he was back to being Officer Thorne to her instead of Max. He blew out an aggravated breath.

Annella leaned her elbows on her shopping cart, offering Max a generous view of her cleavage in her low-cut, white tank top. Max held his hands out, indicating his black basketball shorts and faded gray T-shirt.

"I left my ticket book at the station, so I'm going to let you go with a warning this time."

"Oh wow! You do know the word warning," Annella said, her tone still *off* to Max.

He noted the strained look on her face despite the smirk on her mouth, and he felt a piece of his heart snap to attention wanting to figure out why she looked like that.

"Is everything alright?" He asked in a gentler tone, "I thought we had moved past Officer Thorne."

"Everything is fine." She tightened her hair tie, and a stray curl slipped out. She tipped her head back, blowing it out of her face. "Maybe it's not fine. I thought ignoring Travis would make him go away, but he will not stop texting and calling. I guess I'm going to have to spell it out for him to leave me alone." Annella didn't know why she told Max about Travis, but his genuine concern prompted her to open up. She stood up and reached for the cumin that she needed and placed it in her basket.

Max's eyes went wide, and he started scanning her for injuries. "Did he hurt you? Threaten you somehow? Is he harassing you?"

Annella was baffled at the intensity of his question, and the look in his eyes.

She responded quickly, shaking her head "No. Yes. On the verge of."

Max relaxed, slightly, hearing that she was unharmed, "How did he threaten you?"

Annella tucked that curl behind her ear, trying to keep her composure and not be angry at Max for something he didn't do. "I woke up to missed text messages—" Annella started to respond.

"Show me," Max cut her off before she could say more.

She reached into her bright purple bag for her phone, unlocked it and handed it to Max with Travis's text messages pulled up.

"It's not a big deal, Max. I'm just going to send him one final message saying get lost, and that will be it."

Max read the messages twice, and his face turned the color of the Roma tomatoes in her cart. "You can make an official report about this if you want to." Max handed her the phone back, and she slipped it back into her purse.

"Thanks, I'll keep that in mind." Thoughts flooded through her head. *Do I really want to mess with that? Would reporting it set Travis off more?*

Annella's thoughts were spiraling until Max picked up a bottle of seasoning that was salt and pepper mixed.

The melodic sound of Annella's laugh eased the fist that was holding his heart too tight. "Something funny, Annella?" Max raised his eyebrow, challenging her to comment on the bottle in his hand."

She stopped laughing at him long enough to say, "Your choice of seasonings, Max. Very bachelor of you."

Max looked at the bottle of black and white grains and back at her happy that Officer Thorne had been dropped. "What? It's working smarter, not harder. Two spices. One bottle. No brainer."

Annella was still smiling at him as he went to put it in his cart. "It's easier, sure, but your food won't be as good as it could be. You are at the mercy of the bottle. Your food is probably going to be either too salty or too peppery. With separate bottles, you control exactly how much of each spice you use, making your dish much more balanced in flavor."

Max continued to place the bottle in his cart, Annella's mouth dropped open, and she stopped breathing. Max chuckled at the look on her face and the stillness of her chest. "Breathe, Annella. I'll put it back."

Annella heaved in a breath. "I thought I was going to have to remove that from your hand myself."

Max looked at her and down at himself, thinking of the way her body would feel on his as she tried. He was a bit sad to put it back.

"Now that we have that settled, I suggest actual salt and pepper grinders. So much better." Annella picked up two glass bottles with built-in grinders and handed them to Max.

"You don't mess around with your spices, do you?" Max took the bottles and put them in the basket.

"Food isn't just my job. It's my life. Everything makes sense when I'm in the kitchen."

Max could understand that. It was how he felt about police work and protecting the citizens of Green Lake.

Annella felt the tension from Travis's text messages, and the cart crash dissipate the longer they talked. She found that when he wasn't giving her a ticket, she enjoyed talking to Max. They were just starting to talk about the upcoming Muscles for Money event when Max's face hardened, and his body tensed. Annella was curious about the sudden change, but she soon figured it out when Travis's annoying voice sounded behind her.

He was walking down the aisle, his cart full of salad making ingredients she assumed were for the restaurant.

"What the hell, Annella?" Travis said, his voice rising higher on her name, making her cheeks heat with embarrassment. So much for her quick and easy trip to the grocery store. "Is this why you've been blowing me off? You're too busy trying to fuck Thorne?"

Max was about to respond, but Annella was faster.

"Max isn't the reason I stopped responding to you, and I'm not trying to fuck him. All you do is talk shit about him and the tickets he gave me, and I'm tired of hearing it."

Travis seemed to shrink at the ferocity of her voice, but Annella wasn't finished speaking. "It's time for you to set your sights on someone else and leave me alone, Travis." Annella glared at him hoping she said enough to make him get the point.

Travis recovered from his stupor at being talked to that way and looked at Max. "I bet that makes you happy, huh?"

Max smiled at Travis. "More than you know, Ashwood." He looked back to Annella. "Think about what I said earlier. See you for lunch tomorrow."

With that, Max walked off without acknowledging Travis. Annella followed behind him, leaving Travis seething in the spice aisle.

Annella went through the rest of the store looking over her shoulder, waiting for Travis to find her and say something else, but she made it out without further incident. She got into her van and breathed a sigh of relief, heading home.

—◈—

She had just finished blending her salsa when her phone went off with a text from Lauren.

Heard you had an eventful trip to the grocery store. Are you ok?

Annella put the lid on the salsa container before responding: *I don't know why anyone in this town bothers with phones. The Green Lake Grapevine is clearly the superior communication method.* She followed that up with: *I'm fine. Max was there so it wasn't like Travis could do anything stupid.*

Lauren was quick to respond with a winking face and told Annella that she would see her tomorrow. She put her phone down and finished her prep work before having a quick lunch while reading more about her fierce female main character and the dragon shifter she was falling for.

Annella read until she started feeling antsy with the need to move, checked the temperature on her phone to see if she would die of heat stroke if she went for a run right now. Her phone showed a decent temperature, so she headed to the park.

Chapter

10

Annella was having a great Monday! Her briskets came off the grill perfectly, she felt great in her black tights and bright purple catering jacket that she would shed if the weather got too hot. She walked out of her house dragging the cooler of cold items behind her as her perfect day ended.

She stopped, glancing at the scene before her. "Well shit," she said, looking at her van.

She left the cooler where it was and walked over to survey the damage. A front and rear tire had been slashed, and down both sides, painted in bright white, were the words "Chef Whore."

She pulled her phone out of her back pocket and dialed the non-emergency number for the police department, hearing Danielle's calm voice on the other end.

"Green Lake Police Department non-emergency line. How can I help you?"

Annella pinched the bridge of her nose to keep the tears back that were threatening to roll down her cheeks. She would not let the jerk have the satisfaction of making her cry.

"Hey, Danielle. It's Annella. I guess I need to report a vandalism."

She heard Danielle gasp from the other end of the phone. "Oh no, Annella, I'm so sorry. Are you okay?"

Annella was pacing up and down her sidewalk, fury raging within her. "I'm fine, but my van isn't."

She heard Danielle clicking away on her keyboard and then heard her call for an available unit to her address on the radio. Annella smiled that she didn't even have to give her address.

A few seconds later, she heard a deep voice that was beginning to cause her heart to flutter, saying that car seventy-nine was en route to her location. Danielle came back to her, saying that Max and Cal would be there soon.

"Thanks, Danielle."

Annella sat down on her cooler to wait and stew.

"No problem, honey. Do you need me to stay on the line with you until they get there?"

Annella checked her watch to see how behind schedule she was and started thinking about how she was going to pull today off.

"No, I'll be okay. But can you let all the officers know that if they want lunch today, they'll need to come to the house to get it? I'm not letting all this food go to waste. I'll make sure to send a plate with Max and Cal for you."

She could hear Danielle giggle through the phone.

"Aren't you the sweetest. I'll let everyone know. You call me back if you need anything while you are waiting on Max and Cal."

Annella hung up the phone and sent a text to Lauren with a picture of her van, figuring she should tell her best friend before the grapevine did it for her. Two seconds later, she answered the phone without even looking at the caller ID.

"Hey, Lauren."

Lauren didn't even say hi back before she dove right in. "Travis is such an asshole. Just because you gave him the boot, he did this?"

"To be fair, we don't know for sure it was him. Would he really be this petty?" Annella said, loving the support from her friend.

"We know it was him, and yes. He's the equivalent of a two-year-old whose blankie is in the dryer at nap time when he doesn't get his way."

Annella looked at her watch again. There was no way she was going to be able to salvage the birthday lunch. She had walked out of her house with just enough time to get her ice and the cake before she needed to be at the clinic.

As if Lauren could hear her thoughts through the phone, she asked, "What do you need? Large glass of wine? Shoulder to cry on? Travis held down while you punched him repeatedly. But I bet Max beats us to that one."

Annella blew out her breath and bit her bottom lip. She hated asking for help, but she saw no other way to get her day back to an even scale.

"I hate to ask, but is there any way you can come get the food, grab the cake, and set up Abigail's birthday lunch? I'll split the commission with you for saving my ass."

She could hear Lauren walking and then telling Ginny where she was going.

"I'll be there in eight minutes. No, you're not splitting the commission with me. This is what friends are for."

"Thanks, Lauren. I'll call Dr. Sullivan and tell her of the change of plans."

Annella scrolled through the contract on her phone and called Dr. Sullivan hoping that the cheerful nature she always showed would be there now. The good doctor's voice came on after two rings, "Hi Annella. Are you here already?"

"Hi Dr. Sullivan. No, I'm not there yet, and I won't be able to make it personally. I'm so sorry."

Annella heard the exasperated huff come from the other side of the phone and hurried on. "My van was vandalized last night. Someone painted the sides with inappropriate language and punctured two of my tires so I can't drive it."

"I'm sorry about that Annella. I can see about sending someone to get the food and cake."

Annella released her own breath knowing that Dr. Sullivan wasn't super upset with her. "Thanks, but Lauren is on her way to my house to pick up the food. She'll stop and get the cake as well. Lunch will only be a few minutes late. I'll discount the total remaining balance for the inconvenience."

"You'll do no such thing. We agreed to a price and this situation is out of your control." Dr. Sullivan reassured her. "You just let me know if I can do anything to help."

"Thanks so much for being so understanding. Max and Cal are pulling up now, so I'll speak to you soon."

Annella heard Dr. Sullivan say goodbye as she pulled the phone away from her ear. Max and Cal pulled up with the lights flashing. It was strange, but they were a comforting sight when she wasn't seeing them in her rear-view mirror.

Cal got out of the driver's side without his normal happy smile and came around the front of the SUV. "Hey, Annella."

She raised her hand in a wave. "Hey, Cal. Thanks for getting her so quickly."

Annella looked behind him as Max stepped out of the passenger seat, jaw clenched, stern cop face firmly on display.

There was no sign of the easy-going, smiling Max she bumped into yesterday. This Max stalked toward her with a fire in his eyes that frightened her and excited her at the same time.

"Hey, Max," she said.

"Are you okay?" He surveyed her, the muscles in his jaw releasing when he saw no visible injuries. Annella turned and looked back at her van.

"I'm fine, but the van's another story."

Max sent Cal to take photos of the damage, and he pulled out a notebook from his back pocket to write down whatever information he was going to need.

"What time did you last see your van yesterday?"

Annella closed her eyes, thinking back to what time she got home from her run at the park. "About four o'clock."

She told him about the run and coming home to find it perfectly fine. Max wrote as she talked so that he didn't do something stupid like go punch Travis in the mouth.

"And you didn't see anything wrong or off at that time? No cars on the street that aren't usually here?"

Annella was about to answer when she heard a horn beep twice and looked up to see Lauren pulling up. She got out of her car and ran over to Annella sweeping her up into a big hug. Lauren stepped to Annella's side, keeping her arm around her, and looked at Max.

"Hey, Max," Lauren said.

Max was jealous of her touching Annella so casually. He wanted to be the one to comfort her. Wanted it to be his arm she was protected under. "Lauren, what are you doing here?"

Annella leaned her head on Lauren's shoulder and smelled her friend's lemon-scented hair.

"I asked her to come get the food for Abigail's party since I can't drive. I can't cancel and miss out on the money from the party. It will only take a minute to get the food loaded, and then we can get back to your questions."

Max tucked his notebook into the back pocket of his tan uniform pants as the two headed inside.

Annella started talking, giving Lauren all the instructions that Dr. Sullivan had passed on to her. Lauren asked her three more times if she was okay and what she was going to do about her lunch crowd.

"Ginny is good at the shop. If you need me to set up and work the lunch rush at the picnic area I can."

Annella put her box of chips on the front floorboard as Lauren put the meat and taco shells in the back. "Thanks, but I'm just going to set up and serve lunch from here. I'm going to make a post here in a minute. Danielle is telling all the officers, and the clinic staff will be eating tacos, so they won't miss me being right across the street."

They walked back into the house and grabbed the cooler with the vegetables, salsa, and sour cream. They were coming back out when Lauren said, "I would caution against that saying that people don't need to know where you live, but everyone already knows. You text me if you need me to come help."

Annella pulled Lauren into a hug after they had everything loaded into the car. "Thanks, Lauren. You are the best. Can you make a post about lunch being here today? I know your reach is farther than mine with the people."

Lauren gave her one last squeeze. "Absolutely!"

With that, she jumped in the car and waved, heading for the clinic.

Annella went over to where Max and Cal were talking at the back of the van. She put her hands on her hips and tipped her head back, feeling the warm sun on her face. The sent of Max's cedarwood soap mixing with her roses was a comfort to her frazzled emotions.

"No," she said.

Max and Cal looked at each other, wondering what she was saying no to.

"No, what?" Max asked, pulling his notebook back out.

She brought her head down, opening her eyes. "You asked earlier if I saw anything off or cars that didn't belong, I didn't."

Max wrote that down without taking his eyes from her.

Cal watched Max writing and picked up the questioning trying to take the personal factor out of his tone. "Can you think of anyone that would want to do this to you?"

Annella looked at him and raised an eyebrow. "Just the same person you're already thinking. I know Max told you about the grocery store and texts already."

Cal tried and failed to act like he didn't know what she was talking about, but Annella's snort told him he wasn't fooling her. He started walking down the driveway.

"I'm going to start asking neighbors if they saw anything."

They watched in silence as Cal went to Brock and Olivia's house first. Olivia was at work, but Brock was there. The problem with questioning neighbors in a small town was that everyone answered the questions then wanted the gossip *and* to catch up on life.

Annella turned back to Max who was still staring at her. "Can I get into my van? I need to set up for lunch."

Max's eyes widened in shock. "You're still going to work today?"

She tilted her head at him like she didn't understand his question. "Yes, I'm still going to work today," she snapped. "I don't have the heart to let my food go to waste. I'm also not going to give this jerk-off the satisfaction of costing me a day of profits."

Max held up his hands in surrender. "I got it. Yes, you can get into your van."

Max helped her set up for the lunch crowd while Cal was still making the rounds. "For what it's worth, you're handling this extremely well, and I'm proud of you for not being a crying mess in your bed."

Annella's face brightened with Max's praise. He leaned into the van to pull out a table, the hem of his pants came up enough for her to see his one lime green and one yellow sock. "Isn't there some regulation that says your socks have to match?"

Max set the table down in front of his feet blocking them from her view. "You're in the middle of a mild crisis and you want to talk about my socks?"

"I just don't understand how you can go through life with mismatched socks," Annella said helping him set up the table he was using as a shield.

"My police handbook was conveniently missing guidance on what color my socks had to be. What does it even matter? I'm usually the only one that sees my socks." Annella rolled her eyes at him and opened the cooler with her potato salad. Max was keeping busy putting the silverware in her bright yellow basket trying to replicate how pretty she always made it, but looked up at her when she slammed the lid.

"What's wrong?"

"If I don't get this potato salad on ice soon, I'm going to have to toss it out, or it will make everyone sick."

Max brightened, excited that this was something he could fix for her now.

"How much ice do you need?"

"You don't have to do that. I'll figure it out. I'm sure you have something more pressing to do."

Max looked into her eyes seeing the stress she wasn't conveying to anyone, he admired her strength. "Look, it's going to take Cal a while to do those questions so it's not a big deal. I'll be right back."

"Thanks, Max. Let me go get you my debit card."

She turned to go into the house for her purse, but Max stopped her with a hand on her arm.

"Don't worry about it. I owe you for that first meal since I still gave you the ticket."

Annella smiled at him. "I can't argue with that logic. Five bags will be fine."

While she waited on Max, she checked her phone. Lauren had texted a photo of the lunch setup, and she responded: *It looks perfect! Thanks again for saving the day.*

Lauren responded with: *What are friends for?*

Max pulled back up to her house with the ice, and she loaded down her potato salad to make sure it stayed good. She put the rest of it in the cooler that she would fill cups with.

Max watched the familiar routine and witnessed the stress leave her face as she made three plates. His own shoulders tried to loosen with relief, but he was still too pissed at the situation. Max rolled his neck imagining the workout he was going to put his body through later to get rid of his pent up anger. Cal would cry, but he'd survive.

"Who are those for?"

She closed the box she was working on and looked at him.

"These are yours and Danielle's and Cal's lunches."

Max pulled out his wallet to pay for them, but she waved him off.

"You're not paying for these; they are on me. My way to say thank you."

Max still pulled his debit card from his wallet. "You're not giving us food to thank us for doing our jobs. Please let me pay for them."

Annella shook her head at him, not taking his card, and slipped the containers into a bag as Cal came back up the driveway. Annella turned her head to him and Max slipped the only bill he had in his wallet in her purple tip jar. She would never know the $50 was from him.

"No one saw or heard anything strange."

Cal saw the bagged food as Max picked it up. He clapped him on the back.

"Thanks for lunch, man."

Max picked up two of the drinks, leaving Cal to carry his own.

"I would love to take credit for that, but I didn't pay for them."

Cal went to pull out his own wallet, but Annella shook her head at him, too.

"Nope, it's on me today. Thanks for being awesome." Annella tried to put some enthusiasm in her voice, but she missed the pitch.

Cal smiled at her then. "Thanks, Annella."

Max gave Annella his business card and told her to call him if she thought of anything else or noted any strange activity in the next few days. They headed to the cruiser as more customers started showing up. Max climbed into the passenger seat and set the bag of food on the floorboard.

"Let's drop Danielle's plate off with her and go see Travis."

—m—

Cal and Max sauntered into The Black Tie and asked the hostess to see Travis. She led them to the back office where he sat with his feet on the desk scrolling through his phone ignoring the work for the restaurant that he would inherit one day. *Typical* Max thought.

He dropped his feet to the floor with a thud as the hostess backed out of the office closing the door. "What do you two want? Can't you see I'm busy?"

Max rolled his eyes and swept his hand to the chair that Travis was still sitting in. "Clearly, we've caught you in so much work. We just have a few questions about where you were yesterday after four PM."

Travis looked at his nails picking some imaginary grime from underneath them. "I had an early dinner with my parents and then went home alone where I stayed all night."

Max didn't believe him for a minute and knew that asking the Ashwoods to confirm Travis's story would be a waste. They'd lied for him in the past so they wouldn't have a problem doing it again.

"So you didn't vandalize Annella's van last night for revenge at what she told you in the grocery store?"

Travis's face shows shock, but Max isn't buying it. "Why would you think I had anything to do with Annella's van being vandalized? It's not like she's the first woman to tell me off." Cal snorts and covers it with a cough as Travis's nostrils flare in anger.

Cal and Max exchange a knowing glance. They know that they won't get any more information from Travis. Max gives him one last scalding glare as they turn and walk out without a goodbye.

Chapter

11

Annella's sitting in her home office, earlier than usual, calculating her profits for the day. Her tip jar was overflowing, and it made her feel warm to know how much the people of Green Lake supported her and her food.

Mostly, everyone bought extra meals to take home. "For later," they all said causing Annella's heart to swell with gratitude. They had bought her out of everything by two o'clock with her scraping the bottom of the brisket pan for the last wrap.

She'd be able to get back to her normal spot if business kept up like this, but for now she would keep serving from home. Neal had even volunteered to bring ice to her in the mornings before he started his shift.

Annella leaned back in her crisp white office chair and looked at the ceiling, preparing herself to do the research on how much fixing the van was going to cost her. She'd made a list of everything that needed done:

1. Put the spare on the back tire so that a tow truck can tow it to the tire shop.
2. Two new tires.
3. Paint removal or new paint?

She opened the browser on her computer to search for a tow truck when she heard the doorbell. She expected Lauren to come check on her after she closed the shop, but it was too early for her. Annella came out of the office and did a double take seeing Max through the glass of her front door.

She unlocked the door and opened it, the cedarwood scent that had become her comfort enveloping her. Annella took a moment to appreciate his athletic body in long silky basketball shorts, a T-shirt that was mostly green but had so many stains and paint splatters it could be any color. His still mismatched socks with gray running shoes on. He stared at her for a second as if he hadn't just seen her a few hours ago.

"You know you're the only one in town that locks your doors?"

She chuckled and stepped back, gesturing for him to come in out of the heat.

"Yes, Lauren loves reminding me. What are you doing here? Did you need to ask more questions or take more photos?"

Max rubbed the back of his neck looking everywhere but at Annella. "No, I wanted to come take care of you."

Annella's mouth gaped open at his directness, and Max's hand moved from his neck to his face.

His voice was muffled as he said, "Shit. Van. I meant I wanted to come help take care of the van." He dropped his hand, and Annella smiled at him, trying not to laugh at his distress.

"That's nice of you, but I haven't even done the calculations to see how much this will cost me to know when I'll be able to afford the repairs. I'm just going to keep serving from the house in the meantime. And shouldn't you still be working?"

Annella hugged her arms to her chest trying not to feel overwhelmed with the way the day had turned out. She hadn't broken down yet, and she was going to try and keep it that way. Max bounced on the balls of his feet nervous about how Annella would take what he had to say next.

"I've already called Phil down at the tire shop, and he has some take-offs that he's agreed to let go of at a good price. If you can't afford it, he'll take payments. I've got blocks in my truck to set the van on until we get back with the tires, so there is no need for a tow. Also, we keep cans of paint remover at the precinct for this time of year when the seniors tag buildings around town. I called in a favor another officer owed me and used some time off."

Max shrugged like it was no big deal rearranging his day for her and taking care of the thing that was her lively hood, but it was a very big deal to her.

Annella wasn't used to people being so helpful. In Pure Springs everyone only looked out for number one doing whatever it took to advance solo. "You're serious. You want to help me? Are you trying to atone for the ticket after I fed you or the second ticket after I gave your partner free food?"

He pointed a calloused finger at her and Heaven help her if she didn't wonder what it would feel like stroking her cheek. "You deserved both of those tickets, and yes, I'm serious. This is what communities do for each other."

Annella was sure there was a catch somewhere, he was going to ask her to cook for him and a date or cater a birthday party for free later, but right now, she needed help, so she relented.

"Fine. I'll accept your offer to take care of me. I mean the van."

Max glared at her with a grin. "Not going to let me live that down, are you?"

Annella walked past him outside. "Not a chance."

Chapter

12

The late afternoon sun had burned away the morning clouds and left the sky bright and warm. Annella pulled on her sunglasses and felt lighter than she had even thirty minutes ago.

She took a deep breath smelling the cedarwood soap she'd come to associate with Max and smiled. She might have to find a candle that smelled of cedarwood, just for the calming qualities, not to remind her of Max or anything. Max followed as she walked down the porch steps and over to the van.

The floor jack and two bright yellow jack stands were already sitting in the driveway, waiting for use.

"You were this confident I was going to say yes, huh?" Annella asked, sweeping her arm towards the tools.

Max moved the jack under the back passenger side then moved to loosen the lug nuts just a smidge before jacking up the van, pumping the gray handle. "I was hopeful that you would say yes, and if you said no, I would have just charmed you into agreement."

Annella watched Max's biceps as the jack finally reached the axle and began raising the van.

"Man, I should have said no so I could see what Max Thorne's idea of charming is."

Max gave her a devilish grin. "Oh, chef, you couldn't handle me being charming."

Max got the van up high enough to loosen the lug nuts the rest of the way and remove the tire while Annella's heart was beating triple time at the nickname. She had never had anyone give her a nickname before. Even her parents had always used her full name.

She heard a snap in front of her, along with her actual name, and shook her head. She looked over at Max, flush creeping up her face.

"What did you say?"

Max chuckled and Annella had to force herself to not get lost again at the way his soft lips pulled up into a smile that crinkled his temples. "I said, can you please bring that jack stand over here?"

Annella picked up the yellow stand and carried it over to Max admiring the sheer manliness of him working on something of hers. He positioned the stand and moved the jack to the driver's front tire to repeat the process.

Annella stayed grounded, proud of herself, and was ready when he asked for the second stand. With the van secured on the stands, Max finished removing the rims, and Annella helped load them in the back of his truck.

"I need to grab my purse and wash my hands then I'll be ready to go."

Max looked down at his own hands covered in black grime. "I need to wash up, too, if you don't mind."

Annella shook her head and led the way to the kitchen. Max let out a low whistle. "Wow. You keep your house spotless." He turned a circle in the room noticing how nothing was out of place.

Annella stood at the sink, watching Max judge her space. *Is he thinking I'm crazy? An annoying perfectionist? OCD?*

But what he asked wasn't what she expected.

"Just a guess, but your favorite color *is* purple, right?"

Annella laughed and tucked a stray curl behind her ear. "Is it that obvious? I was trying so hard to hide it. Yes, I like purple, and everything operates better when my space is clean."

Max scratched his jaw smearing grime in the process. "I wish I was more organized. One look at my place, and you'd run screaming. I used to do better at cleaning when Cal still lived with me, but now that it's just me, I've let it get away from me. You want to know why my socks never match? It's because I grab the first two I can find from my floor."

"After seeing your spice choices, I'm not surprised that your house is messy."

Max glared at her playfully

Annella ignored his glare and clapped her hands. "That's how I'm going to repay you for today! Sunday, I'm coming to your house and cleaning for you."

Annella nodded and turned on the water for it to warm up. Max leaned against her counter, letting her wash up first. "Annella, I'm not doing this to get anything in return, and I didn't tell you about my house to make you feel like you had to do something about it. I'm a grown man. I just need to stop being lazy."

Annella finished washing and moved so Max could have the water. "I repay kindness with kindness, so you can either take free food for a week or let me clean your house." Annella smiled at him, waiting for his answer.

Max would give this woman whatever she wanted if she never stopped smiling at him like that. He debated her offer for a minute while he washed the grime from his hands and chin. He knew she wouldn't budge. He had to pick one, and he'd be damned if he took money from her with any more free food. He shut off the faucet and accepted the purple checked towel from the still-smiling Annella.

"Alright. I accept your offer to clean my house, but you can't judge."

Annella beamed and Max's world shifted on its axis.

Annella grabbed two to-go cups from the shelf by the fridge and turned back to Max. "Tea, lemonade, or water for the drive?"

Max hung the towel over the stainless oven door remembering that was where she pulled it from. "Lemonade sounds amazing right now. Thanks."

Annella opened the freezer and put a scoop of ice in each cup then filled them from the pitcher in the fridge. She put lids on both and opened her straw. She handed Max his straw and cup then headed to pick up her purse and keys. Max popped his own straw in his cup and followed Annella out the door. She locked it behind them and headed down the steps.

"You know, I don't even know where my house key is," Max said as he followed her down the sidewalk to his truck.

He opened her door and admired the shape of her ass wrapped in her black bike shorts as she climbed inside. He shut the door and walked the long way around the bed of the truck, shutting the tailgate to take extra time for parts of his anatomy to cool down.

He got in and noticed Annella looking around. "What are you looking for?"

She turned back toward him, and that one curl slipped from behind her ear. "I'm trying to understand. You say your house is messy, but your truck is immaculate."

He gave her a lopsided grin. "It's guy logic. None of my friends are going to judge if my house is a wreck, but if my truck isn't clean, I'll never hear the end of it."

Max could feel Annella's mood shift as he pulled away from the curb. He turned down the radio. "What just went through your head?"

Annella took a drink of her lemonade baffled at how this man could read her like a book. "I'm just thinking of where we're going and the reason we have to go there. I'm getting pissed all over again."

Max stopped at the stop sign, knuckles gripping the steering wheel so tight they were shaking. He was pissed, too, probably more so because of all the things Travis had done in the past and gotten away with. He was trying to think of something to say other than, I'm sorry, but Annella started talking again.

"He couldn't even just exit gracefully." Annella threw her hands up. "We weren't officially dating, and we never slept together."

That made the knot in Max's stomach loosen a little.

She continued, "You didn't see me act like a child when I left my entire life for a job that I didn't get because of *his* parents. No. And for him to mess with my business like that!"

Annella drank more of her lemonade to try and cool down. "Sorry I went off like that. Apparently, I needed to get that off my chest."

Max unclenched his jaw. "Don't apologize for your feelings. Yell, scream, throw something. Let it out. No one has more reason to hate Travis than I do, and I wish I could arrest him right now, but I can't. I can promise you, though, that he will slip, and Cal and I will be there when he does."

Annella noticed Max's eyes go distant and waited for him to continue.

Max blew out a long breath "Just a lifetime of him being an entitled ass."

Annella felt like there was more that Max wasn't saying but left it alone. She was imagining them liking the same girl and her going for Travis.

"Where did Grace Squared Catering come from? Are you a twin?"

Annella, still thinking about why Max hated Travis so much, was lost for a second as she processed Max's subject change. When her brain caught up to her ears she smiled at Max. She loved the name of her company. "My first name, Annella, is Gaelic for Grace. My middle name *is* Grace, so my name is literally Grace Grace. That's where Grace Squared came from."

Max pulled into the parking lot of Phil's Tire Repair and backed up to the first open bay door. "Grace Squared. I like it." He cut the engine and came around to open her door and help her out.

Annella grabbed her purse from the floorboard and accepted Max's hand down to the cracked pavement. They walked through the open door, and Annella looked around. It smelled like oil and the boys' locker room after practice.

Annella cringed at the sight of tools all over the place, half-drank sodas, and resisted the urge to straighten up. Max called out to Phil and a man in his mid-fifties with salt and pepper in his hair and mustache came out from a back room. He had kind eyes and a soft smile that put her at ease.

Max shook his hand. "Hey, Phil. This is Annella."

Phil held out his hand, and Annella shook it. "Hey, Phil. It's nice to meet you. Thanks for helping me on such short notice."

"My pleasure, Annella. I'm a big fan of your chopped brisket sandwich, and those cookies are top-notch."

Phil dropped her hand and started walking to the back of Max's truck to unload the rims.

"I'm pretty good with faces, but I don't remember you eating with me."

"You wouldn't remember. I can't get away from the shop for lunch, so I usually send someone after my order."

Max and Annella watched as Phil removed the slashed tires and then put on the two new-to-Annella tires all while chatting with Max hardly looking at his work. Phil led Annella into the office part of the shop which she noticed was only cleaner because of the lack of tools. Phil walked behind the counter to a cash register that looked like it belonged in the eighties.

"Well, they aren't brand new, but they'll keep you going for a while."

Annella smiled and pulled out her wallet as Phil showed her the invoice with the price.

"Phil, are you sure? I don't know tires, but I'm pretty sure that's too low. I know I can't afford to pay the whole thing right now, but Max said you'd be open to payments."

"I appreciate that, but that's the price for you. I'm not going to charge you an arm and a leg for two tires that aren't on my inventory and a bit of my time. Not everyone in this town is like the Ashwoods."

The rollercoaster of emotions from the day finally caught up with Annella and tears started to flow from her eyes. Phil came around the counter to wrap her in a fatherly hug. He pulled a bandana out of the back pocket of his red coveralls and handed it to her.

"This is my clean one."

Annella used the red fabric to wipe her eyes and nose before trying to hand it back to Phil.

"It's okay, honey. You keep that one. Bandanas are a very useful tool."

Max walked into the office, confused as to why Annella was crying.

"It's okay, Annella. You don't need to waste tears on Travis Ashwood. He'll get what's coming to him. Max will see to that, won't ya?"

Annella pulled out of Phil's arms and gave Max a reassuring smile. She pulled out the money and handed it to Phil who went back around the counter and placed it into the register.

"Thanks, Phil. Sorry I cried on you. It's been a long day."

Phil handed her the receipt and clasped her hand in both of his. "Not to worry. A few tears aren't gonna hurt me. Probably helped to wash some of the grime off these old coveralls."

Annella put her wallet back in her purse and moved to Max's side. "The next time you send someone for your lunch you make sure they tell me it's yours and it's on me."

"Thanks, Annella. I'll do just that." Phil came back around the counter and shook Max's hand.

"Thanks, Phil. Say hi to Lily for me."

Phil dropped Max's hand and pulled a stained red rag from his other back pocket, wiping his hands. "You're welcome, Max. You take care of that pretty little lady."

Max nodded to him as he held open the door for Annella to walk through, following behind her, thinking, *I'll do just that.*

Chapter

13

Max was glad to see Annella smiling on the drive back to her house. She turned the radio up to sing along, apologizing for her bad singing voice, but Max was sure he had never heard those old country songs sound better.

They pulled up to her house as the sun was going behind the tops of the trees. Max backed into the driveway in front of the van and shut off the truck.

"Let's go ahead and get the paint off before it gets dark so we can see. I can put the tires back on by flashlight if I have to."

Annella nodded in agreement and picked up her empty cup and purse before getting out. "Don't want to be the reason your truck's dirty."

"Thanks," Max said and got out to come around and open her door.

"I'm going to take this stuff inside. I'll be right back. Do you need anything from the house?"

Max held out his empty cup to her. "I wouldn't mind a refill."

Annella took his cup and went inside while Max unloaded the box with cans of paint remover.

Annella came back out and handed Max his cup.

Max took it setting the cup down on the bumper of the van and handed her a black can of paint remover. Annella's hand brushed Max's and she looked up into his eyes captivated by their color.

Max held her stare trying to convey the feelings that were just beginning inside him when Annella's phone rang. She answered, breaking the captivation, to Lauren on the other end.

"Hey, Lauren. Thanks again for working Abigail's lunch."

She listened to Lauren for a minute, then hung up and turned back to Max.

"Sorry about that. Where were we?" Max took a swig of his lemonade before setting it back down on the bumper. "All good. It's easy to use; just spray it on, wait a few minutes, and then wipe it off. We'll work in small sections so we don't leave it on too long and strip your pretty, purple paint off."

"Should we have the hose and a bucket with soap nearby?"

"We should."

Max moved to get the hose while Annella went back in the house to retrieve the bucket and soap. When she came back out, Lauren was there talking to Max.

"Hey, Lauren! Thanks for coming to help. Got the bucket and soap." Lauren rolled the sleeves of her T-shirt up and took off her shoes and socks.

Annella dumped some soap in the bucket and Max started filling it up with water. All three looked up at the sound of a door closing to see Brock and Olivia coming outside waving at them. Instead of sitting and enjoying their evening the couple came walking across the yard.

"Hey, neighbors," Annella greeted. Brock reached out and gave Max's hand a shake while Olivia hugged Lauren and then Annella.

"Hey, neighbor. We saw you guys about to start working and we wanted to come help."

Annella and Olivia toed off their shoes by Lauren's, and Max handed out more paint removers.

"How about you ladies work on the driver's side, and we'll work on the passenger." Lauren pulled out her phone and put some music on, and the group got to work.

They worked, talked, sang, and laughed together, Annella's stress slipping away with the paint. Lauren, Annella, and Olivia finished their side quickly taunting the guys that they were more efficient.

Lauren picked up the hose to give the van one last rinse and "accidentally" sprayed Annella and Olivia. The girls shrieked, and Olivia grabbed the hose, spraying Lauren back. Max and Brock came around the back of the van to see what caused the shriek and walked into the crossfire. They called a truce after everyone was soaked and laughing. Max couldn't take his eyes off Annella.

Her gray T-shirt clung to her body, showing off all her curves. Water was running down her thighs, and he wanted his hands to follow the path of the rivulets down her toned legs.

Brock's voice cut into Max's daydream. "How about since you ladies are so fast, you finish our side, and we'll put the rims back on." Brock squeezed Olivia again and kissed her temple, then joined Max at his truck, grinning. "You like her, don't you?"

Max's head whipped up, ready to deny Brock's statement, but he couldn't.

"Maybe a little. I didn't want to. I swore off women after Brenda left town. I can't go through that again."

Brock grabbed one of the rims and heaved it to the ground. "Look, man, I know Brenda screwed you up, but not every woman is the same. We've come to know Annella since she moved in, and she's great. She doesn't strike me as the type to leave when things get tough."

Max lifted his own rim, sat it down beside Brock's, and looked at Annella, laughing with Lauren and Olivia.

"I think you're right."

Brock started rolling his tire toward the van. "My favorite phrase."

Annella's van was back to right as the last skeins of sunlight faded from the sky. The first stars were twinkling to life as Max dumped the water into the yard, and Brock rolled the hose back up.

"Thank you all so much for the help and keeping my spirits up. You are all amazing friends." Annella pulled everyone in for hugs, saving Max for last. She let herself linger and bask in the comfort of his arms for a second longer before stepping back.

"Is anyone hungry? Since Phil gave me such a good price, I can spring for burgers and fries from Happy's."

Brock slung his arm around Olivia's shoulders. "Thanks for the offer, but…we've got chicken in the crockpot that's waiting for us…we'll see you later."

"Okay, we'll rain check. Enjoy your chicken."

Olivia's arm snaked around Brock's lower back not caring that her friends saw her pat his ass.

Annella looked at Lauren. "You up for burgers and fries?"

Lauren sat on the cool, soft grass, putting her socks and shoes on. "I would love to, but…I need to get the receipts and money for the shop from Ginny."

Lauren bounced up and hugged Annella, then slugged Max in the arm. "See ya later, Max."

Annella walked Lauren to her car and picked up the box of serving items from the birthday party.

"Are you sure I can't pay you for working Abigail's party?"

Lauren got in the car and buckled up, sticking her head out the window. "I'm sure. It was a blast to chat with everyone about things other than my blood pressure."

"Tell Ginny thanks for holding down the shop today. Drive safe."

Lauren started the car and waggled her eyebrows at Annella. "You have fun tonight."

Annella backed up and waved as Lauren put the car in drive and headed down the street. She got the feeling that her friends were playing matchmaker.

Chapter

14

Annella suddenly had butterflies in her stomach at being alone with Max. She had spent most of the day with him and felt normal, but now it felt like something in their dynamic was different...more.

She walked over grabbing the bucket and empty box to take inside. Max came up behind her, grabbed the box from her hands, and followed behind her. Annella showed him where the recycling bin was for the box, and she put the bucket in the laundry room.

"What about you, Max? Burgers, fries, and milkshakes at Happy's, or do you have other things to do? I completely understand if you need to get going. I mean, you've practically been helping me all day," Annella rambled, barely stopping to breathe.

He smiled at her and damn it if her stomach didn't flip over itself twice. "It's fine. I don't have anything else going on, and Happy's sounds good, but I'm buying."

Annella patted herself down on the way out of the house pausing to lock the door and to see if she needed to go change. Max's eyes followed everywhere her hands touched, wishing his lips were doing the job instead. She determined that she could get into Max's truck without ruining it and sat down on the concrete to put on her socks and shoes.

"I'm supposed to buy you dinner to say thank you."

Max shook his head, trying to focus on what Annella was saying.

"First, you're already cleaning my house to say thank you, and I have a feeling I'm going to be in your debt when you're through. Second, my mother would smack my hands with her wooden spoon if she learned I allowed a woman to pay for my dinner. Third, you already gave me free lunch earlier, so it's my turn." Max helped Annella off the step and kept her hand in his as he led her around the truck and opened the door.

He climbed in and started the truck, pulling out of the driveway toward Happy's.

They drove in peaceful silence, listening to the radio with the windows down to let in the cool night breeze. He noticed Annella was humming, a soft sweet sound. She must only do that when she's happy, he deduced as he pulled into the drive-through instead of parking.

Max looked at Annella confusion showing in the tilt of her soft lips. "I thought we could go down to the lake and eat under the stars." Annella smiled and nodded her head. She told Max what she wanted, and he ordered.

They got to the lake and found an empty picnic table with a view of the glossy smooth water far enough from the crowded fire pit so they could enjoy their food in peace. Annella unpacked the food, as Max's stomach rumbled. Just like the first time she couldn't stop laughing. "It does that a lot, doesn't it?" She gestured to his midsection with a fry.

Max slung a long muscular leg over the bench of the picnic table and set down their shakes, "It takes a lot to keep me full."

The purple black of the night sky provided a beautiful backdrop to the brightness of the full moon. Annella watched the moon ripple as something disturbed the lake and thought this was a scene paintings were attempted of, but no canvas would be able to capture the magic.

She took a bite out of her burger moaning as the juicy patty mixed with the sour pickles and tart mustard.

"Do you always moan when you eat?"

Max couldn't help but wonder what other noises he could get her to make.

"Only when it's good food, and I've only eaten a banana with yogurt all day."

Annella thought she saw a flash of anger cross his chiseled face, but it was gone before she could be sure. Max finished his burger before Annella even had half of hers gone, and he started on his fries dunking a few into his milkshake before slipping them past his lips.

"You're one of *those* wierdos?" she asked as Max chomped his food and swallowed.

"Yup. Don't tell me that you've never eaten milkshake-soaked fries."

Annella shook her head and stuck out her tongue. "Never have and slightly judge the people that do as wierdos."

"Aren't you a chef? Isn't trying new things part of the job description?" He dunked another fry into his shake and held it out to Annella.

The chocolate ice cream dripped down his thumb as she locked eyes with him and closed her mouth around the fry, sucking the chocolate from his fingers. Heat flooded Max's senses and he wanted nothing more than to taste that chocolate from her lips. She closed her eyes and savored the salty-sweet crispiness.

Max arched his brow. "So?"

"It's amazing! Where has this been all my life?"

"Welcome to the wierdo club, chef." Max chuckled as she popped her own lid off and started dunking her fries. They finished their meals and threw the trash away on the way back to the truck.

Max opened Annella's door before getting in to drive her home.

"Thanks for dinner. I'm glad you are safe from your mother's spoon. Did you have many encounters with it growing up?"

Max had one hand on the wheel, and the other rested on the door.

"Plenty. Only when I deserved it, though. She was tough but fair."

Annella leaned her head on her arm, letting the wind flow through the curls that were coming loose from her ponytail.

"Tell me more about Cody and Sadie. Anything specific I need to know ahead of their tasting?"

"Nothing that I can think of. Cody just wants to make Sadie happy, so whatever she wants, he'll go along with."

Annella smiled. "Sounds like he's already mostly figured out marriage."

"Yeah. He had a good role model. Our mom and dad are still crazy about each other."

They pulled up to Annella's house, and the butterflies that had refused to leave her stomach tripled in size. She grabbed her purse to hop out of the truck, but Max turned the truck off and came around to open her door.

"Thanks," she breathed when Max took her hand to help her out. He didn't drop it as he walked her to the front door his hawk eyes scanning the area while they walked up the steps.

Max tucked a stray curl behind her ear and stooped down enveloping Annella in his signature scent hovering over her mouth. He allowed her a split second to move or speak before he placed a gentle kiss on her lips. Hints of chocolate and salt lingered on her skin and Max had to stop himself from exploring her mouth more.

Annella blushed from her forehead to her toes and didn't even try to hide the smile spreading on her face. Max was rubbing her knuckles, his calloused thumb raising goosebumps on her arm. Max started talking, and it took every brain cell she had left to concentrate on what he was saying.

"I've asked the night shift to do some extra rounds through the neighborhood just as a precaution."

"Thanks for that. And also for everything else today, Max," she said.

Annella had her keys in her hand but hadn't made a move to drop Max's hand and unlock the door. *Just one more time* he thought and leaned down as she rose up at the same time. Their mouths crushed together this time and Max circled his arms around her lifting her clean off her feet to his level. Annella wrapped her arms around his neck and held on reveling in the weightless feeling. Max took his time to explore the softness of her lips and his ego grew at the moan that escaped when his tongue tangled with hers. Reluctantly, Max set her down. When they finally broke apart Annella had to hold on to Max's arm for balance.

"You're welcome for everything. If you see or hear anything unusual, just call me. You don't have to call the station."

Annella nodded, smiling so wide, Max thought she was brighter than the moon. He turned around and walked down the steps, pausing as he reached the bottom.

"Goodnight, chef."

Annella opened the door, and the entryway light created a halo around her. "Goodnight, Max."

He waited until he heard her click the lock into place before heading to his truck and driving home lighter than he had felt in a while.

Chapter

15

The rest of the week passed without incident, and it was finally Sunday. Annella was looking forward to cleaning Max's house and seeing him again. She had served him lunch every day this week, but there had been no talk of the kisses they shared after he brought her home from the lake on Monday.

They exchanged casual conversations while she prepped his food. He had started texting her during the day about the weather and upcoming events, and he always made sure that she ate all three meals each day.

The sun was already shining through her windows making Annella's step light, her lips forming a smile. She loved the sunshine and being warm. Everything just got better as the days got longer.

She went into the kitchen to pack up something for lunch and a couple bottles of water since she didn't know what she would find at Max's house. She pulled a container of grapes out to eat for breakfast on her way, then picked up her keys and purse from the entryway table before stepping into that glorious morning.

Annella texted Max: *Heading your way. See you soon.*

Max texted back immediately: *See you soon. Remember, no judging my house. I'm a bachelor.*

Annella wondered if he would stay a bachelor or if the kisses they shared would lead anywhere. He sent her the address and she pulled out of the driveway, snacking on her grapes. Max didn't live far from Annella, only a five-minute drive, she liked knowing that he was so close if anything crazy happened to her again.

She pulled up to the front of Max's house and took in the site before her. The white siding looked like it could use a good power washing, but it was cute.

It had a large front porch with tipped-over chairs and a low table that held half drank bottles of water. She got out and opened the back of the van to pull out her mop and bucket loaded with rags, cleaners, and a toilet brush. She heard the screen door close and glanced up to see Max on the front porch, looking rumpled and delicious.

His dark brown hair stuck out at all angles, and Annella wanted to run her fingers through their silkiness while feeling his lips meet hers in another kiss. His GLPD shirt looked like he found it wadded up on his floor, his black basketball shorts had a red paint stain on them, and once again, his socks didn't match.

Did he buy them at a special store that sold mismatched socks? she thought as he came to help her carry everything inside.

Max smiled at her, and good grief, if his smile didn't make the sun shine brighter. "Morning, chef." Max leaned in and kissed Annella's cheek like it was something he did all the time.

"Morning, Max," Annella said as she handed the mop and bucket to him so she could get her lunchbox and purse out of the front seat.

Annella followed Max up the steps and then proceeded into the living room while he held open the screen door. He followed behind her, blocking the exit so she couldn't run when she saw the state of his house.

She surveyed the living room, making a list in her head of all the things that she needed to do—dust, clean windows, pick up dirty laundry, bring dishes to the kitchen, and vacuum the couch and carpet. They moved through the house with Annella making lists and Max making apologies as they went.

When they came to his bedroom, Annella tried her hardest not to think about waking up next to Max in his large bed with the soft green blanket wrapped around them. She didn't succeed because soon she was imagining his facial hair tickling her cheek as he kissed her good morning. She looked from the bed and noticed piles of clothes all over the floor and a vital piece of furniture missing.

She turned to Max. "Where is your dresser? Is it in your closet?"

Max ducked his head as he leaned against the door frame and rubbed his neck. "A dresser wouldn't fit in my closet in its current state, and it never seemed important. Why put things in a dresser to only have to pull them out later. This way," Max pointed to the piles on his floor, "My stuff is already out."

Annella walked over to the nightstand pointing at the light wood piece with a drawer. "You have a nightstand, not a box by your bed, an actual nightstand, but you don't own a dresser? In what man universe does that logic make sense?"

Max pushed off the door frame and stood at the foot of his bed. "It's simple, I needed a place to put my phone when it's charging and a drawer to secure my service weapon in."

Annella pulled her phone from the side pocket of her shorts and texted Lauren.

Hey! Do you happen to have any dressers at the shop?

She knew her best friend wasn't awake yet, so she didn't wait for a response before putting her phone away. Annella looked up at Max and started stripping the bedding from his bed.

"You don't have to stay with me if you have things to do."

Max moved out of her way as she rounded the bed to undo the fitted sheet from the other side. She smelled like coconut, and he suddenly wanted to see her in a bikini in the lake.

"I normally go for a run on Sunday mornings around the lake, but I don't want you to feel like I'm abandoning you to this. It's my mess."

Annella gathered the dirty bedding and headed to the laundry room back down the hallway.

"It's totally fine. I have a system, and I don't want to keep you from your run."

Max was right behind her, watching and enjoying her doing homey things in his house. Annella brushed past him on her way out of the room, walking back down to start in the living room.

"Go run, Max. I'll see you when you get back."

Max moved to the door, holding the screen open instead of going to Annella, wrapping his arms around her, and kissing her until she forgot about cleaning.

"Call me if you need anything," Max said and let the screen door slam behind him.

He knew they needed to talk about a lot of things, the kisses after the lake, why he had been mean to her when they first met, and what he felt for her, but he wasn't ready to break the bubble. He wasn't in deep enough that it would hurt too much to just go back to friends.

He let the screen door close behind him and stretched in the front yard before going to wake Cal up to join him.

Annella pulled out her phone and put on her cleaning playlist letting her body find the comforting feeling of cleaning and organizing the living room.

It felt odd, not in a bad way, being in Max's house alone. It brought her the peace she had been searching for since the vandalism. Sleep had been eluding her, coming in brief periods between waking up and checking outside to make sure her van was still okay. Every sound outside caused her to jump awake, leaving her with dark purple circles under her eyes. If this kept going, she would have to invest in a concealer company.

Once the laundry and dishes were out of the room, it looked like a whole new area.

Typical man, she thought as she dusted the gigantic TV. He had spent more money on the TV than the couch.

Annella wiped something sticky from the black end table, where she left a pile of mail for Max to sort through later. Annella felt her skin crawl as she walked into the kitchen and looked around. She couldn't believe that Max had prepared food here. A ping on her phone interrupted her music and saved her from starting the kitchen. Lauren had texted her back about the dresser.

I just had one brought in last week. It's a dark wood, six drawer piece and is selling for $200. I'll let it go to you for $100 though.

Annella's phone went off before she could reply.

Why do you need a dresser? Are you redecorating?

Annella texted her back: *Not redecorating. I'm at Max's cleaning and the man doesn't own one! When can I come get it?*

Annella thought about her budget while waiting for Lauren to text her back. She had some wiggle room because tips this week had been way up. People still felt bad about what happened to her van, and they wanted to show their support. Lauren texted back.

I'm on my way to the store now to do some rearranging and cleaning. I'll be there in 12.

Annella texted that she would see her then and walked out the door.

She felt guilty for leaving Max's door unlocked, told herself it would be fine. It was getting hot already, so she turned up the AC to cool off on the drive. When she pulled up to the storefront of Twice is Nice, Lauren was outside watering her flower boxes.

111

Annella loved the main street of Green Lake. All the shop owners took pride in the appearance of their stores. Flowers and US flags lined the sidewalk. Cute window displays adorned the shops, making Annella want to buy everything.

Annella walked over and hugged Lauren. "Hey, bestie," Lauren said, wrapping her empty arm around Annella. "How's it going at the bachelor pad?"

Annella let go of Lauren and leaned down to smell the blossoms. "It's not as terrible as I was expecting. It's mostly needing to throw away trash, laundry everywhere that needs washed and put somewhere, and general cleaning."

Lauren watered the final box with the last of the water in her can and moved past Annella into the shop. "I can't believe that Max doesn't own a dresser," Lauren said.

Annella followed her through the shop, skirting around clothing racks, home goods displays, and bins of toys to the back, where Lauren kept the little bit of furniture that came into the shop. The shop smelled like coffee and sugar cookies, giving it a cozy feel.

Lauren got to the dresser and started moving piles of folded T-shirts from the top so Annella could see the whole piece. It would be perfect. It was masculine, and a few scratch marks marred the top, giving it a bachelor look.

Annella ran her hand over the top, looking at Lauren. "It's perfect."

Lauren put the folded clothes down on a nearby chair. "Awesome. Let's ring it up, and I'll help you load it."

Annella followed Lauren back to the front of the shop and pulled out cash from her wallet for the dresser. They went back and pulled out the drawers first to make the piece lighter.

Five minutes later, Annella was driving back to Max's with her treasure. Maybe if her food van business flopped, she could sell her services as a professional organizer.

She pulled back up to Max's and opened the back to unload the drawers. The base would have to wait until Max got back from his run, but she could at least get the drawers in and start sorting clothes. She carried a drawer up the steps and let herself into the house.

She thought about Max's comment of not knowing where his house key was and wondered if she would find it somewhere strange while she cleaned. She put the drawer on the floor in Max's room, used his bathroom making sure her butt didn't contact the seat since she hadn't cleaned that room yet, and started back for the others. As she turned the corner out of the hallway, she saw the back of a person she didn't recognize.

Annella screamed, causing the stranger to jump and turn to her, and ran back into Max's bedroom. She locked the door and then sat in front of it to add an extra barrier. She pulled her phone from her side pocket and called Max. Her heart beat faster as she heard footsteps in the hallway in one ear and Max's voice in the other.

"Hey, chef," Max said, sounding a little out of breath. "Is everything okay?"

Annella spoke so fast that Max could barely understand her. "There's someone here, and I didn't recognize them. Why don't you people lock your doors?" Tears were streaming down her face as she tried to focus on Max's words.

"We're on the way. Stay on the phone with me. Tell me what's happening. Where are you in the house?"

Annella's panic kicked into high gear as the doorknob jiggled. "I locked myself in your bedroom, but they're trying to open the door." She heard a tentative "Hello" from the other side of the door.

"Max. He's right outside the door."

Her breath was coming in short pants, causing her head to spin.

"Annella, sweetheart, I need you to take a deep breath. Everyone in town knows that that's my house so I doubt the person is there to cause trouble. I'm right down the road, just hang on. I can see the house."

Annella tipped her head back against the door. The cool wood felt good on her pounding head as Max started talking again. "Put me on speaker phone and slide your phone next to the crack at the bottom of the door."

She did as Max asked and tried to take deeper breaths.

Max's police voice filled the room when he said, "Hello. Who's there?"

Annella heard the male voice on the other side of the door. "Max. It's just Cody. Why is there a woman locked in your bedroom?"

Annella heard Max's sigh of relief as she put two and two together. "Cody?" Annella shouted. "As in your brother?"

She heard the chuckle in Max's voice. "Yes, Cody. My brother. Your future client."

Annella groaned and buried her face in her hands, embarrassment washing away the panic. She heard the screen door slam and hurried footsteps down the hall.

Max's voice came from both her phone and the other side of the door, "Cody, stop frightening your caterer."

Max knocked on the door.

"Hey, chef. It's okay. You can open the door now."

Annella wiped the tears from her cheeks and stood. There was nothing she could do about the embarrassment tinting her face red, so she opened the door. She opened her mouth to offer an apology to Cody and Max when Max scooped her up in a tight hug lifting her off of her feet.

She let herself be comforted by Max's embrace and the smell of sweat mixed with his cedarwood soap. Cody moved down the hallway to allow them some privacy and smiled. It looked like his brother had finally opened himself up again after Brenda.

Max sat on the bed with Annella in his lap and cradled her head to his chest. He placed a gentle kiss on the top of her head and took deep breaths until he could feel both of their heartrates slow down. She pulled back from him and looked down at her lap. "I'm sorry I panicked and called you."

Max put his fingers under Annella's chin and lifted her head so he could look down into her eyes. "I told you, don't ever be sorry for the way you feel or for calling me. You used your instincts and did fine. Most people I would tell to call 911 first, but in this case, I kinda am. You did exactly what I would want you to do in this situation if it wasn't just Cody." Max ran his hands up her arms, leaving goosebumps in their wake.

Annella had calmed down enough that she registered a second voice in the living room talking to Cody. "How did Cal know to come over here when you were on the phone with me the whole time?"

Max chuckled and let her go immediately missing the feel of her body wrapped around him. "I made him go run with me this morning. We were finishing our last lap when you called. Cal kept up for a bit, but I took off at Rose Street to get here. Are you okay now?"

Annella took a breath and nodded. "Thanks for getting here so quickly."

"I'll always be here for you, whatever you need. Now would you like to go meet my brother, who almost got tackled and handcuffed for scaring you?"

"I just hope he still hires me now." She wandered down the hall into the living room and smiled at Cal. "Hey, Cal."

Cal stood up from breathing hard hunched over his knees. He looked her over in that cop way, making sure she was okay, and smiled back.

"Hey Annella. I've never seen Max run that fast."

A warm feeling spread through Annella's chest, knowing that Max was concerned about her.

Max came up behind her and laid his hands on her shoulders. "Annella, meet Cody. Cody, Annella."

Now that she could process thoughts Annella saw the resemblance between the brothers. They both were over six feet with the same sharp nose and wide eyes. Cody's hair was a lighter version of Max's chestnut, and he wasn't as defined in the muscles, but she could tell they were related.

Cody spoke first, holding his hand out to Annella. "Hi Annella. It's nice to meet you in person. I'm sorry for scaring you."

Annella shook his hand, noticing the softness as opposed to Max's calloused touch.

"Hi, Cody. It's nice to meet you, too. Sorry for screaming. I wasn't expecting anyone to be here when I got back. I don't always scream when I meet potential clients."

Cody and Annella dropped their hands as Max looked down at her. "Where did you go?"

Annella tipped her head back and smiled at Max.

"It's time you owned a dresser. I would lose sleep at night knowing that your method of laundry included piles of 'clean' clothes on the floor."

Cal and Cody laughed at the shot Annella took at Max, and he glared at them both.

He looked back at Annella. "You didn't need to do that. I'll pay you back for it."

Annella walked out from under Max's hands and toward the front door. "Max, you were perfectly fine with your no-dresser life, and I changed it, so I paid for it. You don't need to pay me back. You can help unload it, though."

Max walked past Annella and looked back at Cal and Cody while holding open the screen door, "You two can help." Max and Cal brought in the body of the dresser while Annella and Cody followed with the drawers.

They put the dresser up against the wall facing Max's bed and placed the drawers inside. Max stepped back and put his hands on his hips. "Thanks again for getting me this. You really didn't have to." Annella moved to the first pile of clean clothes and sat on the floor to sort and fold them while Max, Cody, and Cal stood there staring at her.

"Unless you all want put to work, I suggest you find something to do while I finish."

Max looked over to Cody and Cal. "Lunch and then the driving range?"

They both nodded and walked down the hall when Max gave them the *get out of here* look. He squatted down so he could look into Annella's beautiful green eyes.

"Don't forget to eat lunch," he said.

Annella looked up at him with a T-shirt in her hands, and he pictured her wearing only that, lying next to him.

"As soon as I have your clothing situated, I will take a break to eat. Have a fun afternoon with Cal and Cody."

Max stood upright, his knees cracking with the run he had just pushed them through to get to Annella.

"Don't make any plans for dinner either," Max said as he leaned down to kiss the top of her head. The flowery scent of her hair filled his nostrils as she tipped her head back, leaning into his kiss.

"And what if I already had dinner plans?" Max leaned her back against the bedroom wall so he could kiss her full mouth.

After hearing the panic in her voice earlier and the visceral need he felt to protect her from whatever was making her cry, he knew now what he wanted. Annella met his lips, swallowing the moan that came out. Cal and Cody were in the living room, probably listening to the whole thing. Max pulled away a hungry look in his eyes.

"Cancel them," he said. He kissed her nose and proceeded out the door, leaving Annella's head spinning and her heart doing backflips.

Chapter

16

Max walked out of his bedroom and snatched his clubs from the hall closet on his way to the living room. When he walked in, Cal and Cody immediately stopped talking.

Max looked between the two and asked, "What?"

Cody looked at Cal who had found a sudden fascination in his shoes, then turned back to Max. "It's good to see you interested in someone again."

Max let out an exasperated sigh and hoisted his clubs higher on his shoulder. "Don't get too excited. There's still time for me to fuck this up."

Cal snapped his head and pointed a finger at Max. "If you are referring to Brenda leaving, you didn't fuck that up. She had one foot out of this town since she was born. Nothing was going to keep her here. She was a coward who used a shitty situation as an excuse to leave. You can't keep blaming yourself for something you didn't do. Now man up and take the chance."

Max rubbed the back of his neck and looked between his brother and best friend. "I'm working on it." He shoved through the two and went outside, leaving them to either follow him or stay and help Annella clean.

Max heard footsteps coming down the porch stairs as he put his clubs in the back of the truck. Cal climbed into the back seat so that Cody could ride up front. Max started the truck and backed out of his cracked, grass-grown driveway.

"Was Sadie freaking out about something today, or did you just miss your big brother?" Max asked Cody.

"Sadie is good. I wanted to get out of the house for a bit. I'm sorry again for scaring Annella. It'll make a funny story, though. Cody, where did you find this amazing caterer? I scared the shit out of her at Max's house."

The three laughed and Cal commented from the back.

"You won't be disappointed. Her food is amazing."

Max glanced at Cal in the rearview mirror.

"You would say that about anyone's food if they gave you extra cookies."

Cal flipped Max a rude gesture in the mirror. "No way. If the food wasn't good, extra cookies would not make up for it."

"Sadie and I keep meaning to meet at the food van and have lunch to at least taste her food, but something always comes up. We're grateful that Annella is doing our tasting on a Sunday, so there's no way work can get in the way."

Max pulled into Happy's so they could have lunch before getting to the driving range. After the run and adrenaline spike of Annella's phone call, Max was starving.

They piled out of the truck, and Cal looked at Max. "What's this? We have to eat inside like commoners? We don't get the picnic by the lake in the moonlight?"

Cody laughed at the thought of the three of them on a picnic by the lake, and Max put Cal in a headlock.

"Shut up, Cal, or I'll put you on the overnight shift for a month." None of the officers ever wanted to work the overnight shift in Green Lake. It's where they always put the rookies to get their feet wet and in a town of families and retirees, it was a slow shift. All of Max's deputies claimed watching paint dry was more exciting than that shift.

Max let Cal out of the headlock but kept his arm around his friend, then threw his other around his brother. "Let's eat and talk about a bachelor party."

The trio headed inside Happy's to the sounds of meat sizzling on the grill, order numbers being called out, and old-time rock on the radio.

Max had to foot the bill since neither Cal nor Cody had their wallets, conveniently. They sat at a table next to the window, looking out at the bright afternoon.

Max pulled out his phone to text Annella: *Did you eat lunch?*

Cody and Cal were bickering about who was going to hit the longest drive at the range when she texted back.

Yes, I did. Once I'm finished, I'll head home and relax in my sweats the rest of the day since I don't have any plans tonight.

Max chuckled at his phone before responding.

Thanks again for cleaning my house. I'll see you tonight for dinner OUT. It's up to you if you go in your sweats or not.

He put away his phone and joined Cal and Cody's conversation, saying he was going to hit the longest drive. They bet on it with the loser having to buy the next time they went anywhere together. They turned the talk to the upcoming bachelor party, and Cody quickly told Max what he didn't want.

"No strippers and no clubs. I had enough of that in college. I want a laid-back night, cards and food, and the guys."

Cal frowned at the no strippers order but couldn't say much as it wasn't his party. He was just glad to be invited since he wasn't an official member of the wedding. Just then, their number was called, and Cal went to get their burgers and fries.

"I was thinking that if you like Annella's food, I'll ask her to set us up a spread at my house. BBQ sandwiches, sausage, sides, junk food. Buffet style so we can snack as we want."

Cal sat the tray down on the table and asked, "Will you ask her to make cookies?"

Max smiled, his dimple popping up in the right corner of his mouth. Sometimes, he wondered if his best friend was thirty-five or ten.

"Don't forget," Cody said to Max, "you have to be fitted for your tux still."

Max wasn't happy about wearing a tux, but for his brother, he would. He pulled his phone back out of his pocket and set a reminder on his calendar for that. "Done. What else do we need to work on?"

Cody took a bite of his burger and savored the greasy, cheesy delight. "Besides finalizing the caterer, that's all that was on my wedding list. Sadie has most of her stuff done, too, so all that's left is waiting."

"That's the worst part," Cal said, taking a drink of his soda. "I hate the waiting."

After the guys finished lunch, they hit the driving range to settle the bet. *It doesn't get any better than this,* Max thought. *Relaxing Sunday with my two brothers AND a beautiful woman going on a date with me tonight. It's a great day.*

They hit balls until their arms were sore and Max came out the winner with the longest shot and Cody with the shortest.

"Looks like the future guys' night is on Cody," Cal said as the guys walked back to the truck. They piled inside and drove to Cody's to drop him off first.

They pulled up, and Cody got out of the truck. He walked around to the driver's side while Cal got into the front seat. "Don't forget about your tux. That's all I need is the best man showing up in something purple."

At the mention of Annella's favorite color, Max wondered if he could find purple flowers to take her tonight.

"Don't worry, little brother. I'll take care of it this week and let you know when I'm finished." Cody rubbed the back of his neck. "Thanks, Max. See ya, Cal."

Max put the truck in gear. "No problem. Tell Sadie I said hi. See you later, bro." Max waited for Cody to make it around the front of the truck before driving away to drop Cal off.

Cal watched the manicured lawns and white picket fences pass as Max drove away. Max shocked him when he asked, "Where should I take Annella on our first official date?"

Cal stopped staring at the scenery and looked at Max, recovering from the shock. "First date? Isn't this technically your second date?"

Max glared at Cal before looking back at the road. "The moonlight picnic wasn't an official date. At that point it was just friends eating together and kissing at the end. I can do better than that."

"Thanks for the clarification although I would still call it a date. Why don't you take her to the clubhouse at the golf course? It's romantic without being over the top, and it's supposed to be cooler tonight."

Max used the hands-free system in the truck to call the clubhouse and secure the last reservation available for the evening. "That was a genius idea, Cal."

Max pulled up in front of Cal's house a few minutes later. He texted Annella while he was waiting for Cal to get out.

I'll be there to get you at 5:40. Still your call if you wear sweats or not.

Annella texted right back: *See you then.*

Cal got out of the truck and shut the door but stuck his head through the open window. "Don't have too much fun tonight."

Max put his phone down and reached up for the gear shift. "I'll try not to overdo it. See you tomorrow, partner."

"Later," Cal said and turned to head inside only a little jealous of his friend having a date.

Max turned up the radio as he drove away from Cal's. He took his truck through the carwash on his way home to get ready. His truck wasn't dirty, but he thought back to his dad always reminding him to wash your truck before you go pick up a pretty girl. He pulled into his driveway sad at the lack of a purple van.

He surveyed her work as he walked up the porch steps. The chairs were straightened, the little glass-top table was clean, and all his half-empty water bottles were gone. He went inside and took his first good look at the living room. He didn't notice a lot earlier in his rush to get to Annella to assure her that everything was okay.

Now, he noticed that it smelled better. The dirty laundry and dishes were put away, everything was free of dust, and his mail was piled nicely on the end table with a note scrawled out in her cute, loopy handwriting on top.

> *Max, this is your homework.*
> *I will be checking on it at dinner.*
> *- Chef*

Max set the note down and picked up the stack of mail, walking to the kitchen so that he had easy access to the trashcan. He stopped short in the entrance taking in the clean space. It looked like a completely different room. No goopy grease on the cabinets, the handle to his fridge was white, the dishes were clean, and he could see the countertops.

He pulled water from the fridge, making sure he didn't leave a mark on the handle and sat on the counter to go through the mail.

Homework complete he went to check the rest of the house. He walked from room to room, noticing the difference a few hours and hard work made. Max loved how comfortable his house felt now. He walked into his bedroom and stared at his bed. It was neatly made pillows were actually in cases—where had those come from?—and there were no piles of laundry on his floor.

He turned around to look at his new dresser. He still couldn't believe she had bought this for him. There was masking tape on each of the six drawers, letting him know what was inside each one. This woman thought of everything.

Max opened the appropriate drawer for fresh socks that Annella had matched and boxer briefs. A whiff of freshness hit his nose, and he smiled. He could get used to "woman clean" laundry instead of "bachelor clean." He closed the drawer and went to shower for dinner.

—◊—

He stood in line at the grocery store two people behind fucking Thorne seething. The dick was buying a bouquet of flowers and bragging about taking Annella on a date. He was so oblivious that there might be people that would use this information against him standing a mere ten feet away. Some cop he is.

Chapter

17

Annella arrived back home, unloaded, and put away her cleaning supplies then headed straight for a shower. She worked up a good sweat while cleaning and didn't want to go to dinner smelling like one of Max's socks.

She texted Lauren: *Thanks again for the dresser. It was so much of a success it got me a dinner date.*

Lauren texted back immediately: *A date with Max? Where are you going? What are you going to wear?*

Annella thought about her options. She didn't want to wear anything that she had worn out with Travis, and since she didn't know where they were going, she had no idea what to wear. She sent Lauren a text back: *No clue where we are going or what to wear. Come help me pick something? If you aren't busy.*

Her phone pinged as she turned on the shower. *Fashion show. I'll be right there!*

Annella took off her sweaty cleaning outfit and stepped into the steamy water.

Feeling more like a human and less like the sweaty bra she just took off, Annella turned off the water and toweled herself off right as the doorbell rang. She threw on her rich, purple, fuzzy robe as she walked downstairs to open the door for Lauren.

Lauren stood on the porch, arms crossed over her chest, waiting. "You know, if you would leave your door unlocked, I could have just walked in."

Annella moved back so Lauren could come in. "And have you scare me just as badly as Cody did earlier? No thanks."

Lauren came in and wrapped her in a hug. "What did poor Cody do to scare you?"

Annella shut and locked the door, then led the way upstairs, telling Lauren about how Cody was at Max's when she got back from getting the dresser and scared ten years off her life. Lauren's bubbly laughter filled the stairwell as they climbed to the second floor.

"I was mortified when Max told me who it was. I can't believe I called him. I must have sounded so pathetic." Annella pulled a fresh bra and underwear and stepped into the bathroom to put at least some clothing on. She came back out, and Lauren was sitting cross-legged on her bed.

Lauren picked up their conversation. "If there's one thing all men love it's to feel like the brave knight rescuing the princess. I'm sure Max didn't find it pathetic at all. I bet his ego grew twenty points." Lauren hopped off the bed and went to look through Annella's clothing selection.

"All you own are chef jackets and black pants," Lauren yelled from her closet over the sound of the blow dryer.

"You really have no idea where he's taking you," she said coming out of the closet clothes in hand.

"I have no clue. I joked that I was coming home to put on sweats."

Lauren laughed and grabbed Annella's hand, pulling her into the bedroom to try on the outfits she had pulled out.

The first option was black capri pants with a white flowy blouse that had a square neck. She put it on and did a few turns to show her friend.

"It's cute, but not for a date," Lauren said shaking her head.

Annella took that off and laid it to the side to put away and tried on outfit number two. Feeling summery in a beige pleated maxi skirt with a black sleeveless cowl neck top she spun around fast so her skirt flowed out.

Lauren looked over the outfit with a critical eye, tapping her finger to her lip. "Still not right, but I loved the twirl."

Annella was about to take off the outfit and lay it with the first as her phone pinged again. She was hoping it was Max telling her where they were going so she and Lauren had more of a direction for the outfit, but it was from an unknown number.

Did you like my message, Chef Whore?

Lauren watched the color leave Annella's face. She got off the bed and guided her friend to sit down. "You look like someone just walked over your grave. Who was that text from?"

Annella handed Lauren her phone and hugged her knees to her chest.

Lauren read the brief message and looked to see if she knew the number. She sat down beside Annella and drew her into a side hug. "Are you okay? How long have you been getting these types of messages?"

Annella leaned into Lauren's hug and rested her head on her shoulder. She tried to ground herself by feeling the soft cotton of Lauren's shirt, smelling the sweet scent from the air freshener that Lauren had in the shop earlier and answered.

"This is the first message like that, but not the first crazy message. I got a bunch from Travis after I told him off in the grocery store, so I blocked his number." Annella pushed off the bed and picked up the first outfit to hang it back in the closet.

She heard Lauren come in behind her. "Are you going to tell Max?"

Annella put the hangers on the rod and turned to Lauren. "I will, but after. I just want to enjoy my night and have a good time."

Annella put a smile on her face and rolled her shoulders, trying on the third outfit. It was a sky-blue dress that fell to her mid-thigh and hugged her body perfectly. She paired it with kitten heel nude sandals that strapped up her ankle. She didn't have to worry about being taller than Max, no matter how tall her shoes were. She walked the length of her bedroom, letting Lauren survey her. Lauren started clapping.

"Yes! Absolutely perfect!"

They picked out simple gold hoops for her ears and a teardrop necklace with a stone that matched her dress to complete the look. Lauren sat back on the edge of the tub and watched Annella apply her makeup, having to stop a few times to steady her shaking hand.

They talked about town gossip. Annella was able to know pieces of it and who Lauren was talking about now since starting her business and overhearing people talking. Annella popped mauve-pink lips in the mirror, thinking she didn't look half bad when she heard the doorbell.

Lauren jumped off the tub. "I'll get it so you can make an entrance."

Annella looked over herself one last time and tried to calm her nerves. *It's Max. You know him. You've already kissed him.* But she wasn't nervous about just him.

Max felt like he was going to fly into a million pieces as he walked up Annella's porch steps. He smelled the daisies in his hand mixed with the scent of Annella's roses, and his head spun a little.

He was trying to remember all the things he practiced on the way over. Tell her she looks pretty, thank her for doing such an amazing job cleaning, tell her she smells like a summer day on the beach. Max rang the doorbell and twisted the stems of the daises in his hands until the door opened.

Instead of Annella staring at him, it was Lauren, and she was holding back a giggle. Everything Max was going to say went out of his head, and all he could do was exhale slowly.

"Hey, Max," Lauren said, slightly giggling at him. "Those are beautiful flowers; Annella will love them." Max finally recovered from the wrong person opening the door enough to say hi before his cop brain took over.

"Is Annella alright? What are you doing here?" He was moving into the house, about to hurry up the stairs, when Lauren stopped him with a hand on his arm.

"Relax, Officer Thorne. She's perfect. She didn't know what to wear, so she texted for backup. I told her I would get the door so she could make an entrance down the stairs. Annella," Lauren called up the stairs. "You might want to come down before Max rushes up, and you two don't even make it out of the house."

Lauren stepped back and made herself as small as possible in the corner of the living room and pulled out her phone.

She snapped pics as Annella came down the stairs, some of Max's awed expression as he watched her, and one as Max took her hand as he helped her down the last step. Annella would love to have these. She put her phone away and watched as Annella and Max locked gazes like the world started and stopped with one another.

Annella spoke first, and her voice amplified the magic flowing in the room. "Hey, Max. You look very debonair."

And he did look debonair, all 6'7 of him. He wore his pressed jeans like a second skin, polished black cowboy boots, and a pristine white shirt that Annella didn't remember seeing in his closet.

She wanted to run her hand through his chestnut locks and mess up the perfect style he had. Max stood a beat longer before he found his words. "I was going to tell you that you looked pretty, but that would be an insult to you. There is no word for your beauty. The closest I can come up with is exquisite."

Annella blushed to the same color as the largest daisy Max still held. "Thank you. Are those for me?" Annella pointed at the cellophane-wrapped flowers, causing him to stammer.

"Yeah. Yes. These are for you. I figured you could enjoy roses anytime you wanted right outside, so I wanted to get you something different. The store didn't have anything purple, so I opted for colorful."

Annella took them, feeling the buzz when her fingers brushed Max's. She smelled the sweet aroma with just a hint of Max's sandalwood soap.

Lauren snapped one last quick photo of Annella's euphoric look, smelling her flowers, and moved to Annella's side. "Why don't I take those and put them in water for you so y'all can get going?"

Annella handed the bundle to Lauren and took Max's outstretched hand.

"Thanks, bestie."

Lauren hugged the flowers to her chest wishing a "Max" would bring her daisies one day. "You're welcome. Have a great time!" Annella picked up her keys and purse as they headed out the door. Lauren found a peach-colored vase with blue flowers on top of the fridge and watched through the window over the sink as Max opened Annella's door and helped her inside. She put the flowers in the vase and set them on the coffee table and headed out the door herself.

Chapter

18

Max followed Annella out of the house and took her hand to help her down the front porch steps. When they reached the sidewalk he refused to let go as he escorted her to the truck.

He opened the door and kept her hand in his while she climbed inside, relishing the softness of her skin even with a career that had her washing her hands at least 100 times a day.

He let go after placing a light kiss on her knuckles and went around to drive them to the restaurant.

When he got situated behind the wheel, he noticed Annella's smile and loved knowing that he was the one to put it there. "Flowers, clean truck, polished boots, you're pulling out all of the stops."

Annella flipped down the visor to check her makeup and keep the sun out of her face.

"It's been a while since my last date, but I remember the rules," Max said, starting the truck and reaching for his seatbelt. "And before you ask, yes, I did my homework."

Annella turned to Max as he pulled away from her house. "Yay! Now my brain can rest easy knowing that's finished."

Max smiled back at her as he guided the truck through downtown and out to the golf course. Annella sighed with contention.

"I'll never get tired of how cute downtown is. It's a nice change from the city with trash piled up everywhere and everything smelling like a dumpster."

"Is that what made you leave the city?" Max asked, turning toward the opposite side of town from the lake.

"It's one of the reasons. It was time for a change. I was so tired of the city, the lights, the noise, not knowing anyone really. I wanted to go somewhere I could feel like a part of a community. I needed to find my place, and the city wasn't it."

Max reached over and squeezed her hand. "And did you leave a string of broken hearts behind when you moved?"

Annella rested her chin in her hand, looking out the window as they passed the tall oak trees.

"Nope. The last guy who showed interest in me was the head chef at the restaurant I worked at. He offered me the sous chef position, but it came with 'stipulations,'" Annella air quoted, "When I made it clear on our first date that I would not be sleeping my way into a job, he paid the tab and left me to find my own way home. It's probably been longer since my first date than yours."

Max clenched his jaw so hard he was surprised he didn't crack a tooth. He couldn't believe the jerk would just leave her like that, not caring if she made it home safe or not.

"I promise to try and keep the house clean, but I may have to hire you for a refresh occasionally."

Annella gave a small smile at the change of subject. "You don't have to hire me to do that. I love to clean you love to make messes. It's a win-win situation in my book. I often have to create messes in my house to have something to clean. This way, your house gets clean, and I don't have to think of a mess to create at home."

Max chuckled. "You create messes? That makes no sense. Do you know what a day off is?"

Annella lightly swatted his arm. "Don't make fun. Yes, I know what a day off is, but I can still clean and call it a day off since I'm doing something that I enjoy."

Max turned the truck into the parking lot of the golf course for the second time that day and parked in the same spot as earlier.

"We're going to have to agree to disagree on that. One day, when all the messes are cleaned, I'm going to show you what an actual day off is. Now, let's see how the food measures up to the best chef in Green Lake."

Annella laughed at that, and his heart tripped over its next beat as he got out of the truck.

She took Max's hand after he opened her door and stepped down from the truck. "It's so beautiful here."

Max memorized Annella's face as she stared at the beautiful surroundings and looped his arm around her lower back because he couldn't stop touching her. They walked through the parking lot and up the stone steps to the part of the clubhouse where the restaurant was located.

"This place looks like it belongs in a fairytale," Annella said as she took in the rough stone, two-story structure that looked like a Scottish castle from a forgotten century. The shrubbery and red poppy flowers surrounding the building added whimsy to the sturdiness.

Annella walked in as Max held the door for her, and she marveled even more at the interior of the space. It was classy without being fussy. She didn't know how The Black Tie stayed in business, with this place being an option for fine dining. The tables were covered in navy blue cloths, and a single red rose sat beautifully in a yellow bud vase. It was light and airy whereas The Black Tie was dark and moody.

The hostess greeted them as Max came up behind Annella. "Hi, Max," she said to him and then held out her hand to Annella.

"Hi, Annella. I'm Penelope. Your food is amazing."

Annella smiled at the bubbly young woman with bouncy blonde curls and bright blue eyes. "Chopped sandwich, plain chips, and a lemonade," Annella said, shaking her hand.

"Sorry, I'm better with food than with names. It's nice to officially meet you now."

Penelope laughed. "Nothing to be sorry for. That's impressive. If you'd like to follow me, your table is ready." She stepped out from behind the hostess's desk and glided through the tables like a swan on a lake.

Annella was looking everywhere trying to take in as many of the details as possible. One whole wall was taken up by a stone fireplace that she bet would be amazing in the colder months. For now, it sat cold with logs piled in for decoration. People stopped Max on their way by, wanting to catch up or complain about a noisy neighbor, but he kept the conversations short and told the complainer to call the station because he was on a date.

Penelope stopped at a table in a glass-enclosed patio, looking out at the water hazard on hole nine. Max pulled out Annella's chair, filling his nose with her tropical scent before taking the chair across from her.

Penelope handed them menus and told them to enjoy themselves before gliding back to the front. Annella stared at the small fountain of water in the middle of the pond, and Max could see her eyes sparkle.

Annella turned away and locked eyes with Max. "I'm glad I didn't wear sweatpants."

Max unfolded his cream-colored linen napkin to have something to do with his hands instead of pulling Annella across the table and kissing her senselessly.

"Chef, you could be in a flour sack and still be the most breathtaking woman here."

"I can't believe Travis never brought you here."

Annella made a face at the mention of Travis's name, and the earlier text message came rushing back to her. Since she couldn't prove it was him, she didn't say anything to Max about it.

"We only went out on a few dates and always to The Black Tie. I think he thought that he was showing off, but all I could think was that the food sucked, and my date was cheap. I'm glad I didn't get hired by the Ashwoods."

Their server arrived, and they both selected white wine and a calamari appetizer.

"I'll second that," Max said as their server backed away to put in their drinks and appetizer.

"So, I told you about my dating past. Tell me about the string of broken hearts that led to Max Thorne sitting here with me looking handsome as sin." Max cringed. Luckily, he didn't have to answer right away as the server reappeared with their wine.

Annella's heart raced as she picked up her glass trying for an easy tone. "If you don't want to talk about it, that's fine. We can change the subject."

Max took a sip of wine, his large hands making the glass look like a champagne flute and waited for the guilty feelings to come flooding back to him. Surprisingly, they didn't. Maybe Cal's pep talk worked earlier.

"It's okay. I'm honestly surprised no one's told you about it yet. The list isn't as long as you might think."

Max rubbed the back of his neck and looked out over the pond. Guilt and dread churned Annella's stomach and suddenly calamari didn't sound so good. *I shouldn't have asked him that. He probably wants the date to be over now* she thought.

Before she could change the subject, Max continued, "There was Sarah in second grade. She was my girlfriend for a whole two days until Scott Hawkins gave her his candy bar at lunch and she dumped me."

Annella stuck out her bottom lip, feeling sad for the little broken-hearted Max. "You wouldn't share your candy bar with her?"

"It had peanuts in it, and she was allergic. I came home from school very upset, but my dad told me, 'Son, one day you're going to find a girl that loves peanuts in her chocolate so much that she eats your whole candy bar. Then, you'll have to start taking an extra one.'"

Annella looked at Max with a little mischievous grin. "I happen to love peanuts in my chocolate."

Max smiled at the memory of their first encounter when she offered him chocolate-covered peanuts.

"After that, I swore off women until freshman year when Brenda Green took an interest in me. She was the town princess, and everyone wanted her, but for some reason she wanted me. We dated all through high school, and I thought she was the one. I should have known she wasn't for me when she didn't like peanuts in her chocolate at all. She left town saying she didn't want to be stuck in a small town with a guy who only wanted to be a police officer."

Max gulped down the rest of his wine in one long drink.

"What a bitch," Annella said, causing him to nearly spit his wine on the table. "I can't believe she would pull that crap."

Warmth spread through Max at her defending him instead of saying that he should have been a better man and kept her happy like some people.

"Now you're all caught up until this gorgeous caterer with a lead foot caught my eye."

The waiter arrived with their calamari heaped in golden strings on a white platter. He took their food order of the special; grilled white fish with a lemon cream sauce paired with roasted vegetables on a bed of rice.

Max picked up a small plate and served Annella first smiling as her hand brushed his.

"Thank you, Max. You could have the first plate though. I'm used to eating after serving." She set the plate down and forked a bite into her mouth.

"Ladies first," Max said fixing his own plate.

The squid was perfect, herby in flavor, not slimy, and fried to a crispy golden brown. They finished the platter not even worrying about having enough room for the rest of the meal.

Their food arrived, and it smelled magnificent. Annella forked a bite of fish dripping with light-yellow sauce into her mouth, eyes wide with excitement. Max couldn't tell you what he ate and only that it tasted like lemon. He was getting more enjoyment out of watching Annella study her food.

"What are you doing?" Max asked as Annella dipped her fork in just the lemon sauce for the third time.

"I'm learning the flavor profile of this sauce so I can attempt to recreate it later."

Max kept watching her as she slowly took bites of the vegetables and rice, surprised that she didn't have a pad and pen taking notes.

When they finished their entre, Max asked, "Was the food up to your standards?"

Annella dabbed at her mouth and took a sip of her wine. "It exceeded them. The mildness of the fish was really enhanced with the lemon and herbs. The potatoes, squash, and carrots were tender without being mushy, and I very rarely enjoy plain rice, but mixed with the sauce it was divine. I give it a ten."

"Hopefully, I get an invitation when you try your hand at the sauce," Max said, looking at the setting sun.

The talk turned to movies, music, and books. The last topic sent Annella down a rabbit hole about her current read with the badass female warrior and her addiction to coffee.

Max confessed to not being much of a reader but listened intently as Annella talked more about her book. He could picture the scenes in his head as she talked about the female warrior training with individuals who were bigger but still besting them.

When she finally quieted down and Max paid the tab, he asked, "How are your shoes?"

Annella looked down at her sandals and then back at Max her eyebrow quirked. "I wouldn't run in them, but they're comfy enough. Why?"

Max stood and came around the table to help her out of her chair. "There's a walking trail through part of the course. I thought since the night had cooled off and no one is golfing now, we could walk for a bit."

Annella looped her arm through the crook of Max's elbow and felt the cotton of his shirt rub against her bare skin. "A walk sounds nice."

They walked through the lush green golf course on the red brick path in comfortable silence. Even though Annella's shoes were comfortable, she still took them off, opting to go barefoot. Max found a purple golf ball on the path, picked it up, and handed it to her.

"Looks like you're not the only one that likes purple."

Annella sat on a low stone bench to put her shoes back on but before she could even get one shoe on, Max scooped her up and began carrying her toward the truck.

Annella squealed. "Max, I can walk. I just need to put my shoes on first."

Max just held her closer, enjoying her body pressing against his and her head on his shoulder so he could smell more of her coconut shampoo.

"I know you can, but I prefer this."

They got to the truck and Annella grabbed the door handle hanging on it as Max pulled backward to open the door. He put her on the seat and thought, *what the hell*. He leaned in and kissed her soft lips deeply but quickly. He practically floated around to the other side of the truck, knowing that he was crushing this date.

Max started the truck and drove them back to Annella's, listening to her sing along to the radio. He never wanted her to stop singing. He pulled up to her house and cut the engine.

"It's still early and I have the cookies for tomorrow to bake. Want to keep me company?"

Max grinned at her as he unbuckled. "Always."

Annella got out when Max opened the door and told him that she could walk since he had parked with her side on the sidewalk.

He had to touch her still, though, so he took her hand again as they walked up the steps. Annella pulled out her keys and went to open the door noticing that the lock didn't need to be unlocked.

"Lauren must have forgotten to lock the door when she left," Annella said to Max as she swung the door open.

"It's okay. Now you're officially one of us."

They walked in and Annella flipped on the living room light. Her hand flew to her mouth with a gasp, dropping her shoes at the scene before her.

Chapter

19

A deep growl tore through Max's throat as he looked over Annella's head into the living room. It was enough to make his blood boil and set his senses on alert.

Scattered around her pristine area rug were shards of peach and blue porcelain, flowers shredded and strewn all over the room. He pulled Annella behind him and started backing toward the door, listening for any sign someone was still in the house.

Max had his phone calling the station before they even made it down the first step. Amber, the night dispatch, answered on the second ring as Max walked to his truck for his badge and weapon.

He put his keys in Annella's hands then placed her in the driver's seat of the truck. He leaned over her and retrieved his badge and holster from the center console.

Max listened as Amber keyed the information before calling for a unit to respond.

Amber came back on the line as he clipped on his badge and secured his holster to his jeans.

"Dawn and Hall responded and are heading there now. Do you need EMS?" She asked.

"No, everyone is fine. I'm going to sweep the house and make sure the perp isn't still here. Thanks, Amber."

He put his phone back in his pocket and then crouched down in front of Annella, running his hands up the smooth skin of her arms.

"Hey, chef," he said in a light voice. "I'm going to make sure there's no one still in the house. If you hear anything, drive to my house and stay there. I've already got back up on the way."

Annella nodded. Max stood up and kissed the top of her forehead before he jogged back to the house. Annella pulled out her phone and called Lauren.

"Hey!" Lauren answered on the second ring. "How was your date?"

Annella blew out her breath and watched Max through the window. "It was amazing, He took me to the country club, and we walked around the grounds after dinner."

Lauren noticed the flat tone of her friend's voice, "You don't sound like a girl that had a great date. Did something happen?"

"Yes. Do you remember locking the door when you left?" Annella chewed on her fingernail hoping that her tone didn't come off as she was accusing Lauren of anything.

Lauren was silent for a second. "I don't think I did. I just put the flowers down and walked out. What happened?"

Annella tipped her head back. She was prepared for that answer but was hoping for a yes that Lauren did lock the door.

"Between you leaving and Max and I coming back, someone went into the house, smashed the vase, and destroyed my flowers."

She heard Lauren's intake of breath before she started talking so fast Annella had to strain to keep up.

"Annella, I'm sorry. It's a terrible habit, and I should have been more thoughtful about it on my way out.

Annella didn't want Lauren to worry or feel guilty. It was an honest mistake, and she wasn't mad. "Lauren, It's okay. I only wanted to see if you locked the door and if you noticed anything strange when you left."

Lauren's voice leveled out. "I didn't. When I left, everything looked like it normally does."

Max walked out of the house, anger twisting his face as he reached the truck. She leaned into his warmth as he wrapped his arm around her.

"There are two officers on their way to investigate with Max. They may have questions for you too. Do you want to come here so they can ask everything at once?"

"You got it bestie. I'm on my way." Annella heard Lauren's keys jingle as she told Lauren she would see her in a bit.

"Which side of the bed do you sleep on?" Max asked with a stone set to his face.

Annella ran her hands through her hair not sure why he asked, but she said, "The side closest to the window. Why?"

Max locked his jaw and watched as his backup arrived. "Because the pervert left an intact flower on your pillow." Max stalked away from the truck to greet Officers Dawn and Hall.

That sent Annella spiraling. She had never slept with anyone in her bed, so how did they know which side of the bed to leave the flower on? Were there cameras in the house? She had never really worried about closing her blinds since her room was on the second floor, but maybe it was possible for people to see inside when she lay down at night. The thought of someone watching her while she slept and not in a cute way sent a shiver down her spine.

Annella rocked in the seat and watched as Max gave directions to the other two officers. She couldn't help but think he looked hot in his 'cop boss' attitude, using acronyms she didn't fully understand that had Officers Dawn and Hall moving into action.

Lauren showed up a few minutes later with more apologies and wrapped Annella in a tight hug. Max told them it was clear, so they went to sit on the porch swing. The first Annella assured her weren't necessary, but she did enjoy her friend's hug. She wasn't mad at Lauren, but she was pissed at whoever did this to her.

The vase wasn't expensive or sentimental, just something pretty she had found in a thrift store in Clear Spring, so no loss there, but for someone to hate her that much enraged her more than bad food.

How did anyone even know about the date or the flowers?

Was someone watching her?

Had she become so comfortable in Green Lake that she had forgotten to be aware of her surroundings?

The feeling of someone staring at her even now had her shivering again.

Lauren went inside and came back with Annella's fuzzy purple blanket. She wrapped it around her and sat back down. "What's going on in your head?"

Annella pulled the blanket tighter around herself. "I'm thinking, how did this person even know about the date or the flowers? Are they watching us now, enjoying the show?" Annella turned her head to look behind her, but all she saw were the soft glow of lights in houses.

Lauren toed the swing into motion. "If the dumbass is out there watching right now, they better run. Max is on the warpath. He has poor Dawn and Hall collecting every piece of the vase and the flowers."

The two officers came out of the house and walked over to the swing. Max was right behind them with a look that could kill. He held back as the two deputies began their questions for Lauren. She confirmed the time she left, that she couldn't remember locking the door, and that she didn't see any strange people or cars.

Officer Dawn turned to Annella. "Can you think of anyone that would want to do this to you?" she asked, holding her pen over her black leather journal.

"I can't think of anyone. I hardly know people in town well enough for them to be this vindictive. The date was also pretty last minute, so the grapevine couldn't have worked that quickly. I only told Lauren."

Dawn turned to Max. "Who all knew about your date and the flowers on your side, Lieutenant?"

Max knew they were only doing their job, but he didn't want to answer questions. He wanted to punch someone in the face.

"Cal and Cody knew about the date, but not that I was getting flowers. I suppose anyone that was in the supermarket when I bought them could have overheard when I told the clerk who I was buying them for."

Lauren looked at Annella. "What about that text from earlier?"

Max looked over Dawn's head. "What text?" Max asked more sharply than he meant to, causing Annella to flinch and making him feel worse than he already did.

"It was a creepy text that came in while I was getting ready. I have no idea who sent it. I was going to tell you while we were baking cookies, but then all of this happened."

She picked up her phone and unlocked it, holding it out for the officers. Max moved between his deputies and took her phone. He read the message three times and looked at the number. He didn't recognize it, so he pulled out his own phone and scrolled through the numbers he had to see if it matched any of his contacts. When he didn't find a match for anyone on his list, he handed the phone to Dawn to put the number in her notes.

Max stomped down the stairs with enough force to cause the wooden steps to groan. Annella followed him with her eyes as his long legs ate up the distance between houses.

"He's going to see if any of your neighbors saw anything suspicious," Dawn said as she handed Annella her phone back. "Was this the first threatening message you've received?"

Annella set her phone down on the wicker table. "From this number, yes. I was getting harassing messages from Travis Ashwood for a while, but then I blocked his number."

Dawn added that to the notes she had already taken. She closed her notebook.

"Thanks, ladies. If you think of anything else, please let us know."

Annella stood up, laying the blanket on the swing, and walked down the sidewalk with Hall and Dawn. Max was coming back up the walkway and he stopped the two. "We're heading into the station to write this up and run the number to see if it matches anything.

Max rested his left hand on his holster and rubbed his face with the right. "Nothing out of the ordinary for a Sunday in Green Lake, according to the neighbors. Call me if that number comes back with a match."

"Yes, sir," they said in unison and headed for their car.

Max caught up with Annella at the bottom of the stairs as Lauren stood up from the swing. "I'm going to head home."

She came down the steps and hugged Annella tight. "I really am sorry."

Annella squeezed her back. "It's okay, really. I'm just glad you weren't here when they came in." Lauren smiled at her, gave Max a one-armed hug, and walked to her car.

Annella and Max waved as Lauren drove away. She looked at Max, who looked down at his boots and then back up to her eyes.

"I'm sorry for snapping at you earlier. I was—am—pissed. It's my *job* to keep everyone in town safe and it seems like I'm failing you. Can you forgive me?"

Max held open his arms for her to either hug him back or turn around and head inside. He wouldn't hold the latter against her. He had been an ass, and he deserved it if she turned away from him.

Annella stared at Max's outstretched arms long enough that she could see them tremble from effort, and she couldn't stand the silence any longer. She wrapped her arms around his middle, using the connection to convey that she was no more upset with him than she was with Lauren. Neither of them was to blame for a sick person's actions. Max enveloped her and kissed the top of her head.

They stood like that for a moment longer until Max spoke, "Pack a bag. You're staying with me tonight."

Annella tipped her head back and cocked an eyebrow at him. "I can't just leave everything and stay with you. I need to clean up what's left of the mess and bake the cookies for tomorrow. Plus, I can't smoke the meat for lunch on your grill. I won't let this d-bag think that I'm too scared to stay in my own house."

Max loved the fire in her voice. It meant that she wouldn't let this get her down. Still, he needed to be near her tonight for his own peace of mind, and he wasn't taking no for an answer.

"Fine, I'll stay with you."

Annella wanted to tell Max that she was more than capable of staying by herself, but she recognized the stubborn set of his jaw from the tickets he had written her. He was not letting this go.

"You better not snore." Annella said. Max sighed in relief and held Annella a moment longer. "Come with me to get an overnight bag?"

She nodded against his chest and walked inside to retrieve her purse and keys. Annella shut *and locked* the door, then walked hand in hand with Max to his truck.

After they were buckled in, Max made a U-turn, heading in the opposite direction from his house.

"Where are we going?" Annella asked as Max continued driving.

"We didn't get to eat dessert at the restaurant and what happened tonight sucked, so we are going to get chocolate shakes because chocolate makes everything better."

Annella smiled and leaned her head back, closing her eyes. "That's always been my motto."

—⚭—

Max hit the drive-through at Happy's and handed Annella her chocolate shake. She took the first sip and moaned at the sweet, cold treat, causing Max's pants to get tighter.

Nope. Not going there, he scolded himself. She's had her safety and privacy violated tonight. She doesn't need sex. She needs chocolate, to laugh and to know that she is safe with me.

He kept his mind out of the gutter all the way back to his house where he packed his bag and showed Annella the neat pile of his bills on the counter. They drove back to Annella's, apprehension radiating from her as her leg bounced quickly.

He reached over and gave her hand a reassuring squeeze. "It's going to be okay," he told her. "I won't let anything happen to you, and I've told Dawn and Hall to make extra patrols down your street."

"Thank you for everything, Max. This was the best date I've ever had. Could have done without the extra police involvement, but still a great night."

Max came to a stop in front of her house. "Anything for you, chef." He cut the engine and grabbed his bag from the back as Annella got out and started up the sidewalk.

She climbed the steps, not feeling the normal happiness that her charming house with the smell of fresh roses usually brought her. Now, all she could see was a smashed vase and destroyed flowers, even though Max's deputies had done a great job removing it all.

Before Annella could take one step inside, she felt Max's arms under her knees and behind her back, lifting her effortlessly.

"What are you doing, Max? I can walk." Annella didn't protest all that hard and wound her hands around Max's neck as he moved through the living room.

"I know you can walk, chef, but there's probably still shards of porcelain in the carpet, and you still have no shoes on." Max continued up the stairs before letting her down.

Annella looked around, feeling awkward at having this very masculine man in her very feminine bedroom.

"I'm going to change and put shoes on then I'll clean and make the cookies for tomorrow. The remote is on the coffee table if you want to watch TV."

"The TV is not what I want to watch tonight." Max ran a finger down her cheek, causing the hairs on the back of her arm to stand up. "I'll see you downstairs," he said and walked out.

Happiness, anger, and nervousness all warred in Annella as she removed her dress and slid into comfortable clothes and shoes. She wasn't going to be run out of town. Not when things were finally going well in her life. She just had to trust that Max and the rest of the officers would keep her safe.

She didn't see him in her living room, so she went looking. She found him in the laundry room, searching for something.

"What are you looking for?" Annella asked with her arms crossed. Max spun around, bumping into the washer.

"I was looking for the vacuum. I'm not going to sit down while you do the work. It may not have looked like it at my house, but I do know how to vacuum."

Annella moved further into the laundry room and shut the door, revealing the black and silver vacuum.

"Thanks," Max said as he reached around her and grabbed it then headed for her living room.

Annella followed Max out and started the oven preheating for the cookies as she heard the vacuum hum. She didn't have a huge living room, so it wasn't long before he put the vacuum away and joined her in the kitchen. He hopped his sexy ass on her counter by the sink, and his phone rang. He looked at the caller ID, seeing Cal's name.

"That took longer than expected," he said when he answered.

Annella could hear Cal from where she stood, placing the cool cookie dough on the sheet. "What the actual fuck? Please tell me we have evidence that it was Travis so we can go arrest him."

"Sorry, partner. I went over every inch with Dawn and Hall and there is nothing here tying him to it, unless he left prints on the flowers. No one saw anything out of the normal either."

"Shit," Cal said, and Max knew he was scratching his chin in frustration. "How's Annella holding up?"

Max looked her over and could see all the same emotions he was feeling. Anger, worry, and exhaustion, but she kept going. "She's holding up. I'm watching her bake enough cookies for the whole town."

"She's one tough woman. Most people would be getting out of town as fast as possible. I'm glad she's sticking to her guns. Call me if anything happens."

"I will. See you tomorrow, Cal." Max ended the call and slid down from the counter.

He waited for Annella to put two large pans of chocolate chip cookies in the oven before he crossed to her and placed his hands on her arms. He stared down into her eyes.

"How are you doing? And I mean, really doing? Don't just say you're fine."

Annella met Max's intense gaze and felt like he was staring into her soul. "Truthfully, I'm annoyed. I don't understand why they did this. Travis couldn't have read that much into the few dates that we went on to react this harshly. I know we don't know for sure that he did this," she pointed to the living room, "or my van," she pointed outside, "but I don't see how it could be anyone else."

Max prided himself on knowing what to do in most situations, but right now, he felt helpless. He could understand her anger and had plenty of his own to work out in the gym tomorrow, but tonight, he wanted to make her laugh.

She baked and showed Max how to put the cookies in bags and tie the purple ribbon after they cooled, which he cussed, saying his fingers were too big for such a small ribbon.

While they worked, Max told her stories. Mostly of him and Cal and the mishaps, they found themselves in when they were kids. He didn't stop until she finally laughed at Cal being chased by a goose at the lake one summer day when they had been trying to fish.

She laughed so hard she was crying when Max told her he threw his rod at the goose, and that only seemed to anger the animal more, so Cal ran and didn't stop until he was home. Max's body relaxed by degrees hearing the lilt of her laughter. They packed the last of the cookies and Annella put the pans in the dishwasher while Max went around the house checking the doors and windows.

Max could already feel his back hurt from how cramped he'd be on her couch, but he wasn't going to push sleeping in her bed.

"Do you have a spare pillow? I don't want to sleep on your decorative ones and ruin them."

Annella looked at her couch and then back at Max, chuckling at the image of him trying to fit on the small couch.

"Max, you aren't sleeping on the couch. My bed is big enough for both of us. You might hang off a little, but not as much as if you slept there."

Max opened his mouth to protest, but Annella held up her hand to stop him.

"Don't argue with me, please. I'm tired. I want to shower and then lay down next to you while I sleep. So, we are either both sleeping on the couch, or you can join me in bed."

Max thought about the pair trying to fit on the couch and thought he might enjoy that more than the bed, but tonight, he only wanted to make her feel safe. If this was what she wanted, he would gladly oblige.

"Whatever you want, chef." He grabbed his bag from the floor and followed her upstairs.

Chapter

20

Max took his boots off and unbuttoned his shirt, revealing his glorious abs to Annella. Her mouth dropped open. "Seriously, how many crunches do you do in a day?"

Max chuckled. "Not sure. I lose count after five hundred."

Annella rolled her eyes and disappeared into the bathroom. He stretched out on her bed, using the time alone to check on the phone number match—nothing there—and price security cameras. Tomorrow, he wanted to talk to Tom and Paula about installing some.

He wasn't sure how Annella would react to having cameras around the house, but he didn't really care. It was either cameras or he was moving in until they caught whoever was doing this. He would enjoy hearing her sing in the shower at night and waking up to her each morning.

The water turned off, and he tried his hardest not to think of her slim, warm body still dripping water and smelling like coconut. Tried and failed.

Annella stepped out of her steamy, relaxing shower and thought about the hot cop lying on her bed. She really hated that their beautiful night was—not ruined; that wasn't right. She had a hot man who made sure she didn't walk on busted porcelain waiting for her, and she was going to sleep next to him, but it had been overshadowed by the jerk that destroyed her flowers.

She toweled off and applied her nightly lotion, still thinking about the hot cop in her room. Did he sleep naked? Only in shorts? Would he be a gentleman? Did she want him to be? Annella was so busy with her thoughts that when she reached for her pajamas, her hand hit the counter.

"Crap!"

She had been so thrown off by Max's abs that she forgot her pajamas.

Annella wrapped her towel around her and opened the door a crack. "Close your eyes," she said to Max, causing his head to snap to her.

"Why would I need to do that, chef?"

Max was intrigued by her request. He still wasn't going to push sex from his side, but if Annella initiated it, who was he to deny a beautiful woman wanting him?

Annella groaned. "Because I didn't bring any pajamas into the bathroom with me, so I need to get them from my dresser."

Max did as she asked. "Okay. They're closed."

Annella opened the door more and checked to make sure. "No peeking."

"I swear I won't," Max said with a smile on his face.

Annella was focused on Max to make sure his eyes stayed closed that she didn't see the boot he left in the middle of her floor until she was heading down.

"Oh shit!" Annella cussed, losing the battle to keep her towel around her and control her fall as her ass hit the ground.

Max jumped up and came to the end of the bed, eyes wide open, and found Annella scrambling to cover herself. His eyes roved over her slender legs, her thick hips, and her magnificent chest. She was stunning.

He picked up her towel and handed it to her turning his head towards the ceiling "I might have peeked."

Annella snatched her towel feeling a heat in her face that had nothing to do with her shower. "You were supposed to keep your eyes closed."

"I did until you hit the floor cussing," Max snapped back. "What if you had been knocked unconscious, and there I sat, not able to see? I wasn't willing to risk it." Max re-closed his eyes and held out his hand to help Annella up.

"I think it's a little late for that now," she said, taking his hand and standing.

"Are you hurt?" Max asked, dropping her hand and turning away from her.

"I'm fine." Annella grabbed her pajamas and hastily headed back into the bathroom.

She could still hear Max's soft laugh as she dressed and put curl cream in her hair. By the time she came back out, Max had straightened his boots so they were out of her path.

"I'm sorry my boots were in your way. Are you sure you're alright?"

Annella tossed her clothes into the hamper and walked to the other side of the bed, sliding between the soft sheets next to Max.

"I promise the only thing damaged is my pride. Thank you for picking up your boots."

Max got up from the bed and picked up his bag.

"Your pride shouldn't be damaged at all. You look like a godess. And you're welcome. I should have done that when I took them off. How would you feel about security cameras?"

Annella looked at him, and she stammered, "Um. I. Do you really think they're necessary?"

Max sat his bag on her bed and went through the reasons he thought that they were a good idea. "They are necessary for peace of mind while the house is empty, while you're at work, and while you're sleeping. Also, hopefully, the jackass that's harassing you doesn't learn about them until after he attacks again, and he will, but this time we'll have proof of who it is."

Max pulled out his phone and showed Annella the options he had found. She scrolled through the pictures and read the price, and her jaw dropped.

"Max, I can't ask Tom and Paula to spend this much because of two incidents, and I can't afford the extra cost. Maybe after the commission from Cody and Sadie's wedding, if I get the job, but I'm hoping this person is either caught or just stops by then."

Max took his phone from Annella's outstretched hand and tossed it on the bed. He walked around the foot of the bed and sat beside her, taking her hand in his.

"Sure, the attacks have been small, but what happens when the next one isn't? What happens if this creep decides to come for *you* next time, not just your stuff? With the cameras, we'll know. Please, Annella, let me do this."

She looked at Max and saw the pleading in his gaze. He was trying to make sure she was safe.

Annella nodded. "Talk to Tom and Paula, but if they don't want them or can't afford them, then it's a no."

Max kissed her forehead and stood up. "Thank you. I feel better already."

Annella smiled, feeling better herself, and asked, "Has there been any update from the station?"

Max looped his bag strap over his shoulder. "I checked while you were in the shower, and no. Speaking of the station, you still need to pay your speeding tickets."

Annella crossed her arms, giving Max another view of her chest, and rolled her eyes. "What happens if I don't?"

Max bent over her, placing a hand on either side of her. "You'll have a warrant out for your arrest and could possibly be handcuffed and frisked by someone other than me." He kissed her nose as she gasped.

"You wouldn't."

Max looked her dead in her eyes. "I would, and if it happens to be anyone other than me, I will put them in a holding cell next to you." Max gave Annella a wide grin and headed for the bathroom.

Annella's phone pinged as Max shut the door. She picked it up and read Lauren's message.

Sorry again. I hope these make up for your lost flowers.

Pictures flooded her phone, and she smiled. Looking back at her from her screen was a girl looking the happiest she had ever been. She had almost forgotten Lauren was even in the room.

Max, holding the flowers that were now in police custody, looked at her with an awed expression on his face. And Max as he took her hand when she reached the bottom of the stairs like she was a princess. She saved them all in her phone and added the picture of Max to his contact information then responded to Lauren.

I love them all. You are the best friend ever! You have nothing to be sorry for. See you tomorrow.

Lauren responded: *See you tomorrow.*

Annella put her phone down—after looking at the pictures three more times—and picked up her book. She was reading about the most decadent cup of coffee the main female character had ever had when Max came out of the bathroom in only a pair of basketball shorts, his chest glistening, still damp. Well, that answered the question about what he slept in.

He dropped his towel on the floor next to the hamper, and Annella raised an eyebrow at him. He bent over, giving Annella a perfect view of his firm, muscled ass, and picked up his towel, putting it in the hamper.

"Better?" he asked, moving to the bed to lay down.

Annella nodded her approval and asked, "Are you normally a 'go right to sleep person,' or do you do something to unwind?"

Max hooked an arm under his head. "I normally go to sleep, but if you want to read more, I can look at more security cameras."

Annella set her book back on her nightstand and made sure her alarm was set then turned the light out. She rolled over and snuggled close to Max. She was glad he brought his own soap instead of using hers. The smell of it and the feel of his skin were driving her crazy. She placed her hand over his erratic beating heart, and he wrapped his arms around her. One under her head and one slung across her midsection.

She was in control of this situation, but Max thought he would be safe kissing her. He touched his lips to hers tentatively, listening for any sign that she was uncomfortable. When she arched into him, he deepened the kiss, running his tongue along her lips until she opened them for him.

They kissed passionately, letting the fear and anger out from the night. Their bodies and mouths tangled until Max didn't know where he ended, and Annella began. She rolled on top of him, her feet barely hitting his shins. Max didn't move or even breathe as she leaned down to trail kisses from his ear to his collarbone.

"Max, make me forget the bad part of today," she said in a sultry, smooth voice.

Max found his voice, and it came out in a husky whisper, "Are you sure? You've been through a lot—"

Annella silenced him with a soul-stealing kiss. "Yes. Let's replace the bad memory with an amazing one."

Max didn't have to be told again as he flipped her under him and made sure this was the way she remembered their night.

Chapter

21

Annella's alarm went off bright and early. She stretched, feeling sore in places that hadn't been sore in a while thanks to Max's efforts to make her forget the night. Her gaze traveled over Max's still form and she bit her bottom lip. He was glorious to look at. Muscles for days, tan skin, thick chestnut hair that she relished running her hands through repeatedly.

She kissed his stubble-lined cheek, and he groaned. "I don't hate mornings, but this is early even for me."

He moved to grab her and pull her back to his side, but her reflexes were faster.

"I just have to go put the meat on and then I get to lay back down while it smokes." Max lifted his head, eyes only half open. "Do you want any help?" She stuck on her house shoes and headed for the door. "I've got it. You go back to sleep." Max put his head back on the pillow, and Annella slipped out the door.

She went down the steps as quietly as possible in case Max was already back asleep. She forced her mind to see Max with her fresh flowers at the bottom of the stairs instead of the busted vase and shredded stems.

Annella put the meat on and set her app. Normally, she would do some yoga, but normally, she didn't have a sexy man lying half-naked in her bed. A few extra hours of sleep next to Max won out over downward dog.

Annella finished her water and threw the bottle away before climbing back upstairs. She used the bathroom and crawled back under the covers that were still warm from Max's body heat. She tried not to disturb him, but he must have been waiting for her.

He pulled her to him, then pressed a gentle kiss to her temple and fell back asleep. Annella didn't think she would sleep, but with Max's breathing and heartbeat in her ears, she found her eyelids heavy as sleep overcame her.

Max was on a tropical island feeling happier than he ever had. He took in the sight of the sun setting into crystal blue water, smelling coconut mixed with a smokey scent that didn't fit the atmosphere. He saw auburn curls as the gorgeous woman holding his hand led him into the water, she turned towards him with a sultry grin. The beeping of an alarm brought reality crashing back to him.

Once the jerk harassing her was captured, Max was going to make that dream come true. He gave her one last squeeze, then let her get up.

"Is this your life every morning?" Max ran his hand down his face and sat up. Now he knew how Cal felt whenever he woke him up on Sundays for a run.

Annella pulled clothes from her dresser and looked back at Max. He examined her looking for any signs of regret about what they did last night, but happily didn't find any. "No. I usually stay up once I'm awake, but something about my bed this morning was irresistible."

Annella went into the bathroom to get ready, and Max checked his phone. Nothing had come up on the number trace and there had been no fingerprints. He had suspected that, but it still got under his skin that this person was likely someone he knew and saw on a regular basis, but he couldn't pin them down.

She came back out of the bathroom in a purple Grace Squared Catering T-shirt, denim shorts that showed off her long, tan legs, and tennis shoes.

"Absolutely stunning," Max said, getting up and walking to her. He pulled her in for a hug, wishing he could keep her cocooned there so that nothing else would happen to her.

One of the reasons she moved to Green Lake was to feel more independent and live her life on her terms. He settled for a kiss on her cheek, so he didn't subject her to his morning breath and then headed for the bathroom.

Annella made the bed and then went back downstairs to make breakfast. She figured Max would want more than yogurt and fruit, so she fixed him an omelet with leftover brisket, sausage, bell pepper, and tons of sharp cheddar cheese.

She set his plate in the middle of the sun ray that was sneaking through the window as he sauntered into the kitchen. Her eyes roamed over his body appreciating the way he filled out his uniform. A sly grin spread across his face as if he already knew what she was thinking.

The corner of his mouth turned up. "You keep looking at me like that, and this omelet will be eaten cold."

Annella blushed and went to the fridge for her breakfast of an apple and key lime pie yogurt. She sat them on the table opposite Max's plate and asked him, "Orange juice or water?"

Max looked from the king's omelet on his plate to her meager breakfast. "Water. Thanks. There's no way I'm eating this," he pointed to his plate, "when all you are eating is that." He pointed to her apple and yogurt.

Annella pulled two waters from the fridge and tossed one to Max. She joined him at the table as he held out her chair.

"If I ate all of that this early in the morning, I'd go right back to sleep. You, on the other hand, need fuel to fight the crimes of Green Lake. Plus, if you don't eat it, you'll hurt my feelings."

Max pulled out his chair and sat down. His giant frame dominated her tiny vintage table.

The smell coming from his plate made his mouth water and the first bite of the omelet with the cheese stretching to his fork from the plate tasted like something from heaven. He shoveled down the rest before Annella could even finish half of her green apple.

"That was amazing." Max leaned back and patted his stomach.

"Cal will have to do all the heavy crime-fighting today. I'm going to be as useless as the g in lasagna." Annella beamed at his praise and the fact that he cleaned up his plate and put it in the dishwasher.

She finished her own breakfast, watching Max go through his bag, making sure he had everything he needed for his day. It brought her comfort to watch him move around in her space so easily. She got up and threw away her trash, Max wrapping his arms around her from behind as she rinsed her spoon.

She let out a happy sigh as her head rested on his chest. "Promise me you won't take any unnecessary risks today. We don't know the next level of crazy this person will escalate to in order to get to you." Max had only lost one other person in his life that he had cared about by not saying something sooner and he refused to let it happen again.

Annella turned in Max's embrace and looked at him in his piercing brown eyes. "I promise I'll be safe. Just the usual day. Work, grocery store, and then my run. Lots of people around me."

Max smoothed his hands down her back, resting them on the dip of her hips. "Don't go for the run by yourself. Wait, and Cal and I will go with you. You may have to bribe him with an extra cookie at lunch, but I'm sure he won't complain too much." Max kissed her forehead and took a step back. "I'm going to talk to Tom and Paula first thing this morning about the cameras." Max picked up his bag and headed for the door.

"Thanks," Annella said, following him.

Max paused with the door open and leaned down to Annella. He kissed her with a fury as if he was afraid he would lose her like he lost Heather. He shut that thought down. He would find this person, and they would be punished to the full extent of the law.

Annella sank her fingers into Max's hair and matched his tongue thrusts with her own, not wanting to think about the criminal hurting Max to get to her.

They broke apart, gasping for air. "I'll see you at lunch," Max said rubbing her bottom lip, swollen from his kiss, with his thumb. "You know where I'll be."

Annella grazed her hands across his chest, pausing over his heart, and rose on her toes to kiss his cheek. "Have a good morning."

He groaned and walked out the door before neither of them made it to work. Annella shut the door and locked it, suddenly feeling vulnerable.

—m—

Max pulled into his parking spot just as Cal was getting out of his own truck. He watched his partner shut the door and headed toward him. Max turned off his truck and got out as Cal rounded the hood.

"Morning. You look well rested despite the night you had. I'm thinking you didn't go home after you watched Annella bake cookies, did you?"

Max couldn't hide the grin spreading across his face, and Cal slapped him on the back. "I knew it!"

Max slung his bag over his shoulder. "Morning, Cal," was all he said as they went to work.

The daily sounds of the station generally calmed Max's nerves, but today, it only elevated them. Every time the phone rang, Max's heart sped up, thinking it was Annella. He needed to get to Tom and Paula quickly to talk about securing her house. They put their bags in their lockers, got their assignment for the day, and took off in the cruiser.

"Let's stop by The Buttered Biscuit first thing," Max told Cal. The sooner he could get that ball rolling, the sooner he could breathe again.

Cal took a left, following orders. "Didn't have time for breakfast?"

Max gave him a brotherly smack to the back of his head. "I had an amazing omelet for breakfast with brisket, sausage, peppers, and cheese. I want to talk to Tom and Paula about a security system for Annella's house."

Cal parked at the curb in front of the white brick storefront with the red mahogany door and large display windows full of pastry props. The bell dinged as they walked inside, the smell of cinnamon and sugar filling the quaint space.

"Morning, Max. Cal," Tom greeted from behind the glass display case. A blue baseball cap over his mostly salty white hair. A tan apron covering his white shirt had remnants of dough on it.

"You boys needing breakfast?" Tom and Paula didn't have any children of their own but always treated everyone like their kids. Max could remember helping Tom with yard work, and the only payment he would accept was a lemon square or two from Paula.

"No thanks, Tom. I need to talk to you and Paula about the house Annella is renting. Is she busy?"

Tom looked at the pass-through window into the back and saw Paula perched on a stool with a cold soda. He waved her to come to the front and turned back to Max and Cal.

Cal punched Max in the arm. "Just because you aren't hungry doesn't mean the rest of us aren't. I'm getting a cinnamon roll before we leave and you're driving while I eat it."

Max rubbed his arm where Cal struck him.

"Okay," he said as Tom and Paula came from the back of the shop.

Paula came out first, a smile on her face. Her frame was small, and her black hair had some gray, but she was stronger than she looked. She could throw around the fifty-pound bags of flour with no help needed.

She hugged Cal and Max before sitting at one of the black tables with a bright white daisy in the middle. Max looked at the flower thinking he needed to replace the destroyed bouquet.

"I need to talk to you about Annella," Max said as he took his own seat across from Paula.

Paula reached over and squeezed his hand. "Of course, Max."

Max had too much energy to stay seated, so he stood and paced. Cal leaned up against the counter, eyeing the sweets with the colorful icing.

"I don't know how fast the rumor mill is running today, but someone keeps attacking Annella. We have no leads now because this person has only struck while they have no way of getting caught. Her, your house was entered unlawfully and vandalized yesterday while we were out at dinner."

Paula gasped and covered her mouth with her hand. Tom's eyebrows shot up to his hairline.

"We had heard about the van but not about last night," Tom said. "What happened?"

Max gave them a rundown of the events that happened. Tom's nostrils flared in anger.

"Poor Annella. What can we do to help?" Paula asked fiddling with the white gold chain she always wore.

"I'm glad you asked. How would you feel about putting in a security system with cameras? This jerk is going to keep coming,

I know it, and this way, we can always be watching the house. You won't have to pay for anything. I'll take care of it..."

Tom held up a hand to silence him. "Max, we appreciate that, but we'd be more than happy to do this. We want Annella to feel safe at that house, and if this is what it takes, we'll do it. I never would have thought that a security system would be needed in Green Lake, but I guess anything is possible."

Max let out a heavy sigh, "Thank you both. I feel better."

Tom and Paula stood up.

"I'm going to call the company now. I'll schedule the installation for the first available appointment." Tom walked to the back of the shop where the office was located.

Paula moved behind the counter, wringing her hands. "I hope they can get here today. I'll feel better knowing Annella is safe. She's such a sweet girl." Paula looked at Cal still locked in on the treats. "What would you like, Cal?"

Cal pointed at the largest cinnamon roll with the most icing dripping from it. "That cinnamon roll right there, please." Cal paid for his breakfast, and they headed for the door.

"I'll have Tom call you with the details once he knows," Paula said as the bell tinkled.

"Thanks," Max said following Cal out to the warm summer day, his mood finally lighter. He drove the rest of the morning so Cal could eat.

Chapter

22

Annella was acting paranoid. She knew it, but she couldn't help it. Eight days had gone by since the flower fiasco, and everything was fine. There hadn't been any new attacks or text messages, and it was making her crazy. She was hardly sleeping. Each day instead of waking up rested she just wanted to cry and go back to sleep.

Tom and Paula had personally come over the same day Max spoke to them about the cameras to check on her and oversee the installation. She thanked them repeatedly and told them that they could raise her rent to compensate for the added cost, but they waved her off. They just wanted her to feel safe and would do whatever they could to make that happen.

She saw Max every night after work. They would go for a run, eat dinner, and then unwind with him, watching TV and her reading her book. Max only went home when she went to bed.

The morning was already warm, the sticky humidity from the lake dampening her skin as she got out at her spot to start setting up for the day. Max had reminded her last night and again this morning via text that her window to pay for her tickets was rapidly closing.

Apparently, sleeping with a police lieutenant didn't get her out of paying tickets. She locked her van and walked over to pay Danielle so that Max didn't have to handcuff her. Unless she wanted him to.

Danielle greeted her when she walked in, pink curls bouncing as she talked. "Morning, Annella." The station house was exactly as Annella pictured it from listening to Max's stories. Metal, utilitarian desks and chairs, gray metal door that led to the locker rooms and gym, and Captain Booker's office off to the left in the corner.

"Come to pay your speeding tickets?"

Annella rolled her eyes and blew out a huff. "Hi, Danielle. Yes, I don't want to end up behind bars. Orange is not my color."

Annella and Danielle laughed while Danielle pulled up the information on the tickets. Annella paid her, grumbling that Max owed her dinner now. She turned to leave and heard her name bellowed from Chief Booker's office. She shared a look with Danielle, not sure about the tone that he used, and walked through the maze of desks.

Chief Booker was a thicker man but still muscular, built like a linebacker, with bright blue, sharp eyes that didn't miss a thing. His shaved head gleamed in the fluorescent lights, and his white starched shirt popped off his deep olive skin. Annella had served him plenty of lunches so far and each time she fidgeted, afraid that he would arrest her if his brisket touched his potato salad.

"Have a seat," he said, gesturing to a metal chair with worn green cushioning on the seat and arms.

Annella twisted her fingers with worry, not knowing what possible topic the chief could have to discuss with her.

"Annella," he began in his no-nonsense tone, "have you heard about the Muscles for Money event from Max at all?"

Annella smiled and stopped wringing her hands together. "Yes. He told me that it's a great fundraiser for the first responders."

Chief Booker nodded and scratched his chin. "It's our largest fundraiser of the year. Something about the thought of seeing us in a state of undress brings people together with their wallets out."

Annella blushed at the thought of seeing Max shirtless and doing multiple rounds of pushups.

"How would you like to be a part of it? The food offerings in years past have been limited, but with you we could have a whole meal. I'm sorry it's last minute that I'm asking, but Max just came to me with the idea."

Annella clapped and bounced in her seat. "I'm in! I love giving back to the community and I have a vested interest in the police department."

The chief held out his bear-sized hand Annella shook it. "Great. I'll have Danielle email you the details."

Annella hopped up from her seat. "Sounds perfect." She walked out of the station on clouds, her panic momentarily forgotten.

Her tickets were paid, she had a new food event coming up, and it was almost time to see Max for lunch. Her good mood kept up while she served lunches, the citizens of Green Lake keeping time like a Swiss clock.

As if her thoughts summoned him, Max pulled into the parking lot with Cal in the passenger seat, causing her stomach to flip and a smile to cross her face. Max got out first, carrying a large bouquet of bright pink stargazer lilies and a box of her favorite chocolate covered peanuts. He set the flowers and chocolates down by her drink area and then kissed her temple.

"Hey, Cal," Annella said as she gloved up to serve them lunch. "Tell the truth, were these your idea?"

Max glared at Cal, fire in his eyes. "I wish I could take credit for them, but all I was observe."

Annella smiled at Cal and looked back to Max. "What's the occasion?"

Max hooked his thumbs in his pockets and kicked a pebble under his foot. "No occasion. I just thought since you didn't really get to enjoy the first flowers that I brought you, I would try again."

She fixed their plates, making sure to give Cal an extra cookie, then took her gloves off to feel the silky petals.

"How is your day going?" Max asked, picking up the bag with their food.

Annella was vibrating with excitement, but she could feel her exhaustion underneath. "It's great. I paid my tickets; the chief asked me about serving food at Muscles for Money, and a handsome man brought me flowers and chocolates. How's your day going?" Annella followed Max and Cal to the picnic table to visit with them while they ate.

"It's slow this morning, but something is about to happen. I can feel it. I'm glad the chief lined you up for that."

Max's statement brought back the paranoia and feeling of being watched. She looked over her shoulder but didn't see anything strange.

"Are you really alright? Not to sound like an ass, but you look worn out." Max asked when she turned back around.

"I'm pushing through it. A little caffeine later and I'll be good." Annella took her sunglasses off her collar, not mad at Max for pointing out what she saw in the mirror, and covered the bags under her eyes that her concealer didn't hide.

She was about to say fuck it and ask Max to start sleeping at her house to see if that helped, but she didn't want to make him change his life just so she could sleep.

Max and Cal finished eating and headed back to work with Max kissing her deeply and promising to see her later. Annella finished her lunch service and then began cleaning and packing up. Her phone pinged with a new text.

I see you have new flowers for me to destroy.

The color drained from her face, and her hands shook so badly that she dropped the phone, cracking her favorite purple case. Annella started shoving things in her van, not caring about organization. She threw tables and her trash in the back, jogging around to get in and get home.

She took off from her spot, heart pounding, breaths short, gripping the steering wheel with sweaty palms. She didn't notice that she was speeding down the hill until she saw the familiar red and blue lights in her rearview.

Max pulled in behind Annella, half angry and half afraid. "What the fuck?" he asked Cal. "Does she think she's getting out a ticket because we're dating?"

Cal glanced at Max playing devil's advocate. "Maybe she has a good reason. Don't say anything you're going to regret."

Max took some deep breaths, trying to calm down as he walked to the van.

"What are you doing?"

Annella flinched. *Maybe that wasn't the best opening,* he thought, noticing the panicked look on her face.

Max was about to open his mouth to try again when Annella cut him off. Her exhaustion making it difficult to control her emotions, as she yelled. "It doesn't matter." She pointed a finger at Max, "All you care about is the fact that I was going over the speed limit. What is your deal?"

Max softened his voice and tried again. "Annella, talk to me. What happened? We've only been away from each other for two hours."

Annella blinked rapidly trying to keep her tears from falling. "The jackass that can't be caught is watching me. He texted me about the new flowers that you just gave me. I freaked out and wasn't watching my speed."

Max held out his hand. "Let me see your phone."

Annella pulled up the message and slapped her phone in Max's hand, taking deep breaths, trying to calm her racing heart. Max read the message, his anger rising to match hers.

He checked the number, comparing it to the first one. It was the same unassigned number that he knew wouldn't turn anything up in a trace. Max handed her back her phone, and she tossed it into her purse. She held out her hand for the ticket she knew was coming.

She heard the paper rip from his book and felt it hit her hand. She pulled her arm back into the van as she read the ticket. Scrawled in Max's precise handwriting were the words "I'm sorry."

Annella bit back a sob and got out of the van, throwing her arms around Max. She lost herself in the comfort of his embrace and the smell of his soap.

"I'm sorry I snapped at you and said you can't catch this guy. I know you are trying. You can give me a ticket. I understand that I broke the law, and it's your job."

Max squeezed her tight, his insides warring with each other. Half of him wanted to keep her secluded until this was all over and it was safe for her. The other half knew that she needed to live her day-to-day life as much as possible, or she would resent him.

"Just don't tell anyone. I have a reputation to protect."

She kissed him until her heart was beating fast for a whole different reason before letting him go. "Thank you. I'll see you after work."

Max pulled her in for one more quick kiss. "I'll see you after work. Don't worry about anything for dinner. I'm cooking for you."

Annella nodded and got back in the van. She didn't know how far Max's culinary skills went, but she was excited to see.

She watched Max's ass in the mirror as he walked back to the cruiser before pulling back onto the highway and driving away.

She felt the exhaustion from her head to her toes. She wanted to take a nap, but knew she would not sleep in her own bed. She pulled up to Max's house and let herself in. She didn't even bother to examine if he had kept the house clean as she changed into one of his T-shirts that fit her like a dress and slipped into his bed. She was asleep before she took the first breath of his sheets.

Max got into the car and slammed the door, causing Cal to jump. He put his head in his hands, letting out a frustrated sigh.

"I hate it when we're right," he said to Cal.

Cal clasped Max's shoulder, feeling his partner shake with rage. "How were we both right?"

Max pulled out onto the road and headed up to Annella's spot to see if there was any evidence left of this creep watching her.

"I was right when I said that something was about to happen. You were right when you said that something might have happened to Annella."

Cal sat forward in his seat, all seriousness. "What happened to Annella?"

Max parked the SUV, and they stepped out to look around. "He was sitting somewhere here watching her today. He texted her about destroying the flowers that I just handed her. It freaked her out, and that's why she was speeding home."

"We've got to do something," Cal said, shutting his door. "We can't keep letting this prick harass her."

"I agree with you." Max tried to put himself in this guy's head and think about where he would park to be concealed but still be able to see her.

The clinic would be an obvious spot. No one would think a vehicle in front of it to be out of place, and whoever this person was had an unimpeded view of Annella serving.

"We just need this asshole to slip up, just once, and we'll catch him."

—∞—

He and Cal finished their shift and then he put them through a brutal workout to sweat out his anger before he saw Annella again. She didn't need his anger and she didn't deserve it. He headed to his house to pack an overnight bag. He didn't care what it took, he was sleeping beside her tonight so hopefully she would actually sleep.

He was confused when he got close and saw her van parked in his driveway. She hadn't told him she was coming here, and he hoped nothing else had happened at her house to make her flee to his.

He walked in and noticed that there were no lights on or noise of any kind. Annella wasn't in the living room or the kitchen or out on the back deck. He was starting to feel a prickle of panic as he stepped into his bedroom and found her in his bed, her body curled around his extra pillow.

Max slipped off his shoes and stretched out next to her trying not to jostle the bed. He combed her hair back from her face and felt his heart swell that not only was she sleeping in his bed, but she was sleeping in his shirt. He kissed her lightly on the temple and rose to go start dinner.

—∞—

Annella woke up finally feeling rested to the sounds of pans hitting the stove. She stretched out her limbs and crawled from the bed to see what Max was cooking for her.

Max moved through the kitchen as she came in and sat on one of the stools. "Hello, Lieutenant." She said causing Max to turn and grin at her.

He walked to her and gathered her in a tight embrace. "Hello, chef. You look well rested."

Annella kissed the stubble on his jawline, then the corner of his mouth, and then his lips melting into him as she wrapped her arms around his neck.

She pulled back as something splashed over the side of the pot and hissed on the stove. Max was across the kitchen in two strides turning the temperature down under the soup.

"Thanks. I feel better. Is it ok that I came here to sleep?" Annella hadn't thought about it being weird earlier she just knew that she wanted to be as near to Max as she could be while she was napping.

Max stirred the soup and turned his soft gaze back to Annella. "Chef, you have complete possession of all of me and all that I have. Sleep here, shower here, meditate here, whatever you need of me or mine is yours." Max went back to making dinner for the woman that was stealing his heart, and his shirt. He didn't know how to cook much and since he knew he would never grill better than her he opted for grilled cheese and tomato soup. His favorite comfort food.

Annella grinned at Max's menu choice, looking forward to a meal she didn't have to plan or prepare. Sure, it was simple food, but sometimes simple just hit the spot.

Max plated their sandwiches and ladled the soup into bowls carrying her food and a bottle of water to her first before joining her with his own.

Annella took a corner of her sandwich and dunked it in her soup savoring the buttery bread mixed with cheese and tomato flavors. She noticed that Max hadn't taken a bite yet and he was rubbing the back of his neck.

She reached her hand over and stroked his thigh. "Are you alright?"

Max blew out his breath and stood to pace the kitchen forgetting the food. "You asked me a question earlier that I didn't answer then, but I do owe you an answer on it."

Annella set her spoon down and turned to face Max, giving him her full attention.

"You asked me what my deal with people speeding was and I didn't respond." Max leaned back on the counter and crossed his arms.

Annella stayed quiet, sensing that she needed to just listen at this point.

"Has anyone in town told you that Cody and I had a sister?"

Annella shook her head, *had* she thought, but she didn't want to interrupt.

"Heather was the youngest. She was eighteen and had just graduated valedictorian." Max began pacing again and Annella wiggled in her spot itching to get up and comfort him.

"She was dating an older guy in the next town over that everyone knew was a jerk, but Heather wouldn't listen. One night she was at his place, and he had been drinking. She asked him to stop, and he backhanded her across her face then threw her to the ground."

Max clenched his fists at his sides, still angry that someone dared to do that to an eighteen-year-old girl. "He moved to stand over her and when he did, she kicked him in the balls, got up, and ran like hell. She made it to her car and called me."

Annella played with the hem of his shirt to give her hands something to do.

"She was crying so hard and telling me how she wanted to file charges against the guy when I heard the crash." Max ran his hands through his hair tugging on the ends.

"I called her name over and over, but she wouldn't answer me. She couldn't"

Annella felt the tears run down her cheeks and used the back of her hand to wipe them away.

"I hauled ass to Cal's house and then we headed to find her. I had made sure that I knew where he lived and the route she took to and from his house."

Max leaned across the counter and gently wiped away one of Annella's tears.

"We called an ambulance on the way, but we still beat them there. I was the first one to see my sister's unmoving body."

Annella couldn't be still any longer. She got up and wrapped her arms around Max resting her cheek to his back.

"I pulled her out and started CPR, but she already had no pulse. The EMTs showed up and took over, but they never could get her back. I had to watch them cover her body in a white sheet."

Max turned around and clung to Annella, burring his face in her hair. The coconut smell comforting him. Recounting that night was never easy, but with time he could finally tell the story without crying.

"I looked around and saw that it was Travis that hit her in his big ass truck. He was speeding and driving drunk. He ran a stop sign and plowed right into her. That's the full reason why I can't stand him. Cal stopped me from murdering him that night, badge be damned, and drove me to my parents' house to tell them and Cody."

Max let go of Annella and helped her back onto her stool before sitting down. "We pressed charges against Travis, but Mommy and Daddy's money got him off with community service. My sister was dead, and he just had to pick up trash."

Annella's heart hurt so much for Max and his family and the life that never got be. "I'm so sorry, Max. I promise not to speed any more unless it's an emergency."

Max picked up his sandwich and dunked it before taking a bite, trying to lighten the mood. "I'll hold you to that."

Chapter

23

Another week had gone by since the last creepy text message, and Annella hated it. Her flowers were still looking beautiful, so the threats had been unsuccessful, but it didn't mean she stopped looking over her shoulder at every turn or that she went longer than fifteen minutes without checking her cameras.

Today was the Muscles for Money event and at this point, she wanted something to happen. Most of the police force and first responders would be here, so if she was attacked, hopefully, they would catch the creep.

Green Lake PD had kept a close eye on her during her lunch service this week, and she was grateful for them all. Max and Cal sat at the picnic tables to eat and keep watch. When their lunch was over, Officers Dawn and Hall would take their place.

Chief Booker ate with her every day, usually as her last customer staying even while she cleaned up. Annella finally felt like part of a family with people caring about her well-being and going out of their way to look out for her.

Annella and Lauren were busy serving chopped sandwiches, sausage wraps, or brisket burritos at the pavilion that had been assigned to her.

The spot was great, with a full, simple kitchen and tables covered in her signature purple plastic. There was a huge awning giving people a break from the sun in the summer heat. Annella had envied the townspeople who had come to her dripping wet from a dip in the lake.

Max and Cal had helped serve for a while claiming it was part of the event that the participants volunteer at the booths. When it was time for them to go to the next booth, Max left her with a quick, deep kiss that curled her toes.

"Have you told him you love him yet?" Lauren asked during a break in customers. Heat that had nothing to do with being in a kitchen in 100-degree temperature crept up her face.

"I haven't told him yet. It still feels too good to be true, and I don't want to jinx anything."

Lauren pulled the cover off the container of tea, checking the level. "But you do love him, don't you?"

Annella searched for Max in the crowd. Spotting him with Cal and Chief Booker wasn't hard with how tall he was. "Of course I do. He's the whole package; tall, tan, handsome, sweet, and not without that undercurrent of protectiveness. He's the type of man that women dream about after they've fallen for him in a book."

Lauren screwed the lid back on the large, orange container. "I understand you not wanting to jinx anything, but you have nothing to worry about. That man is crazy in love with you already."

Annella smiled and gave Max a quick wave when she caught him staring at her while Lauren helped the next customers.

"How can you tell? I mean we didn't get off to the most romantic start and have only slept together twice. Isn't it supposed to take longer to fall in love?"

Lauren handed the librarian her lemonade and turned back to Annella. "Honey, I've known Max his entire life. I've witnessed him think he was in love with Brenda, but that was just a crush compared to how twisted up as he is with you."

Annella blew out a breath, picking at a thread hanging from her shirt. "I wasn't even looking for love when I moved here. I was looking for my place and a community."

Lauren grabbed her hands to stop them from unraveling her entire shirt. "When you aren't looking for love, that's when it's the sweetest kind."

Annella helped a mom she recognized from the mom joggers carry her plates over to a table, making sure they didn't need anything else before she went back to join Lauren.

"So, were you one of the girls Max pined over when Cal called dibs?" Annella had never heard Max mention that either he or Cal had a thing for Lauren, but she knew that everyone dated everyone in a small town now.

"No. It was never like that with Max and me. He was more a brother than a potential boyfriend. Cal and I dated for like a minute. He was a ladies' man, but I thought I could change him into a one-woman man." Lauren huffed out a laugh. "Then, when I saw him checking out Maria Rose Stone, I knew he would never change."

Annella's heart hurt for her friend. She wanted Lauren to find the most perfect man and be as happy as she was. *Hopefully someone comes into town and sweeps her off her feet*, Annella thought.

The day was a success. Chief Booker was standing in front of the raised platform, looking out over the crowd as Danielle handed him the microphone. The man was a born performer getting the crowd hyped up.

"How is everyone doing?" he began. The crowd screamed like they were at a rock concert instead of a small town fund raiser. "Thank you all for coming out to the Fifteenth Annual Muscles for Money fundraiser. I'm pleased to announce that this year has been a record-breaking year."

A round of applause went up and the chief waited for them to settle down before he continued. "With your generous donations and the help of our vendors, we raised a total of sixty-five hundred dollars for the day!" More clapping and whistles broke the air, and the six people on the stage turned ghostly white.

Max and Cal represented the police department, Brock and Cal's brother, Bill represented the fire department, and Casey and Leo represented the EMTs. Casey was the only woman in the group, so she opted to do her pushups in a navy blue sports top along with the guys.

"Since we still need our participants to be able to use their arms tomorrow, we are amending how the pushups will be counted."

Danielle had six children standing next to her, all with big smiles on their faces. "We are going to put our newest first graders on the backs of our team, and each push-up with one counts for four. That's still over two hundred each, but it sounds a lot better than over a thousand, doesn't it?"

Danielle herded the group up the steps while the team stripped and laid chest down. She helped them sit in the middle of their backs and told them not to move too much. Chief Booker gave a 3-2-1 countdown, and the pushup commenced.

The sun was starting to set, making the sheen from the sweat pop under the large lights set up over the stage. Annella and Lauren watched while they cleaned. They had sold out all the food, so it was mostly packing away containers and wiping down counters left to do. She was grateful that there wasn't much cleanup. She wanted to go get a closer look of Max before going home and prepping for Cody and Sadie's tasting tomorrow.

Lauren picked up the two dispensers from the tea and lemonade while Annella was wiping down the counter, watching Max with a little Cabe Thompson on his back.

"I'm going to run these out to the van," Lauren said.

"The keys are in the front pocket of my purse," Annella responded over her shoulder, not taking her eyes off the sexy, sweaty cop in front of her.

Annella needed to shut down the windows and then she would help Lauren load the van, but the final serving window was not budging.

She was balancing on the bottom shelf of the counter using every yoga muscle she had when she heard footsteps behind her.

"Lauren, can you help me close this wind—"

A hand grabbed Annella's curly locks, and it felt like they were all being ripped from her head. Her feet slipped off the bottom shelf, and she landed on her back first, her head slamming into the metal shelf of the island behind her. She heard footsteps run away quickly before all she saw was black.

Lauren came back in for the next load, took one look at Annella lying on the ground, not moving, and screamed. She took off running to the stage, yelling for Max.

Max was on number sixty of his 200 pushups when he saw Lauren rushing through the crowd like the devil was chasing her. Max's heart threaten to beat out of his chest. He stayed on his stomach and tapped Cabe on the leg. "Hey, partner. Better hop off, looks like trouble."

He popped his knees under him and stood, reaching the side of the platform in three powerful steps, not bothering with his shirt on the way down. Lauren was waiting for him at the bottom with a look on her face Max didn't like.

"What's wrong?" Max asked as he hit the ground. Lauren was breathing hard and talking fast.

"A...nne...lla. Not...moving."

Max's face crumpled and the color drained from his skin as he took off running toward the pavilion.

No. No. No, was all he could think as he rounded the back of the white brick building and flew through the doorway.

He skidded to a stop, frozen at the scene in front of him before Lauren crashed into his back, sending him into the action. He knelt to Annella on the ground, looking up at him with dazed eyes.

Annella thought she was hallucinating. Max was kneeling beside her, shirtless, which she didn't hate, but he wasn't supposed to be there.

She tried to sit up, but his strong, sweaty hands held her in place. She tried to speak, but he placed his finger gently against her lips, telling her to be quiet.

"Easy, chef. Just stay down." Max looked at Lauren. "What happened?"

Lauren was trembling, one arm wrapped around her middle and chewing on her other thumbnail. "I have no idea. I went to put the drink containers in the van and when I came back she was just lying there."

Max was trying to keep it together. He heard more fast footsteps as Cal and everyone who had been on the stage with him came in.

"What the fuck?" Cal asked, coming to kneel on Annella's other side. Casey found a place beside Max and started searching for broken bones.

"Lauren, go find Dr. Sullivan." He was sure he had seen her in the crowd at some point, so hopefully, she was still there.

Lauren nodded and left in search of the doctor. Cal moved back to let Leo help Casey while they waited.

Casey looked at Max with sympathy in her emerald green eyes. "No broken bones from what I can tell, but I'm sure she'll have a concussion."

Casey looked down at Annella's face, tense with pain.

"Annella, can you tell me where it hurts and, on a scale of one to ten, how bad?"

"My head and my back and a seven," Annella gritted out. The sound of pain in her voice had Max feeling like he was being raked across hot coals.

Lauren came back in with Dr. Sullivan a few minutes later, and Max was grateful that the good doctor hadn't gone home yet.

Dr. Sullivan looked at Casey and Leo. "What've we got?" she asked in her no-nonsense tone.

"No broken bones, but pupils are unevenly dilated. She said only her head and her back hurt at a seven," Casey reported. Annella gasped as the doctor's quick deft fingers contacted the back of her head, and Max's heart ripped out of his chest.

"I can already feel a lump forming on the back of your head," she said. "Do you feel like trying to sit up?"

Annella barely nodded. Max held one hand while Dr. Sullivan took the other, and they guided her into a sitting position.

A sudden wave of dizziness hit her, and she closed her eyes, leaning into Max's bare chest.

"It's okay, chef, I've got you." Max ran his hand up and down her arms in slow, soothing strokes. She opened her eyes and blinked a couple of times against the bright, white lights.

Dr. Sullivan moved directly in front of Annella blocking some of the lights. "Can you tell us what happened?"

She put her hand on her head to hold off another dizzy spell and told the story of trying to close the window and being yanked down by her hair, her body hitting the floor, and head hitting the island.

Max went rigid when he heard that this wasn't just a slip but another attack that he wasn't there for. He brushed a stray curl from her forehead and leaned to whisper in her ear, "Who did this to you?"

Annella saw the faces staring at her, waiting for something to use to catch the one responsible. "I don't know," she said, feeling like she was letting everyone down. "My back was to the door, and it all happened so fast that I didn't see anything. I'm sorry," she said to Max.

"You're sorry? For what? You haven't done anything to apologize for. I'm sorry I wasn't here to protect you again. I promise you we will find this prick, and he will be in a jail cell once we do."

Lauren came over and knelt. "I'm sorry, too. I shouldn't have left you alone, knowing there's someone out there that wants to hurt you."

Dr. Sullivan looked up and waved Leo and Casey over with the stretcher. She turned back to Annella. "You have a concussion, and I need to look more at your back. We're going to take you to the hospital and keep you overnight."

Annella tried to get up. "I can't stay overnight. I have a tasting tomorrow that I need to prepare for."

Dr. Sullivan put a gentle hand on Annella's shoulder. "You could have more wrong with you than what I can determine on the floor in the pavilion. I think work can wait."

"Everyone back up, please, so we can get to Annella," Casey said as they wheeled the stretcher in with the crisp, white sheets.

Max hated those things. The last time he saw one was when Heather's body bag was strapped down and loaded in the ambulance. He shuddered at the thought.

Everyone shuffled outside except for Max, Cal, and Lauren, who were reluctant to leave. Cal and Lauren at least backed up, but Max could not stop touching her to assure himself she was fine.

After they had the mobile bed in position as best as possible, Leo bent down to pick Annella up. "This isn't going to be comfortable, but I'll be as gentle as possible."

Annella groaned as he scooped her up and stood to place her on the stretcher. A fresh wave of anger flowed through Max.

"Thorne, Roberts," Chief Booker called from the doorway. "Let's start interviewing people. Maybe we'll get lucky, and someone saw whoever did this."

Max looked down at Annella lying on the gurney, conflict warring inside of him. She gave him a tentative smile and squeezed his hand. "Go do your job. I'm in good hands."

Max leaned in and kissed her forehead. "I'll be at the hospital as soon as I can. I'm going to send Officer Dawn with you to stand outside your door." Max held her hand until they got to the doorway, and he had to let go so they could all file out. "I'll see you soon," he said, leaving while he was able to.

Lauren came up behind him with Cal and gave his shoulder a light pat. "I'm sorry, Max. I shouldn't have left her alone."

Max put his hand on top of hers. He knew she was almost as upset as he was and feeling guilty. He wanted her to know that he didn't blame her.

"It's all right. Can you go to the hospital too? I don't want her to be alone in her room."

"Of course. I'll follow the ambulance," Lauren said, taking off toward her car. Max found Dawn and sent her to the hospital in the ambulance before checking in with Chief Booker.

The hospital in Green Lake wasn't fancy by any means, but it served the people well. A small emergency room and six patient rooms were all housed in a single-story building.

Annella closed her eyes against the stark white lights as they wheeled her through the hallway, leaving Lauren and Officer Dawn on the other side of the swinging doors.

Chapter

24

It was late by the time Max got to the hospital to relieve Lauren. He told Dawn to head home when he saw her blurry-eyed with a coffee in her hand.

"Only Dr. Sullivan, Lauren, and the nurses have been in or out of this room," she told him before she left.

"Thanks," Max responded as he walked into Annella's room.

Max was not prepared for what he saw. Annella lay still in the flowered hospital gown, her body looking pale against the white sheets. It took all his senses to keep his composure. The beeping meant that she was alive. The rise and fall of her chest told him she was breathing. Not dead.

Not like Heather, he said to himself.

None of these observations did anything to slow his racing heart. It cracked to see the woman he was in love with motionless, wires and tubes coming from her body. He didn't plan on loving her. Didn't plan on loving anyone again after Brenda. He had built his walls up to get through life with his heart still mostly intact. But seeing her now, completely helpless, told his brain what his heart already knew. He was crazy in love with this woman and would do anything for her.

As he suspected, no one saw anything helpful. His frustration grew with each head shake and look of apology, but he helped his brothers and sisters-in-arms do their jobs before leaving the park, finding a shirt, and speeding to Annella.

He didn't go much over the posted limit, and this was sort of an emergency, so he didn't feel the least bit guilty about it now.

Lauren snoozed in the chair on Annella's right side, holding her hand to comfort them both. Max brushed an auburn curl from Annella's forehead and stared down at her, his heart in his throat. She fidgeted from the touch of his hand, causing Lauren to bolt awake.

"Hey," she said, covering a yawn with her hand. "No updates other than the mild concussion and the deep bruising on her back. Did you find anything to help catch whoever did this?"

Max clenched his jaw and shook his head. "No one saw anything useful. I'm about to hire her a bodyguard so she's never without protection." Max chuckled, only 80% serious.

"Has she said anything that might help? Maybe she remembered something after the fact."

"She didn't. The only thing she was worried about was Cody and Sadie's tasting tomorrow."

Max let out a sigh. That didn't surprise him that even lying in a hospital bed, she would be worried about work and other people. He really needed to take her on a vacation. "I'll call him tomorrow. I'm sure she won't give me a choice on that."

Max watched Lauren yawn again and rub her eyes. "Why don't you go home and sleep? I'll be here the rest of the night."

Lauren gave her hand a light squeeze and then stood. "Text me with any updates," she said on her way by him.

"No problem," Max responded, moving to take up the position that Lauren had left.

Max knew she needed her rest but wanted nothing more than to just hear her say something to him. He didn't even care if she called him every bad name available for not protecting her if it meant he heard her voice. He thought he would get his wish when Abigail came in to take her vitals, but she was so gentle that Annella didn't stir.

He put on classic country, Annella's favorite, just so there was something to distract him from his own thoughts. When that didn't work, he talked to her quietly. He told her stories of growing up with Cody and Heather, trying to set a good example as the older brother but always being the one to come up with the bad ideas instead.

Abigail came in periodically doing her job, which she didn't get enough recognition or pay for, and asked Max each time if he needed anything. Max dozed on and off through the night, the clock moving extremely slowly, in his opinion.

—⁓—

Around 5:30, Abigail and Mitch came in for shift change. He stepped into the hall so that the room wasn't so crowded and wondered if he didn't have a concussion, too. Cal was walking down the hall, looking tired, carrying two coffees and a brown bag of drive-through breakfast.

"I'm dreaming, right? I must be to see you up before the sun on a Sunday, and you brought me food."

Cal handed Max the bag and coffee and then looked through the little glass into Annella's room. "I figured you came straight here after we were done with questioning, so I thought I'd be nice."

"Thanks, man," Max said, sitting in the hard plastic chair and tearing into the bag of food. He took a sip of the coffee, but it did nothing to rid his body of the exhaustion he felt.

"How's she doing?"

Max swallowed his bite of hash brown and slugged some more coffee.

"She slept all night, which Abigail said was good since her concussion was only mild. If she's feeling up to it, they said she can go home later today. Dr. Sullivan should be around to check on her soon."

They stayed quiet while Max finished his breakfast. Abigail and Mitch came out of her room and nodded to Cal. "She's awake and asking for you."

Max stood so fast that he saw black spots and swayed a little. Cal steadied him and followed him into Annella's room after picking up his trash and throwing it away.

When he finally locked eyes with her, his world tilted a little more toward okay. "Hey, chef," he said as he leaned in and kissed her cheek.

She wrapped her arms around him so fast he had to brace himself on the rails of the bed so he didn't fall on her.

"Hey," she said with her head buried in his chest.

Max squatted on the edge of the bed and held her to his chest, needing to hold her. Needing to comfort her. Needing to assure himself that she was going to be just fine. He tried to ignore the wrongness of her smell. Instead of a tropical island, she smelled like antiseptic and sweat.

Annella finally let go and settled back down on her pillow. Cal walked up to the foot of her bed.

"Hey, Annella," he said and gave her a reassuring smile.

"Hey, Cal. Thanks for coming to check on me."

"No trouble at all. I had to make sure you were okay. I brought Max food so that he doesn't turn into a bear on you. I can go get you something if you're hungry."

Annella smiled up at him, rubbing her thumb across Max's knuckles. "Thanks, but I'm good."

She looked at Max and noticed the dark purple bags. "Did you sleep at all last night?"

"I dozed in between nurse checks." Max rubbed his hand across the five o'clock shadow that had grown along his chiseled jaw.

"If you want to go shower and get some sleep, I'll stay with Annella," Cal offered.

"Thanks, bro, but I'm not leaving until she does."

"I figured that's what you'd say. I'll at least get some clothes so you can shower here. Call me if either of you need anything while I'm gone."

Annella pulled her hair tie out and finger brushed her locks before putting it back up. "I need Dr. Sullivan to come release me soon. I have your brother's tasting this evening, and I can still make it work even though I didn't get to prep anything yesterday." As Annella talked, her heart rate sped up.

Max cupped her cheek in his hand and drew her gaze to him. "We'll call him when it's later in the morning. I'm sure he and Sadie will be fine until then. Their tasting is more of a formality at this point, right."

Annella nodded, a little stung at his words, and her heart rate came back down.

Cal came back a while later and handed Max a blue duffel bag with fresh clothes and toiletries. "Go shower. You smell like shit."

Max opened his mouth to reply and then smelled his armpit. "I guess you're right." Max took the bag from Cal and headed into the little bathroom connected to Annella's room.

Cal sat with Annella while Max showered. Even though she said she didn't need anything he still brought her a yogurt parfait and a large water. She ate the yogurt like it would disappear right in front of her and guzzled down some water not realizing how thirsty she was.

"Thanks, Cal. You're a good friend."

Cal wasn't used to being okay with being in the friend zone, but it fit with Annella. She was for Max, and he knew it in his soul. As she moved to get more comfortable, she tweaked her back and made a face. Cal jumped up to help her, but she waved him away.

190

Max was coming out of the bathroom just as Dr. Sullivan came in, his wet hair leaving dots on his gray shirt.

"How are you feeling this morning?" Cal moved to stand beside Max.

"She's in a bit of pain based on the look she just had on her face," he said, and Annella glared at him. If his comment made her stay longer, he would never get another cookie.

"I'm fine. My back is a little sore and stiff, but other than that, I feel good."

Dr. Sullivan read over her chart to see how she had done through the night. "Well, no dizziness, vomiting, or memory loss. I think we're good there. There isn't much we can do for the bruise, so I'm happy to release you if you promise to take it easy for a few days and come back if you feel worse."

"I'll make sure she doesn't overdo it," Max chimed in, earning him a glare as well.

Dr. Sullivan patted Annella's shoulder. "I'll have Mitch come in with your discharge paperwork in a while, and there will be a prescription waiting for you at the pharmacy in case you need it for the pain."

Dr. Sullivan walked out, and Annella tipped her head back, sighing in relief. Max walked over to her and kissed her right on the lips, not caring that they had an audience. They were so wrapped up in each other that they didn't even know Cal had slipped out behind Dr. Sullivan.

They watched an episode of bad reality TV before Mitch came in to discharge her. He removed her IV needle and went over instructions of not lifting anything over five pounds or strenuous exercise for at least a week.

"Fine," Annella grumbled.

Mitch gave her a questioning look, but Max answered him, "She won't work too hard."

Annella changed out of her hospital couture and walked as fast as she could, which wasn't quick at all, to get out of the hospital. She stepped out of the double-sliding glass doors and soaked in the sunshine and fresh air.

Max had pulled his truck into the loading zone while she was changing, and he waited with her door open. It took her longer to get in the truck than she would have liked, but she finally made it, and Max shut her door.

He got in and started the truck, then called Cody, who answered on the second ring. "Hey, Max. How's Annella?"

Small town gossip, Max thought.

"Slight headache and sore back, but glad to be out of the hospital," Annella responded before Max could say anything. "I'm so sorry that I can't do your tasting today, but your brother might tie me to the bed if I try. We can reschedule for one night this week after work if you two are free, or just move it to next Sunday if that's better. I know Sadie is anxious to have this finalized, so I'll do whatever I can."

Annella listened as Cody and Sadie talked about their schedules for the week. "Let's just do it next Sunday. We are both trying to fit as much work in as we can before the wedding so that we can enjoy the honeymoon."

Annella sighed in relief that Cody and Saide were so understanding. "That sounds good to me. Let me know if anything changes."

She could hear Cody chuckle. "You just focus on feeling better and not murdering my brother for hovering over you."

Annella chuckled at the image of little bitty her doing any kind of damage to a man that was more than a foot taller. "Thanks. I will try."

Max ended the call and pulled into Annella's driveway a few minutes later. She opened her eyes, squinting against the bright sun, and felt like she was seeing her house again for the first time.

"How did the van get here?" she asked as Max opened her door and helped her down.

"Cal and Lauren brought it here last night after I relieved her, so it wasn't at the pavilion."

Max helped Annella up her stairs and held the door open for her to walk through first. He made sure to lock it behind them. Annella stood behind her couch and ran her hands across her soft purple blanket, loving being back in her own space.

Max took her purse from her and set it on the entry table, noticing the purple golf ball he had given her during their walk in the bowl next to her keys. He had to keep moving. Had to keep the anger away. It wasn't what Annella needed right now. Now, if he had to guess, she needed a shower, soft pajamas, and uninterrupted sleep.

He walked up behind her and placed his hands gently on her shoulders. "Why don't you go shower and change into some pajamas? Then we can binge-watch whatever you want."

Annell turned in his arms and rested her head on his chest. "Yes, to the shower, but I have to prep for tomorrow."

He backed up and looked at her like she had grown wings. "You've got to be kidding me. Chef, you have a concussion, you can't lift anything heavy, which includes tubs of meat and vats of drinks, and the bruise on your back is going to hurt like hell if you stand all day."

Annella took a deep breath to try and compose herself. "Max, I know you're trying to take care of me, but please stop. I can't afford to miss a day of work."

Max turned from her and ran his hands through his hair, pulling at the ends. He knew he was being controlling, but this whole situation was killing him.

He turned back to Annella. "Look, I'll give you the money you should make tomorrow. Just please take the day off." He realized that he had said the wrong thing when red heated Annella's cheeks.

Annella looked at him like he had struck her. "Max, I don't want your money. I'm not a damsel in distress that needs rescuing. I work hard to make my own way so that I'm not in debt to anyone. Why are you acting like this?"

"Why?" Max asked, not bothering to check his voice. "Annella, I just had to watch as you were loaded on a gurney and spent the night in a hospital bed because I failed. I can't go back and stop the attack, but I can protect you now so you don't cause further harm with your stubbornness."

Max dropped his head feeling completely defeated. He searched his soul for something to say that would make her understand his motive and decided on the truth.

"I love you, Annella, and I just want to take care of you." Max softened his voice and tucked that dang curl behind her ear. "Never control you." Max's breaths were coming in quick pants, and he was sure Annella wasn't breathing at all with her mouth hanging open.

Max was staring at her with what she would describe as longing in his eyes. Annella snapped her mouth closed. How could he make her so mad one minute and so happy the next? She thought about not responding to him, letting him sweat while she was in the shower, but she didn't want vengeance to taint the moment.

Instead, she walked to him, giving nothing away on her face, wrapped her arms around his waist, and whispered, "I love you too, Max."

Chapter

25

They stayed wrapped in each other's embrace, not wanting to break the magic of the moment, until Max started laughing. The man was all out laughing. Two minutes ago, he was yelling at her, and now he was laughing.

A moment of panic waved through Annella. Had he been joking when he said it? Was it a bet between him and Cal to see if Max could make her love him? She wasn't the kind of woman men loved.

Feeling insecure, she started to back out of his arms, ready to hobble up the stairs if he confirmed her fears. "I'm sorry. Laughing like that probably hurts your body. I'm just so happy."

The panic melted away, and her muscles relaxed. She smiled at him and gently kissed his lips.

Max wasn't going to let her go with just a peck. He pulled her in, being careful of her injuries, and sealed her mouth to his. Her soft lips cradled his, and she tasted like the tart berries from her yogurt.

Annella moaned, opening her mouth for Max's tongue to wrestle with hers until a ping from Max's phone interrupted them. She wanted to throw his phone out the window and continue kissing him but smiled when he said it was Lauren.

"She wants to know how you're feeling. She tried to text you but didn't get a response."

Annella moved to the table and pulled out her phone. It was completely dead. "I should probably charge this. You can tell her that I'm wonderful. Sore and a slight headache, but still wonderful."

That made Max chuckle, knowing that he was the reason she was wonderful, but also feeling guilty that she was injured at all.

As if she could read his thoughts, she walked over and cupped his cheek. "Max, this isn't your fault. You had no way of knowing that I was going to be attacked. You're going to catch this jerk soon. I know it."

Max sighed, wresting with the anger inside him. "I hope you're right. We questioned everyone possible last night and combed the pavilion, but still no clues. It's like you're being attacked by a shadow. It's my job to protect and serve the people of Green Lake and I'm failing with the person I love the most."

Annella smiled, thinking of all the fantasy books she had read where shadows were responsible for lots of things, good and bad. She dropped her hand, and Max immediately missed her touch.

"I'm going to plug my phone in and get in the shower."

Max watched her get to the base of the stairs and look up at them with an 'oh fuck this is going to hurt' look on her face.

"Do you want me to carry you, or we could go to my house where it's only one story?"

Annella smiled at his thoughtfulness. "Thanks, but I'll make it." She started up the steps taking it slowly.

"Why don't you just get into bed after your shower? I'll make you something to eat and bring it to you."

Annella paused on the third step. "Your grilled cheese is great, but I have a better idea. I'm going to teach you how to cook my favorite pasta."

A look of terror crossed Max's face at the thought of cooking a full recipe. "It's a good thing you live next door to a firefighter," Max said as he watched her limp the rest of the way up the stairs, taking his heart with her.

Max still had aggression and couldn't stop moving. If he stopped moving and started thinking, then he was probably going to do something stupid. He grabbed Annella's van keys from the bowl on the table and started unloading her equipment. His phone went off again on his last trip inside and he was happy for something else to distract him.

He read the message from Cal, shocked that he hadn't gone back to bed when he got home.

How's Annella? Do you guys need anything?

Max's fingers typed back while he listened to the sound of the shower.

We're good. She said she's sore with a headache, but wonderful.

He saw Cal's typing dots, so he just waited with his phone in his hand.

How is she wonderful? She's got to be in so much pain and still with a mild concussion. Wonderful should be the last thing she's feeling.

Max couldn't help the smile on his lips.

Maybe because I told her that I loved her.

Cal's response didn't surprise Max at all.

She said it back, right?

"Fucker," Max said to the phone like Cal could hear him.

Yes, she said it back.

Cal responded: *Good for you guys! Let me know if you need anything.*

Max heard Annella's footsteps slowly moving down the stairs. He put his phone down after texting Cal *thanks* and went to help her.

She reached the bottom and plugged her slightly alive phone into the charger by the couch. She just wanted to collapse there and sleep the rest of the day, but she couldn't do that. She had to keep moving to prove to Max that she was fine to go back to work on Tuesday. Max looped his arms loosely behind her shoulders.

"How do you feel?" Max started gently walking her backward toward the couch.

"Better. Still tired and sore, but mentally better."

She realized what he was doing and stopped walking. "Oh no. You're not getting out of your cooking lesson that easily. To the kitchen."

Max blew out his breath and changed direction. "Fine, but you're only going to direct. No work for you."

Annella moved her finger in an X over her heart and held up her hand swearing to not work. Max pulled a chair from the table and moved it closer to the counter so she would be able to see better.

She noticed the white tubs and carafes on the counter by the fridge. "You unloaded the van?" She lowered herself gently into the chair, and Max brought her water.

"Yeah. I had to have something to do while you were showering. If I sit still, I get angry all over again." His jaw clenched, remembering her still body on the concrete floor.

She hooked a finger in the pocket of his jeans, drawing his gaze back to her. "Hey." She smiled at him. "I love you, you love me, and it wasn't as bad as it could have been. That's a happy memory. Let's focus on that instead."

Max took her hand from his pocket and knelt in front of her. "Say that again, I liked it."

Annella smiled at him. "I love you, Lieutenant Max Thorne."

Max beamed, knowing he would never get tired of hearing those words and feeling the conviction behind them. He could admit now that he had never felt the words from Brenda. He kissed her nose and stood back to his full height. "And I love you, chef. Now teach me to make pasta."

—ⱲⱮ—

Over the next forty-five minutes, Annella walked Max through making her chicken scampi. Laughing with him after the stress of the last twenty four hours felt good. When it was ready, Max helped her stand and moved her chair back to the table.

He fixed their plates and joined her, watching as she took the first bite. He was relieved when her head dropped back, and her eyes closed.

"It's good?" he asked tentatively.

"It's wonderful. You get a gold star from the teacher." Max took his first bite, shocked that he made something good that was more than cheese and bread.

"You know, if you ever want to give up law enforcement, I think you'll make a great sous chef," Annella said, interrupting his self-congratulations.

"That's high praise coming from you, but I think I'll stick to handcuffs over hand mixers."

They finished eating watching the world go by outside the window, people coming home from church. Families walking soaking in the sweet summer sun. Everyone knew what had happened last night, but no one was letting it stop them from living. Annella wouldn't either.

Annella supervised Max cleaning the kitchen and loading the dishwasher only having to correct his technique twice. She stood and took a step toward the fridge.

Max was by her side instantly. "What do you need?"

Annella checked her tone before she bit his head off. She was already over the hovering. "Water. Please."

Max beat her to the fridge and handed her a cold water. "Let's go get comfy on the couch and watch TV."

Annella took her water and walked to the living room sitting down on the end of the couch next to her phone. Max covered her up with the throw before he sat down at the opposite end and lifted her feet into his lap, massaging them gently.

Annella picked up her phone and read through the messages she had missed while her phone was off. Five were from Lauren before she gave up and texted Max. One was from an unknown number.

Did you enjoy your stay in the hospital? I have no problem putting you back there the next time I see you drool over fucking Thorne.

The color drained from Annella's face, and she felt the anger well up inside her. She was tired, she was sore, she didn't want to deal with this shit anymore. She texted the number back.

Look, I don't know who you are or what I've done to piss you off, but you need to back the hell off.

She hit send and got an instant response that the message couldn't be delivered. She let out a frustrated "Ugh" and dropped her phone on the side table, making Max cease his rubbing.

"Everything alright? Do you need anything?"

Annella didn't say anything. Just picked up her phone, unplugged it, and handed it to Max. What she now recognized as his angry face appeared as he lowered the phone.

"Enough is enough. We're getting you a new phone number today! Do you feel up to going with me or should I ask Cal or Lauren to come hang out with you?"

Annella opened her mouth to inform him she didn't need a babysitter, but Max held up his hand.

As if he could read her thoughts Max responded with pain in his voice. "I know you don't want a babysitter, but chef, I'm barely holding it together as it is. I'm half tempted to try and get you in protective custody, but I know that won't happen so please have mercy on me."

Annella studied his face, noticing the grief and anger housed in the depths of his deep brown eyes.

"If I didn't want to be the officer to finally catch this guy, I would take you to the beach and eat coconut off your body."

Annella waited a minute, giving serious thought to the beach idea. "I'm going with you, but I want a milkshake on the way home."

Max moved in front of the couch and held out a dishwater wrinkled hand to help her up. "As you wish."

Chapter

26

No new threatening messages had come in, thanks to her new number. She didn't even update her website. She had a button that said message me for information.

As much as she hated to admit it, Max, who had only left her side to go to work, had been right about not feeling up to working.

On Wednesday, she told herself tomorrow, *I'm going to work.*

She even went as far as prepping the meat, but Thursday morning came, and she could still barely get out of bed. She smoked the meat, but later in the morning so it wasn't ready by lunch.

Lauren ended up taking it all to the community center for an impromptu community dinner. It shocked and warmed her heart when Lauren came back later with $500 in donations from the town. Even though the move to Green Lake didn't go quite as planned, Annella still felt like she was where she needed to be.

—⚬—

On Sunday, she woke up rested and 95% better. She was ready for Cody and Sadie's tasting. She even let Max help her in the kitchen claiming that he made up the 5% she was missing.

The couple requested herb-smoked chicken, a light garden salad, and mashed potatoes with gravy. Sadie had told her Cody originally wanted French fries, but she was not having that on her wedding plates, so they compromised with the next best form of potato.

Annella and Max had everything ready to plate when her doorbell chimed promptly at noon. She smoothed her purple chef's coat on the way to answer the door, nerves making her heart race.

Sadie, all bubbly and blonde hair with turquoise steaks, smiled at Annella. "Hi! I'm Sadie!

Annella shook the hand that Cody's fiancé held out.

"I'm so happy we are finally getting to do this. It's the last major detail we need to finalize. It's either you or frozen pizza."

Annella could see why Lauren and Sadie were such good friends. They were just alike, except for their physical appearance. Annella stepped back from her and moved further into the house so the other two people could come in.

Wait, two?

Cody shook Annella's hand and went to introduce Annella to the woman standing behind him. Max came out of the kitchen doing it for him.

"Mom?"

Annella felt a confused look on her face but recovered and smiled warmly at the tall woman with gray streaks through her brown tressels. She was dressed in a casual, long floral sundress and white sandals.

Annella held out her hand. "It's nice to meet you, Mrs. Thorne. I'm Annella Lindley."

She shook Annella's hand and returned her smile. "Please call me Wendy. It's so nice to meet you. I've heard a lot about you from Max. I'm sorry to tag along uninvited, but I was impatient to meet you." She moved to Max and gave him a warm embrace. "You don't even have to worry about a plate for me. I'm just here to visit."

Annella liked Wendy immediately and could appreciate her curiosity over the girl dating her son.

"Nonsense. I have more than enough food for everyone, so I hope you enjoy it. This way, please." Annella gestured into the dining portion of her kitchen and stepped to the counter as Cody, Sadie, and Wendy were seated, Max and Cody pulling out Wendy and Sadie's chairs.

Max took a step toward the counter to help Annella, but she waved him back to sit by his mom. She leaned over and patted his cheek. "She's as beautiful as you said, son."

Annella blushed at the compliment, wondering what else Max had told her. Soon, the talk changed to family memories, Cody doing his best to embarrass Max, wedding flowers, and bittersweet recollections of Heather.

Annella plated the food, proud of the golden color of her chicken, and served the family at her table. She held her breath as the first bites were taken, only exhaling when Sadie closed her eyes and made a noise of appreciation.

"This is amazing. Flavorful, juicy, and just the right amount of herb and smoke flavor."

"Thank you. I'm so glad you like it."

Sadie took another bite of the chicken before scooping the potatoes and gravy up and sampling those.

"They aren't French fries, but I guess they'll do," Cody said. He looked at Sadie and got her nod of approval before turning to Annella. "You're hired."

Annella clapped in her excitement and retrieved her tablet from her office. She put the details into the contract waiting for Cody and Sadie to be finished before she handed it to them to read over and sign. They added cookies for guest favors, and after what seemed like forever, occupational hazard Cody claimed, they signed.

Annella was so elated about getting the job she practically floated around her kitchen getting second helpings, refills, and cookies that she and Max had baked last night.

But happiness in Green Lake is short-lived.

Chapter

27

That bitch changed her number. He had been texting her all week, and with each message undelivered response, his fury grew. It was time to confront her and demand that she forget about Max. He may have to threaten Thorne, but he would gladly do it. He knew Annella would do anything to keep Thorne safe, including breaking up with him.

She was scared. She had been hiding all week. That's how he knew this would work. He would use her fear to get what he wanted. He pulled up a little way down from her house in a borrowed car, and looked around for witnesses before he got out.

Of course, Thorne's truck was parked across the street. He was always there when he wasn't at work. At least he'd be able to threaten Thorne to his face. He climbed the steps, ready to ring the doorbell, when he heard laughter to his left.

She had people here? No. She was supposed to be cowering under a blanket, waiting for him to rescue her. He slid his way over to peek into the window. She wasn't scared at all! She was *laughing*. Having a great time with not just Max, but much of the Thorne family.

His vision blurred with anger. She wasn't afraid of what he could do to her. She hadn't appreciated the low level of harm he had caused so far.

In a daze, he walked back down her porch steps, determination driving his feet. He spotted her gray scalloped garden stones and used his handkerchief to pick one up. He threw it through Thorne's windshield on his way back to his car, wishing it was his face meeting the brick. He got back in his car and drove away, plotting his next move.

—ɯ—

After the contract was signed and everyone had eaten their fill, Annella sat down, enjoying the family time with her own cookie. The story came out about how Cody and Annella first met face to face. Wendy laughed so hard she snorted. "I'm sorry. I don't mean to laugh at your fright, but that's quite a meeting."

"It's fine," Annella assured her. "I think it's been long enough. We can laugh about it now."

"Annella," Sadie said after speaking in low voices with Cody, "I know we've already signed the contract, but could you add on charcuterie boxes for the bridal party to snack on while we get ready?"

"Of course. Let me just add that in. Cody, do you want anything for the groomsmen while you all are getting ready?"

Cody shared a look with Max that made her think they were having a whole conversation that only they knew.

"Sure. We'll add in some chopped sandwiches and bags of chips, please."

Annella corrected the contract, had Cody and Sadie initial the updates, and sign for the new price.

"Thanks," Sadie told her, handing the tablet back.

"No. Thank you," Annella said, getting up to start cleaning up.

"Does anyone want food to take with them? Believe it or not, I still have extra."

Wendy stood and walked over to the counter to Annella. "I would love to take some for Glen and I to have for dinner."

Annella grabbed two to-go containers from the laundry room and fixed the plates.

Max and Annella walked outside to bid farewell to his family. Wendy hugged Max and then Annella before heading back to Cody's black sedan. Sadie's hug was next. "Thanks for an amazing meal and for accommodating us on a Sunday."

"You're most welcome. Thanks for choosing Grace Squared Catering for your big day. Call me if you have any changes or questions." Cody bro hugged Max and then shook Annella's hand, "Thanks for saving my ass."

"No problem," Annella said as she stepped back to Max's side.

They stood and waved as Cody drove away. Max wrapped his arm around her waist and kissed the top of her head.

"I'm so proud of you."

She blushed at Max's praise. "Thanks for recommending me."

"Just don't speed on the way to the wedding." Max kissed her nose. "Can I stay here tonight?"

Annella squeezed Max around the middle. "Of course."

"I'm going to go get some clean clothes out of my truck."

Annella turned toward the house as Max walked toward his truck. She made it to the bottom step before she heard Max's angry voice from behind her.

"Son of a bitch!"

Annella turned, her heart dropping to her feet, and jogged back down the sidewalk to see what happened this time.

Annella stopped beside Max, hands on his hips, as he looked at his truck. He paced back and forth for a minute, Annella watching, not able to say anything. He pulled out his phone holding it so hard Annella thought he would shatter the screen just like his windshield.

Danielle answered on the second ring. "Hey, Max. What's going on?" He knew Danielle might have been expecting pleasantries, but he didn't give a shit.

"I need a unit to Annella's now. Someone shattered the windshield of my truck."

He could hear the click of the keyboard and her calling for an available unit. Max knew it would be Soto and Green today. "Is anyone injured?"

"No injuries," Max said, leaning his head back and praying that this would all be over soon.

"Okay. Soto and Green are on their way now."

"Who would do this to you?"

Annella looked up and down the street to see if anything didn't belong. She had gotten extremely familiar with the vehicles of her neighbors after the van incident.

"Whoever this is, they're getting desperate. This isn't the action of an in-control person. Desperate people do dumb shit."

By the time Soto and Green pulled up, Max had cooled down, and his cop brain kicked in. "Hey, Lieutenant," Soto said, coming around to shake Max's hand. He pulled out his notebook asking Max the standard questions.

"When was the last time you saw your truck? Can you think of anyone that would want to do this?"

Max answered them, then stood back as Green took pictures and then gloved up to pull the garden décor from his driver's seat.

Max was on the phone with the insurance company already as he and Annella walked back toward the house. Soto and Green were finishing up their investigation of his truck and asking the neighbors again if they saw anything.

As soon as Max finished with the insurance call, he pulled up the camera footage on his phone. He scrolled through right after his family arrived and started watching. Green came up to the porch, and Annella showed him where the brick had been earlier that morning so he could take a few photos.

"Is that the footage from the security cameras?" Soto asked, coming over from Brock and Olivia's.

"Yeah, with any luck, we're going to see someone. They had to get close enough to pick up the brick." The time on the camera kept going with nothing happening. Max knew they were getting close to his family leaving, so it had to be soon.

Finally, he saw a grainy image in the frame. "Piece of shit cameras. The glare from the sun is making it so you can't make anything out." Max paused the feed and zoomed in as much as he could, but all he saw was a blurry face. They kept watching as the person moved away from the front door toward the kitchen window. It gave Annella the creeps to think about this asshole watching her in her home. She shivered but kept watching as the person left the camera frame.

"I'll get the rock checked for prints and let you know ASAP," Green said as he walked down the steps.

"Do you want us to stay out front for the rest of our shift?" Soto asked, following Green down the steps.

"Thanks, but I doubt they'll be back. Stay on patrol."

"Ten-four," Soto said as he and Green made their way back to the cruiser, taking one last look at Max's truck.

Max turned to walk into the house. "I'm going on a run. Do you feel up to coming with me?"

Annella looked to her dirty kitchen and then to the man who needed her more than the mess. "Loser does the dishes?"

Ten minutes later, they were out front doing warm-up stretches before heading to the park at a jog.

Chapter

28

Summer business was booming for Annella. Family reunions, birthdays, and an elopement party that Sadie threw for one of her fellow stylists. Grace Squared Catering was the first call anyone made when they needed to schedule food and Annella's pride swelled for her little company.

Today was her busiest day yet. Lauren and Max had both hired her to cater for the bachelor and bachelorette parties. Luckily for her, they were both low-key events, a BBQ buffet for Cody at Max's and a grazing table for Sadie at the house she shared with Cody.

She pulled up to the house and had to double-check she was in the right place. The seafoam green cottage structure was not what she was expecting. The only thing that confirmed she was where she was meant to be was Lauren walking out on the front porch and waving.

Annella got out of the van and waited for her usual best friend hug that Lauren delivered as soon as she was close enough.

"Hey, bestie," Lauren said, stepping back and walking with Annella to the back of the van.

"Hey," Annella responded as she reached up to open the door. "This is not what I pictured a lawyer living in." Lauren hopped into the back of the van and slid a cooler labeled Sadie to

Annella. "This is Sadie's house and has been since she moved out on her own at eighteen and Cody left for college. She worked two jobs to put herself through cosmetology school. Cody went from his childhood bedroom to his college dorm to here with Sadie."

Annella helped Lauren lift the cooler down and then she jumped back up for the next one. Annella put a box with pretzels, crackers, and nuts on top so she could wheel it all in at once. "It's a cute house, just pictured his house less colorful."

Lauren got back down and helped Annella lift another box on top of the cooler. She picked up her drink dispenser in her free hand and shut the doors.

They were halfway to the house when Lauren told her, "He just cared about being with Sadie. They plan on buying a bigger house after the wedding."

"That makes sense," Annella grunted as she wheeled the cooler over the steps, careful not to dislodge the box.

Lauren made a similar sound right behind her. "How can cheese, deli meat, and fruit weigh so much?"

Annella opened the white screen door, stepping back so Lauren could go in first. "I wanted to make sure there was plenty of food. I've never been to any kind of sleepover party, so I might have overdone it a little bit."

Lauren stopped in the doorway, gaping at Annella. "You've never been to a sleepover? What about people coming to your house for one?"

Annella looked down at her feet, feeling awkward, and shook her head. "I was mostly a loner in school. I stayed home reading or cooking."

Lauren leaned over the cooler to hug her friend and try to heal the child inside her. "Well, you have friends now. You should come spend the night with us after you get Cody's party set up."

Lauren headed through the door. "I wouldn't want to impose or make Sadie upset that I crashed the party," Annella said, following her through the living room and into the kitchen.

There were so many colors in this one room Annella couldn't take them all in. Deep blue subway tile backsplash, yellow cabinets, white counters, avocado green fridge. The colors continued to neon orange cushions on the bar stools and bright pink daisies in a purple vase on the table.

"I see Sadie's love of color applies to more than just her hair," Annella said as she wiped down the table before setting up. "Yeah, she said the world has too many colors to only use a few at a time." Lauren pulled out the white butcher paper from a box and helped Annella spread and tape it down.

Annella placed the décor pieces first, including a Miss to Mrs. sign and a giant engagement ring centerpiece. "If you don't need my help in here, I'm going to go finish setting up the living room."

Lauren set the box of paper down and turned to Annella. "I'm all set. Shout if you need any help out there." Lauren nodded and headed out of the kitchen.

Annella hummed along to Lauren's playlist and lost herself in her work. She loved serving her customers at the van but loved the quiet hours of prep work before an event, too. She finished just as she heard voices from the front. She stepped back with her hands clasped in front of her to present her display to Sadie.

"Oh, Annella! It's absolutely perfect." Sadie bounded over in her jeans and white, sparkly tank top and hugged Annella. "I'm so glad I gave you creative liberty. This is better than anything I could have come up with."

Annella enjoyed the happiness shining out from Sadie as Lauren came in.

"Nice work, bestie." Lauren whistled through her teeth. "I can't wait to snack on everything. Oh, Sadie! Did you see the drink mix?" Lauren asked, pointing to the counter.

Annella walked over and picked up a mini champagne bottle.

"I know you said not everyone would be drinking, so I made Sadie's Sparkling Punch with ginger ale, pink cranberry juice, and edible glitter. Those that want to can add in the champagne."

Sadie squealed and clapped her hands. "It's too pretty to drink, but I bet there won't be a drop left. Thank you, Annella. It is all amazing." Sadie took the champagne bottle and popped the cork. "Should we give it a sample?"

Annella poured some of the champagne into each of their glasses and then filled them with punch. She held out her glass. "To you, Sadie. May you always be as happy as you are today. You are going to be a beautiful bride."

The girls clinked their glasses together and sipped the pink, sparkly drink. "It's delicious," Lauren said. "Light and summery and fun."

Annella took a small sip and savored the bubbles tickling down her throat. The alarm on her phone went off, signaling that it was time to head to Max's and set up the bachelor party.

"You girls have fun tonight. I've got to go set up your fiancé's party." Annella packed up the few things she didn't use and made sure everything looked perfect once more before grabbing her purse and the coolers. "I hope you enjoy everything and have a wonderful time. You just text me tomorrow when you want me to come clean everything up."

Annella paused in the living room and surveyed Lauren's decorations. "It looks great in here, Lauren. Tasteful but fun. I'll see you both tomorrow."

Annella reached for the door when Sadie called her to wait. "What are you doing after you set up at Max's?"

Annella adjusted the strap on her purse.

"No plans. Just going home to enjoy my book."

Sadie exchanged a look with Lauren that made Annella think they had already discussed what came next. "Why don't you come back here and party with us? You know most of everyone that's going to be here, and everyone else will love you."

Annella looked between the two of them. "It won't be awkward for you? Hanging out with someone you've hired to do a job?"

Sadie grabbed Annella's free hand. "Girl, you are dating my soon-to-be brother-in-law, so to me, you are more than the caterer. If I didn't want you here, I wouldn't have said anything. You'll be here as just a friend, not the contractor. I will stop you if you try to work." Sadie crossed her arms and gave Annella her sternest look, which wasn't harsh.

"I guess I can't argue with the bride. I might be a touch late since I'll need to go change if I'm not here as the caterer." Annella looked down at her purple chef's jacket and loose slacks that she had chosen for the day. "Is there a color that I need to wear?"

Sadie uncrossed her arms and high-fived Lauren. "Anything pink. No need for a dress or heels as we are just having a spa night in. Get here whenever you can."

Sadie headed down the hall, and Lauren helped Annella with the coolers. "You didn't pressure her into this, did you?"

Lauren held up her hands in surrender as Annella opened the back of the van. "I swear I didn't. She asked if I thought you would want to come. Totally her idea, and now you'll get to have your first sleepover!"

Annella and Lauren loaded the back and walked around to the driver's side. Annella got in and narrowed her gaze at Lauren.

"If my hand gets put in warm water and I pee myself, I'm going to be so mad at you."

Lauren barked out a laugh, making Annella stop glaring at her. "I thought you've never been to a sleepover." Annella reached for the door and Lauren stepped back waving as her best friend drove away.

—ɯ—

Annella pulled up to Max's, happy to see that the porch was still clean and tidy and happier to see Max standing on it waiting on her. She cut the engine and hopped out to meet Max at the back of the van. He kissed her like he hadn't seen her in weeks instead of just a few hours.

When he finally let her come up for air, she was laughing and breathing hard. "What was that for?"

Max opened the back door. "To say hi and thank you. It couldn't have been easy to do both parties on the same day." Max stepped up into the back of the van.

He handed her a box with chips and cookies then got down to unload the coolers with Cody's name on masking tape. He shut the doors and followed Annella to the house.

"It's not bad. All about time management and organization. While your brisket was smoking, I chopped and prepped the grazing table meats and cheeses. While it was resting, I threw on the sausage and loaded what I could. When the sausage was ready, I threw it in a pan and headed to Sadie's."

Max held the screen door open and followed her through to the kitchen, which was also still clean.

"I'm impressed the house is still clean."

Max opened the cooler and pulled out covered pans that smelled like heaven. "It's been easy since I've been mostly at your house. I cannot be held responsible for how it looks tomorrow, though."

Annella rolled her eyes and grinned. "I'm going to get the drink dispensers. I'll be right back."

She headed outside and stopped short so she didn't run over Cal on his way inside with a box full of liquor. "Hey, Annella," Cal said, backing up so she could come out.

"Hey, Cal." Annella walked out and held the screen door. "I have a whole basket of cookies inside. You still have time to hide them before everyone else gets here."

Cal grinned, showing his perfect smile. It was easy to see why he was so popular with the ladies. "If you weren't in love with my best friend, I'd go after you myself."

Annella thought about how far they had come since she was first pulled over. "Guess you should have thrown that rock, paper, scissors match."

Cal looked up and saw Max coming from the kitchen. "Yeah, I don't think it would have ended the same, and I'm okay with that. I'm happy for you guys."

Annella walked down the porch and got the drink containers. One for tea and one for in the morning. She knew they probably wouldn't be interested in anything non-alcoholic tonight, but she wanted them to have the option and knew they would want the electrolyte drink in the morning.

Cal helped Max set up the poker table. Then, they helped Annella make sure there were enough pillows and blankets spread out as she told them about going to the bachelorette party.

"You guys have a good time tonight," Annella said.

"We will," Max and Cal responded in unison as Max helped Annella outside. He felt better knowing that she wouldn't be home alone tonight. Max drew Annella into him and kissed her so hard that she wanted to drag him off and forget the parties.

"If you don't tell me to leave now, we aren't going to make it to our parties."

Max's grin told Annella that he had every intention of finishing what he had just started. And a chill crept down her spine in anticipation.

He held open the door for her and kissed her again. "Enjoy yourself tonight. Don't think of it as work. Think of it as a night with your best friend."

"I will. I'll see you tomorrow. I love you, Max."

Max's head spun every time he heard her say those words, still not sure he wasn't dreaming. "I love you too, chef." He shut the door and stepped back so she could drive away, watching until he couldn't see the van anymore.

Chapter

29

Annella went home and changed into a pink workout tank and black yoga pants. She threw some things in an overnight bag and headed back to Sadie's ready for her first sleepover ever. Green Lake had given her a lot of firsts in her life. First business, first time being in love, first true best friend, first sleepover, and first feeling of home.

She parked and walked up the steps to knock on the door, but Sadie opened it before she could.

"Annella!" Sadie squealed making Annella wonder how many glasses of punch she had already drank. "Come on in." Sadie led Annella into the living room and took her overnight bag.

Sadie introduced her to the rest of the bridal party, her older sister Kaitlyn was married to Cal's brother Danny and Nina, her younger sister that was in college in Pure Springs for business management.

Wendy walked in from the kitchen with a plate of snacks in hand. "Annella, it's so good to see you again." Annella returned the smile and hugged Wendy back careful not to make her spill her plate.

"It's nice to see you too. How did Glen enjoy the dinner from the tasting?" Wendy stepped around Annella and seated herself by Kaitlyn. Sadie headed down the hallway with Annella's bag.

"He said it was the best chicken he's ever had and practically licked the gravy off of the bottom of the container."

Annella beamed with pride and looked around for Lauren spotting her in the kitchen with another face Annella didn't recognize.

"Annella, this is Tonya, Sadie's mom." Lauren said handing her a glass.

Annella shook hands with Tonya, "It's nice to meet you. I can see the resemblance between you and your three daughters."

Tonya smiled a warm motherly smile at Annella, "Considering I have some beautiful girls I'll say, thank you. This spread is amazing and such a fun idea with the glitter in the punch."

Annella absolutely loved it when people enjoyed her food. It's what got her out of bed in the morning. Annella fixed herself a plate and second drink, adding only a little champagne to her punch then followed Lauren and Tonya to the living room.

Sadie had stations set up for manicures, pedicures, and chair massages. Annella took part in all three and scheduled a follow up appointment for a full body massage after the wedding.

Annella laughed so hard her sides ached, and she had tears rolling down her face when Wendy told the story of Cody having to sleep on the porch the one time he was out past curfew with Sadie.

The ladies embraced her instead of treating her like an outsider and she landed another grazing table job for Sadie's mother. No one brought up the darkness that had been plaguing her lately even though Annella was sure everyone knew, and she was grateful for that.

Annella and Lauren had shared the queen bed that was in the guest room and woke to Annella's alarm.

"Why did you set an alarm?" Lauren groaned as she tossed a pillow over her head.

Annella fumbled for her phone and silenced it as fast as possible. "I had an alarm set before I knew I was spending the night here and I forgot to turn it off. Sorry."

Annella hopped out of bed, grabbed her bag and tip-toed to the bathroom. She got ready for a day of cleanup and resetting. When she walked back through the bedroom to grab her charger Lauren was sitting on the side of the bed rubbing the sleep from her eyes.

Annella crept as quietly as she could through the house to start cleaning up the kitchen and found Sadie there with her sisters drinking coffee.

"Morning," Annella said as she started cleaning up.

"Morning," they all said as Lauren stepped into the kitchen behind Annella and made a beeline for the coffee pot.

"Thank you so much for the invitation. I had an amazing time."

"You're welcome," Sadie smiled in response and sipped her coffee.

There was no food left and only a smidge of the punch, so clean up was easy. Annella left Sadie's as Lauren mumbled about going back to bed and went home for a shower and breakfast before heading to Max's.

She thought it was a decent hour since it was creeping up on eleven when she pulled up, but when she opened the door, she was met with groans and shouts to "Shut the damn door."

She backed out and texted Max to let her know when it was safe to come back.

—⁂—

The week between the parties and the wedding flew by for Annella. She took Friday off from the food van to check and double-check and triple-check that she had everything ready. The reception venue had its own commercial kitchen with a grill/smoker combo out back, so she would be cooking on-site instead of transporting her food. Score!

Annella knew she was going to need some help, and since Lauren was going to be busy doing the maid of honor duties, she decided to use high school home economics students.

Olivia was the home ec teacher and happily helped arrange for three of her best students to lend a hand. Annella would be paying them and feeding them, which went a long way in getting seventeen-year-olds to work.

The wedding was all anyone could talk about. How beautiful Sadie was going to be. What a lucky SOB Cody was. Where were they going on their honeymoon, and Annella's favorite subject. The food.

Her alarm went off at an hour that shouldn't even exist, and she quickly silenced it so she didn't wake up Max. Annella had delivered everything she would need today to the venue last night before going to the rehearsal dinner. Sadie's parents rented out the banquet room at The Black Tie for the night, and Annella couldn't help the uncomfortable feeling of being there.

She had offered to cook the dinner and serve it at the community center, but Cody and Sadie said they wanted her to just relax and enjoy dinner with Max and the families since she would miss the ceremony. She met Max and Cody's dad, Glen, and liked him right off. He told her he was sorry to have missed the tasting, but he couldn't back out of his tee time. He had asked Annella if she golfed, and she shook her head. He promised to teach her so that she could beat Max on the course.

She texted her first-ever "employees," pleased to see their responses come in quickly that they were up and getting ready to meet her. She shut the door as quietly as possible to the bathroom and stayed nearly silent as she got ready. She kept it simple for the day.

She gently kissed Max on the forehead, tip-toed out of the bedroom, and headed out the front door.

Annella drove through town and noticed that only The Buttered Biscuit had lights on. Tom and Paula were in there preparing their regular baking as well as putting the finishing touches on the wedding cake. She couldn't wait to see what they had put together. She pulled into the back parking lot of the Willowbrook Event Venue as the morning colors kissed the hills on the horizon and basked in a moment of peace.

She stepped out of the van when Shauna pulled up in her little compact car and waved excitedly. A more somber Jordan emerged from the passenger seat glaring at the sun that dared to shine. Jordan only perked up slightly when Adam pulled in, blaring music out of his single cab truck.

"Good morning," Annella greeted the three of them as they walked into the back door of the venue.

Annella handed them each a black polo shirt with Grace Squared Catering embroidered in purple. Annella bent over her tablet, reciting the schedule of events to them until she hoped it stuck, and looked up.

"Questions."

She ate her protein bar as Jordan raised her hand like she was in Olivia's class. Annella nodded at her and drank her water.

"Is there caffeine anywhere?" Annella pointed to a coffee station with a single pod machine and a basket of pods. Jordan selected her flavor and watched the brew like it was life in a cup. She took a tentative sip and perked up.

"She's coming alive now," Shauna said.

"Good. We've got to get moving."

Annella finished her protein bar and checked her watch.

"Alright. Let's build charcuterie boxes."

Annella demonstrated on the first box, then built the second along with the crew giving out pointers, but overall impressed with their work. She found a large box to hold them all to make delivery easier for Shauna and Jordan.

She put the box in the refrigerator and pulled out a small brisket flat she had smoked the day before to make sandwiches for the groom's party. The teens left to make their deliveries as Annella started the smoker.

When she came back in, she was mesmerized by the venue staff laying the tables. Watching as linens fanned out like an aerial silk dance. She loved Sadie's color choice of blush pink and gold. It was just like the bride, bubbly and bold. The food would be served buffet style so there were no large plates on the tables. Only baskets for bread that Tom and Paula would also bring.

Annella tore her eyes from the choreographed chaos when a very handsome police lieutenant walked across the dance floor to her. For a second, she dreamed about a fall wedding with a deep purple and maroon theme, then checked her thoughts before they escaped like someone had left the gate open.

Max reached her and then surprised her by lifting her completely off her feet and kissing her deeply. Annella melted into Max and welded her mouth to his. Their kiss was love and passion with all tongues and teeth that left them both breathless as Max set her back on her feet. Annella kept her arms around his neck as she didn't fully trust her legs at that moment and looked up into Max's fierce gaze.

"Hello, chef. It smells wonderful in here."

Annella giggled like Jordan when she saw Adam that morning, making Max raise an eyebrow at her. He had never heard her make that sound, and it made his heart flutter.

"Hello, Lieutenant. I just put the chicken on. There's no way you can smell it yet."

"I wasn't talking about the chicken," Max said, kissing the top of her head and leaning back against the stainless counter.

"What are you doing here? I just sent Adam to Cody and Sadie's house with food for you all."

"There are more important things than food."

Annella shook her head and slid onto the metal stool at the island.

"Almost nothing is more important than food. It's a good thing I sent extra sandwiches. There might still be one left by the time you get back. Which brings me back to my original question. What are you doing here?"

"I have a gift for you is what I'm doing here." Max pulled a long, black velvet box from his back pocket and handed it to Annella. "Sorry I didn't wrap it. My wrapping skills make my cooking skills look amazing."

Annella laughed and stepped toward him as she slid off the stool. "A gift? What's the occasion? It's not my birthday or Christmas, and we haven't been dating long enough to celebrate any kind of anniversary."

Max took the box back from her and opened it as he said, "Just because I love you." It wasn't diamond or flashy, but it was perfect for her. Inside the box was a sterling silver chain with a purple enamel chef's hat charm hanging from it.

Annella beamed up at Max, smiling with her whole face. "It's perfect! I love it. Thank you."

Max took the necklace from the box and motioned her to turn around slipping the chain around her. He clasped the necklace and sealed it with a kiss on the back of her neck.

Annella spun back around and kissed Max softly. "I love you, Max. I'm glad you pulled me over."

Max kissed her nose, which made her giggle again. "Just doing my job. You know, to protect and serve."

Annella grabbed the charm and slid it along the chain. "Now, you get out of here and let me do my job to cook and serve."

225

"Yes, chef," Max said, walking backward a few steps and winking at her.

He was almost out the door when Annella called out, "Make sure your socks match tonight." Max turned around and saluted her, then walked out the door.

Chapter

30

Max stood at the front of the Willowbrook Historic Chapel in his rented tux that they had to have shipped in due to his height with his socks matching and a pink flower in his lapel smelling sweet. The ends of the seating rows held pink and gold wildflower bouquets tied with white lace making the space smell like an open field on the summer day.

Cody standing next to him in a matching monkey suit couldn't stop moving. Max had watched him in the court room go toe to toe with the best attorneys and not break a sweat, but now waiting for the love of his life to walk down the aisle nervous energy poured off of him.

"What time is it?" Cody asked for the fifth time in the last 3 minutes, pulling Max's wrist up to look at his watch.

"She's late. Did she change her mind?" Cody looked towards the back of the chapel as if willing Sadie to come through the doors. He took off down the aisle. Max caught up with him in two easy strides.

"Relax, man," Max told him steering him back to the front with the rest of the groomsmen. "When have you ever known weddings to start on time?"

Cody tipped his head back and let out a long sigh. "You're right. You're right."

The officiant entered the chapel from the little door behind the podium and gave Cody a reassuring smile and signaled for him to turn towards the back.

The music began and the back doors opened to the little flower girls bouncing down the aisle in their pink dresses with gold trimming tossing pink rose petals in front of them. Nina came in next, her gold gown whispering along the floor already dabbing at her eyes with a tissue. Kaitlyn came in next and Danny, who was standing on Max's other side beamed a smile and winked at his wife floating down the aisle.

The doors closed, the music quieted, and Cody dabbed at the sweat dots on his forehead. The officiant raised his arms out in front of him for everyone to stand as the classic wedding march started and the doors opened again to Sadie and her father.

Cody pinched his lips together and covered his face with his hands for a second. When he lowered them, tears leaked from the corners of his eyes. Sadie glided to him in an ivory and gold trumpet gown with a lace overlay. Her hair was in a cascade of curls, and she carried a small bouquet of pink roses and gold carnations.

Sadie handed her bouquet to Kaitlyn as Lauren straightened her train and the guests took their seats.

The couple exchanged vows that they wrote themselves and Cody had to swipe a tear away from Sadie's cheek as he promised to let her fill their house and his life with as much color as she wanted. Max handed Cody the ring he had been carrying and watched as his brother kissed his bride, hopeful that he wouldn't be too far behind him in that endeavor.

"Family and friends, it is my honor to present to you Mr. and Mrs. Cody Thorne," the officiant said as Saide took her bouquet back and the couple walked back down the aisle to claps and cheers.

—⚏—

Adam, Jordan, and Shauna worked so well together that Annella would have sworn they had been doing it for years. She checked the clock on the wall and turned to address them.

"It's just a buffet, but we are still going to make the rounds to refill glasses and clear away empty plates—just general help. Any questions?"

Shauna's hand flew up this time.

"You guys are not in class you don't have to raise your hand."

Shauna put her hand down. "How is the cake-cutting going to work?"

"Excellent question. After Cody and Sadie do their cutting and take photos, Tom and Paula will take over slicing while we serve. Don't rush. Everyone picks a table and serves the whole table before moving on. Anything else?"

"No, chef," they responded in unison sending an excited chill to flow down Annella.

"Then it's time," Annella said as the first guests trickled in and made their way to their seats.

The guests snacked on fluffy rolls, and soon, the DJ announced, "Ladies and gentlemen, Mr. and Mrs. Cody Thorne." Applause went around the room with some whistles and cat calls.

The wedding party made a hasty approach to the food table and friends and family followed their direction. Annella and Jordan kept their eyes on the dishes, refilling chicken, potatoes, and salad before the pans were empty. They served the tables closest to the buffet while Adam and Shauna worked the tables farther away. Annella had tried to put Jordan and Adam together to play a little matchmaker, but Jordan said she preferred to be in the back.

The reception was a blast for everyone. Max's toast had boisterous laughter filling the room, while Lauren's had more than one woman dabbing their eyes, Annella included.

At exactly 8:30, Cody and Sadie cut the first pieces of the cake. Sadie did the honorable thing and gently fed Cody his slice of cake while Cody dotted a pink bit of frosting on her cheek before he slipped the white cake into her mouth.

They shared a soulful kiss and took their plates back to the table. Tom and Paula started plating the perfectly sliced cake while Annella and her junior chefs passed them out.

When they had their last table served Annella let the kids take over while she started to clear serving dishes out. There was still food left, so if anyone wanted more, all they had to do was ask, but everyone looked completely stuffed.

Annella made up to-go plates for the wedding planner to put in Cody's car in case the bride and groom got hungry...later. She also made plates for the rest of the staff and still had food left over. The dancing was a good mix of sweet, slow numbers and fan favorites. She even spotted Cal and Lauren dancing... interesting.

—ᴘᴘᴜ—

At 11:00, the DJ called for everyone to line up the walkway outside for the sparkler send-off. The four of them hung back and threw away trash while the place was empty. Only a few people came back in to grab purses and coats before heading back out, and the night was over. Annella handed the crew envelopes with their payments and sent them on their way. She was doing a final check when she sensed Max behind her.

She turned from the counter and saw him standing in the middle of what had been the dance floor, looking sexy as sin. He crooked a finger, and like a moth to a flame, she went.

Max wrapped her in a tight embrace and then rested his hands on her lower back. "The food was amazing, and everyone that I talked to praised you and your staff."

Annella rested her head on his chest and circled her arms around his neck. "It couldn't have gone any better if Patton was leading the night."

Max laughed and kissed her soundly. "It was only missing one thing to make it my perfect night."

Annella looked up at him questioningly.

"I didn't get to dance with the most gorgeous woman here."

Max let go of her long enough to pull out his phone and start playing her favorite country song. He held out his hand to her like she was in a ball gown instead of sweaty work clothes. "Annella, will you dance with me?"

Annella placed one hand in his and covered her face with the other. Max pulled her in, removing the hand from her face and pulling it around his shoulders.

They swayed back and forth, not really dancing, just moving in circles and swaying. All too soon, the song was over, but Max didn't let her go until Cal came in whistling loudly. "Sorry. Don't let me interrupt."

"You're not," Annella said.

"Speak for yourself." Max glared at Cal.

Cal came over to Max and handed him a beer. "There needs to be more events in this town where tuxes are required."

Annella let her gaze trail over Max and then Cal.

"You keep looking at him like that, and I'm going to have to forget he's my best friend." Max gently shoved Cal.

"Is that any way to treat the man who brought you a beer?"

Annella kissed Max and one-arm-hugged Cal. "You two enjoy your beers. I'm going to head home."

Max walked her out to the van and then joined Cal sitting in the kitchen. "So, when is this going to be yours and Annella's wedding?" Max took a deep drink of crisp, cold beer.

"As soon as I plan the proposal and give her the diamond ring I bought two weeks ago."

Cal spit out his beer on the counter, and Max threw him a rag. "No shit? I was half joking."

"No shit," Max replied.

They finished their beers and went back into the main room, doing one last sweep for anything forgotten. Max was picking up a tiny bowtie that had been missed when his phone rang.

Chapter

31

Annella drove down the mountain with her windows down, letting the warm summer night flow through the van. She wanted four things in her immediate future. A hot shower to wash away the sweat, BBQ smoke smell. A large glass of red wine to wind down the thoughts in her head. And to make love to Max and sleep in his arms for the next twelve hours.

She was weighing the pros and cons of lighting all the candles she could find in her bedroom as she drove through an intersection, headlights shining through the driver's side window.

—⁂—

Max's phone vibrated against his chest in his jacket pocket. He held it up to Cal when he saw Dawn's name. "She's probably calling about a slice of cake," Max said as he picked up. "Hey, Dawn. I've got your—"

Dawn's police voice cut off the rest of his sentence. Her next three words would haunt Max for a long time.

"Max, it's Annella."

Max was moving at a sprint before she said another word. Cal was right on his heels. Cal grabbed Max's keys from his hand before they got to the truck and jumped into the driver's seat. Max's phone connected to his truck as Dawn gave her report.

"She was in a hit-and-run right into the driver's door. Some folks that were going into The Tavern saw the whole thing. The truck that did it sounds like Travis's."

Max opened his mouth to ask how she was, but no sound came out. Instead, it was Cal that asked, "How's Annella?"

Dawn paused, saying something they couldn't hear, then came back to them. "She was unconscious when I got here, but she's awake now. EMS is here already and is getting her out to take her to the hospital.

Max's leg was bouncing as Cal was flying down the mountain as fast as he could. "Max!" he shouted, trying to snap him out of it. "It's not Heather. She's going to be fine. We have work to do."

Max nodded and found his voice, which sounded gravely. "Did the witness say which way the vehicle went?" Max shut down his thoughts and turned on his cop brain.

"West up Main toward The Black Tie. They're about to load Annella, but she's asking to speak to you."

Everything in Max's body screamed at him to get to Annella as soon as possible. He looked over to see how fast Cal was going, not even caring that he was breaking the limit. He heard the rattle of the gurney wheels on the pavement and then Annella's sweet voice coming out through gritted teeth. "Max, it hurts."

Max couldn't stop the tears that were flowing from his eyes. "I'm coming, baby. I'm so sorry it hurts. I'll be at the hospital about the same time you are."

Cal made it to the bottom of the mountain and floored the truck, fishtailing around the corner towards the hospital.

"No. You go get the asshole that did this to me. I love you, and I'll see you after this is done."

Max loved the bravery and selflessness she exuded. She would make a good police wife. Cal slowed down, barely, and U-turned toward The Black Tie instead of the hospital.

"Yes, chef," Max said.

Dawn's voice came back on the phone. "Do you need backup?"

"No. We've got this. You and Hall stay on patrol in case we don't find him at the restaurant. Thank you for taking care of her. We'll call with any updates."

Cal hit the button to end the call on the steering wheel and glanced at Max.

"How do you want to handle this? We're not in uniform and not in a police vehicle."

The calm grin that spread over Max's face scared Cal more than his rage.

Cal gunned the engine, and the scenery passed in a blur.

—❊—

Travis sat in the parking lot behind his family's restaurant and tried to think, but his head pounded in time with his heartbeat.

"There's no way they're going to know it was me. No one saw anything, and I can pay someone for an alibi easily or pay my way out of this."

Travis was still talking out loud when headlights cut a blinding path across his vision.

When he saw Tweedledee and Tweedledumbass pull into the parking lot, he snapped. He jammed his truck into gear and spun his tires heading straight for Max's truck.

Cal gunned the engine and flipped the steering wheel so that Travis connected with the bed of the truck.

Travis fell out of his truck and started shouting, "Of fucking course, you two are here. Precious Annella gets hurt, and GLPD immediately shows up to question me. Tell me something, is it just one of you fucking her, or do you share?"

Max and Cal walked up and stopped in front of Travis, crossing their arms as if this were any other chat.

"Evening, Travis," Max began. To anyone else, Max looked calm, but Cal could see his knuckles bone white around his bicep.

"I don't believe that's any of your business, and I never said anything about Annella being hurt. Cal?"

Cal shook his head. "Nope. Never said that."

Travis's eyes turned to bloodshot slits and he threw up his hands. "You didn't have to say anything. The only reason Green Lake Police Department deigns to visit me is when that bitch cries. Let me go ahead and answer your questions. I was at The Tavern until ten with Naomi, and we were bored, so I took her home, rocked her world, and then came here to be alone."

"Thanks for that, but I don't trust you are telling the truth. You trust him, Cal?"

"Not since he ratted me out in fourth grade for hiding at recess to avoid going back to class."

Travis roared in anger and let his fist fly toward Max connecting with his jaw.

Max had had enough. His head snapped to the side from the impact. He turned back towards Travis, nostrils flaring and a growl coming from deep in his throat.

Did Max let Travis hit him?

Yes.

Was it going to be put into the report that way?

No.

Travis drew his hand back to swing again, but his drunken state made him slower than Max.

Max clenched his fist and hit Travis so hard that he fell to the gravel. Max grabbed a fist of Travis's jet-black hair and kept hitting him until his knuckles were bloody.

Max pulled him to his feet and tossed him into his own truck. Travis roared with rage and came for Max again fist raised.

Cal caught his arm and jerked it behind his back, "That was quite enough."

Cal had Travis pinned to the bed of Max's truck as lights and sirens filled the parking lot. Max got right into Travis's panting, red face and smelled the alcohol. "Travis, you just assaulted a police officer, and that's a felony."

Cal pulled Travis's other arm behind his back while he recited his Mirandas to him as Dawn and Hall came sprinting out of their car. Travis did not exercise his right to remain silent as Cal walked him to the back of Max's truck.

"That stupid whore. I can't believe she picked you over me. This was karma catching up with her for ignoring me and changing her number. Cal shut the door on the rest of Travis's words, walking to Max, Dawn and Hall.

"I thought I told you two to stay on patrol," Max said as he took a bandana from Hall and wrapped it around his knuckles wincing a bit.

"Well," Dawn started, "We figured when you didn't call saying you couldn't find him that we would come offer encouragement. I mean backup."

Cal threw an arm around Dawn and Hall and nodded to Max's face, "Thanks. Sorry you missed the fun though. That's probably going to bruise."

Max ran his thumb on his jaw. "One can only hope. It'll add to the story. I'm going to call Phil to tow his truck to impound. I can see the purple paint from here on the grill guard. I want it in police custody before Mommy and Daddy Ashwood do something with it."

Max tipped his head back and exhaled long and slow.

"Let's take his ass to jail."

—⁓—

Annella woke up to the sounds of beeps and the hum of the blood pressure cuff expanding. Her left leg and arm felt extremely heavy with their cast enclosures, and the burn across her chest from her seatbelt throbbed every time her gown rubbed against it. The doorknob rattled, and she looked over as Max came in. Anger flashed across his face for a second before he walked to the right side of the bed.

"Is it over?" Her voice sounded small and tired.

"Yes. Travis is in a jail cell as we speak, requesting his lawyer and calling you some not-nice names."

She saw the darker skin on his jaw in the dim light from the bathroom. "What happened to your face?"

"Something else he won't get away with. Do you still think I'm handsome?"

Max bent and kissed her gently. Annella tried to giggle, but the movement had her chest rubbing against her gown causing her to wince.

"You are still the most handsome man I've ever seen."

Max saw her wince and regretted not hitting Travis harder. "Do you need anything?"

Annella squeezed his hand and pulled him to her, kissing him deeper. "I have everything I need."

Epilogue

Annella tapped her good foot against the end of her bed in her flower lined hospital room as she waited for Dr. Sulivan on Monday. Max was sitting beside her trying to calm her down.

He had found out early that morning that Travis was still in jail. The paint matched her van, so he was charged with the hit-and-run. He was drunk when they booked him in, so driving under the influence was added on. He assaulted a police officer, he admitted to stalking her, the vandalism in her house, and breaking Max's windshield.

His parents had tried to bribe his way out of it, but the judge wasn't even allowing bail to be set as Travis was considered a flight risk.

Dr. Sullivan came in, a cheerful smile on her face that only annoyed Annella more as she flipped pages on her clipboard.

"How are you feeling this morning?" She asked.

Annella sat up and scooted to the edge of the bed. "I'm feeling fine. Sore and a little heavy on the left side of my body, but everything else is great." Annella would say whatever she had to if it got her out of the hospital.

Dr. Sullivan handed Annella her discharge paperwork with a card for a follow up visit in four weeks. "Call the office if anything starts to hurt unnaturally or if you experience any laten concussion symptoms."

Annell took the forms and handed them to Max as Mitch came in with a wheelchair. "Sorry, but we don't have a purple one." He said as he got up next to the bed.

Annella's smile widened to her eyes and she laughed sucking in a deep breath around the tightness in her muscles. "That's ok. I've got enough purple on me right now to make up for it."

Max kissed Annella's forehead when she stood with Mitch's help. "I'm going to meet you out front with the truck." He said as he walked out the door.

Annella had her crutches across her lap as Mitch wheeled her down the short hallway and out into the circle drive. Mitch locked the wheels and came around to help Annella up and onto her crutches. "I'm so glad you are ok, Annella."

She hugged Mitch as best she could as Max pulled up. "Thanks for taking such great care of me while I've been here."

Mitch went and opened the door as Max moved to Annella's side to help her in. "You're welcome."

With a little lifting and maneuvering Max had Annella in the truck and her seat belt fastened. Before Mitch shut the door, he looked at Annella, "No offense, but I hope I don't see you here for a while."

"Agreed," Annella said as Mitch shut the door and stepped back.

Max shook Mitch's hand before getting in and leaving the hospital.

Max passed his favorite spot to sit with Cal and radar unsuspecting speeders and pulled the truck over. He got out, came around to Annella's side, and opened her door. Annella looked at him as he squatted down next to her.

"Max, what are…"

Max held up a hand to stop her. "A few months ago, I pulled over a girl right here, ready for it to be like any other stop, but it wasn't. Chef, you sped your way into my life and into my heart, and now I'm asking if you'll stay here forever. I love you so much. Annella Grace Lindly, will you marry me?"

Annella was crying big, sloppy, snotty tears and shaking her head yes as Max slid the diamond ring on her finger. It popped against the deep purple of her cast and sparkled in the late morning sun.

He took her face in his hands and kissed her gently at first and then more deeply when she opened her mouth to him.

Max pulled back and looked into Annella's eyes, seeing the happiness and love that he felt mirrored there. "I love you, Max, but I still can't believe you gave me a ticket."

Max barked out a laugh and kissed her quickly again before closing her door and driving his fiancé home, listening to her sing to the radio.

The End

Acknowledgements

As with the dedication, the first acknowledgement has to go to my wonderful husband, Allen. I literally would not have written this book without your support. I wanted to figure out a way to try and pitch it to an author that I felt could do this story justice. Thank you for pushing me to be that author and for reading/listening to this story at least 3 times in full.

To my parents, thank you for fostering my love for reading and for always cheering me on. To my brother, Eric, and sister, Kayla. Thanks for sharing in my joy for my book baby. Joseph Runnels, thanks for listening as you were the second person behind Allen that knew about my secret. Your insight and advice on the post writing process was a tremendous asset and I appreciate you so much.

To the Moad family: Chuck, thanks for your help with the police questions that I had. Angie and Cheryl, thanks for promising to buy copies before you even read it.

Jen and Jason, thank you for being such awesome supporters of the project and reminding me that it's all about perspective. Also, thanks for my amazing author photos.

To my "Lauren" AKA Betsy, thank you for technically being my Beta Reader. I love you!! Lastly, but most certainly not least, thank YOU for reading my book. If I could reach through these pages and hug you I would, unless you're not a hugger, then I would high five you. Just know that you now hold a special place in my heart, and I am grateful for you.